HIS TO HOLD

QUINTESSENTIALLY THEIRS: TWO

SERENA AKEROYD

G. A. MAZURKE

DEDICATION

To Aunty T,

The original lover of all things Christmas.

Thank you for being a part of my life and for loving me faults and all.

Love you,

Gem

xxx

PLAYLIST

If you'd like to hear a curated soundtrack, with songs that are featured in the book, as well as songs that inspired it, then here's the link:

https://open.spotify.com/playlist/1zCGTVrOo4FUJWQZTrvlHQ?si=928af7886f67439b

FOREWORD

Wishing you all a very happy holidays.
> Much love,
> Serena
> xoxo

PART 1

ONE

BEAU

My gaze was glued to the TV screen.

Heart racing, lungs burning, my muscles were locked with the tension that never seemed to abate when I was watching this godforsaken sport.

Jack Dubois was leading the race.

Of course he was.

This looked set to be his ninth victory of the season and the forty-second in his career.

Winning was what Jack did.

But that never stopped terrifying the bejeezus out of me. Not with the stunts he pulled out there.

There was a reason the crowds called him 'Jumping Jack.'

And there was a reason I couldn't deal with watching him live anymore.

Last year's crash at the Veronian Grand Prix had scared the shit out of me, and I knew that I was *D. O. N. E.* watching him self-destruct.

"Why do you watch it if it scares you so much?"

I turned to my dad who was smiling at me, but looking away from the screen was too painful so I skimmed his smile then returned to the action.

And considering that action was the source of the agony, there wasn't much escape from the torment.

Have you ever loved someone so much that you couldn't be around them when they put their life in danger?

When they constantly battled the need for adrenaline highs and pulled stupid stunts to win big?

That was Jack and me.

He didn't know I loved him, of course.

Well, he knew I loved him as a friend.

Just not that I was *in* love with him.

Which I was.

I had done that stupid thing women did when they fell for their best friends who thought they were the girl-next-door.

Pathetic.

I was so damn pathetic.

"I have to watch," I told Dad gruffly. *Because I was a fool.*

"You look like you're going to have a heart attack."

"By the time Jack's done with this phase, I might."

"Phase? Honey, he's been racing for the last ten years. I think it's more of a career."

I gulped because he wasn't wrong.

Still...

"Don't need you pointing that out right now, Dad."

The newspaper in his hands rustled as he returned his focus to *The Guardian*, and I didn't need to look at him to know he was shaking his head at me.

Hell, I'd shake my head if I were him.

Lifting my legs, I wrapped my arms around them and propped my chin on my knees. Self-comforting, sure, but no one else was going to do that for me.

Dad and I didn't have that kind of relationship. He was the type of guy who patted people on the head or the shoulder. Whether you were forty, ten, or ninety, a pat was about as affectionate as Dad got.

I was usually fine with that.

Really, I was.

Just not right now.

It had started raining.

I blew out a breath.

I was a Brit. Rain was our natural environment, but this was a freak shower.

I gnawed on my cheek, watching as the fractious, multi-million-dollar racing car whipped its way around the track en route for a pit stop.

Truly, this was a driver's best friend's idea of hell.

Jack was used to it.

Only, he wasn't using his set of rain tires yet.

"Jeez, it's really teeming it down, isn't it?"

Understatement.

"Not helping, Dad," I breathed, not even bothering to shoot a glower at him.

Where was the goddamn safety car?

Why weren't they putting a stop to this yet?

He shrugged. "It is."

It was.

It was...

Fuck.

I reached up and rubbed my forehead as the red bullet that was my best friend whipped around the track.

For lap after lap, he'd done this. Endlessly. Tirelessly.

It was the most boring shit I'd ever seen in my life, and I'd seen it more than most because of Jack, but for all that the race was tedious, *he,* the man, was riveting.

Jack lived.

He triumphed.

He burned with an inner flame that drew me to him like I was a moth.

And that was a pretty good metaphor.

I was a moth. Kinda bland, boring, and I only came out at night.

My bottom lip trembled as I watched the camera pan, showing the bleak sky in São Paulo, Brazil.

The gray clouds were growing darker, blacker before the camera returned to the action.

The safety car had pulled out.

At fucking last.

The camera zoomed in on Jack's Sabre, which was both heaven and hell.

He was there.

Alive.

Safe.

So why did I feel like that was the last time I was ever going to see him whole and hale?

Anxiety had tears burning my eyes as I sucked down a shaky breath.

It was stupid. *I* was stupid.

Jack was like a cat—he always landed on his feet.

He was perennially fine.

Until he wasn't.

Two cars collided.

It happened in seconds.

One moment, they were a length apart. The next, they were hugging each other as they drifted around the Pinheirinho turn.

But the chaos didn't stop there.

It took me a handful of seconds to figure out what I was seeing. What I was actually—

The Cotovelo hairpin.

My mouth worked.

My brain slowed down.

My lungs stopped.

No.

"No," I whimpered, hands sliding into my hair as I tugged on the roots.

The pain grounded me, but what broke me was Dad whispering, "Jesus."

I wasn't seeing things.

This was happening.

As we watched a replay of Jack's teammate, John Almsleigh, slaloming around the curve, my eyes blurred as he clipped Jack's car before colliding with a tractor.

Jack went into a tailspin, smashing into the safety car, while other drivers steered to avoid—

"Oh God," I sobbed.

Dad's hand went to my shoulder, so I knew he'd moved. Only he didn't give me his patented pat.

He perched on the armrest of my seat, curved his arm around me, and hauled me into his side.

That was when I knew I'd never see my best friend again.

TWO

JACK

It was bad to hate a dead man, wasn't it?

I was sorry John had died.

I was.

Really.

But—

"You're lucky to be alive."

My mom's waspish tone wasn't lost on me.

I tipped my chin down to avoid her gimlet stare—patented in thirty countries for making her kids feel her disapproval—but was well aware that she was standing in the doorway, my daw, Sawyer, at her side.

He was the only one who came to these events anymore.

I had five dads.

Yeah, you read that right.

Five.

But only one came to every race.

My mom wasn't like your average mom, and not just because she had five partners.

She was an American billionaire, infamous across the pond and in the UK, and was also the grandmother to the next queen of Veronia.

Sawyer, Daw, was a Nobel-laureate statistician; Andrei, *Papa*, was a now-retired stock exchange guru with one foot in his homeland's business, Russia, and the other in Britain. My *Vati*, Kurt, had won Oscars and Pulitzers like they were things to be collected with his family memoirs about life behind the Berlin Wall, and Father, AKA Sean, was a criminologist who'd put The Liverpool Ripper behind bars.

As for my dad, Devon?

Well...

What wasn't he?

Aside from not here.

No one was here apart from Mom and Daw.

Dad had refused to come to my races last season when he told me I took too many risks.

And when he told me that, it wasn't because he was concerned for my safety—which he undoubtedly was—but he meant probability.

I wasn't doing the math, and therefore, Dad didn't approve.

I wondered if 'the math' would have solved today's little incident.

Maybe in all his lessons, Dad would be able to tell me the probability of being sabotaged by my own motherfucking teammate.

"It wasn't my fault."

It was all I could think to say.

Not that it ever mattered.

It was always my fault.

If you'd just listen to the question, honey, and didn't rush to answer—

Are you trying to turn me gray, Jack? It's working—

"Yer grandmother wouldae said the angels were watching over ye," Daw rumbled as he stepped deeper into the hospital room. "Yer grandfather wouldae said she was drinking tae much whisky."

Amid the whites and the greens, the beeping machines and the equipment, both my parents were a rainbow of color that hurt my eyes to behold. Like seeing Technicolor after a lifetime of black and white movies.

I squinted at him. "I could really do with some of that." And maybe a hug.

And Beau.

Fuck, I wished she were here.

Much like Dad, she'd told me she couldn't deal with all the risks I took. An accident on the *Monver* hairpin in Madela late last year had been the final straw for her.

"Aye, me tae," Daw retorted. "I could dae with a whole feckin' bottle of it. I could also dae with breaking yer other shoulder for the hell ye just put us through."

"It wasn't my fault," I repeated, needing them to know that. Even if they wouldn't, *couldn't* understand.

I reached up and scrubbed my forehead, well aware that I was lucky to be alive.

Well aware that it was a miracle I'd only dislocated my shoulder.

In the clusterfuck that was the end of the Brazilian Grand Prix, I'd totaled my car but had somehow only fucked up my shoulder and given myself another concussion.

Somehow I was alive. Not dead. And I'd admit, to no one but myself, I'd thought I was a goner.

Mom's hands went to the bed rail—I saw her French tips bleed white with how hard she clenched down. Probably seeking patience from a benevolent god somewhere.

"You don't have to keep on doing this."

I turned my head away. "It's my job."

Her fingers clutched at the rail some more, so I knew I was in for a lecture.

They didn't understand.

They couldn't.

"This is nae a job," Daw grumbled. "It's feckin' dangerous. Yer not even doin' it fer the money! Where's the glory in watching grown men crash their tinker toy cars and gettin' theirselves killed?"

My mouth firmed at the scorn in his voice. I tried to keep my shit together, tried to because it upset Mom when we fought, but my head was aching, and—

"We can't all be fucking geniuses," I snapped. "Maybe this is the only thing I'm good at? And maybe, just maybe, this is what I want to do with my life?"

"End it in a blazing fire on the Cotovelo hairpin?" Daw snarled, his face turning as red as his hair. "Killing yer mother and me as we watch from the sidelines—"

"Your heart, honey." Mom's fingers traveled to his shoulder which she squeezed.

The lights played over the gems on her wedding ring—the regard ring she'd told all her kids stories about. Five interlocking rings, each one signifying a promise she'd made to the men she loved.

The fathers of her children.

It was easier to look at her hands, that ring, than her eyes.

Disappointment.

I knew that was what I'd see there.

I sucked in a breath, trying not to feel the burn of that. Trying not to feel lesser.

I wasn't like the rest of the family. I wasn't intellectual and book smart.

They just didn't get it.

No one fucking got it.

Not even Beau.

"Did someone tell Beau?" I rasped.

"Even though you scared her off tae, the lassie watches every Grand Prix at home, boyo. I dinnae think she needs someone to tell her what happened."

Mom's hand tightened on his shoulder again, apparently reading my expression and seeing that Daw had winded me worse than whiplash. "He's in pain, Sawyer."

"Aye, well, so am I. Damn near had a feckin' stroke out there." He pointed to the still-bright red hair on his head. "Yer gonna turn me gray, Jack."

"Has she called?" I demanded, ignoring his BS about the hair.

Daw had had streaks of gray for a while, but he insisted each one was tied to my victories.

"No." Mom's gaze met mine. "We're going to arrange for you to come home tomorrow."

"The doctor might not clear ye for travel, but it's tough shite. Yer coming back wi'us."

"It's only a dislocated shoulder," I retorted. "After a few weeks of downtime, I'll be back in the game."

Mom's brow furrowed. "John just died, Jack. Doesn't that make you want to reflect on what you're doing?"

My mouth flatlined. "I didn't like him."

"Doesn't take away from the fact he just feckin' died," Daw boomed.

"He pulled stupid stunts because he hated that I was winning. He hated that I got all the damn press. The only reason he's dead is because he wanted to beat me," I snapped, uncaring that the volume of my voice made my ears ring. "The only reason I'm in this fucking hospital room right now is because he was a moron."

"He died," Mom repeated like I'd forgotten how to speak English.

"I don't care," I said bluntly. "I don't even care if that makes me sound like a heartless bastard. He died how he lived—like the piece of shit he was."

Daw shook his head. "This isnae like ye."

"Isnae like me?" I mocked his Scottish brogue. "It's exactly like me when I was just pushed off the damn track because he careened into me."

Mom shifted her weight and pressed her butt onto the side of the bed. "You're not thinking straight. You need to come home, baby."

"I *am* thinking straight."

And I was.

Pre, during, and post-race, I was always thinking clearly.

More often than not, it was the only time I felt like I was as smart as the rest of my brainiac family.

I'd never utter these words to anyone, but I *knew* John had purposely collided into me.

I knew it like I knew my name was Jack fucking Dubois.

"You mean you think he purposely crashed so that he could derail you—"

"I wouldn't go that far," I muttered grimly.

Even though I *did* believe that, I knew she'd think I'd lost the plot if I verbalized it.

She already had that expression that reminded me of her reaction when Dad—Devon, our resident math genius—was trying to figure out how she baked her cookies.

The recipe always worked.

Always.

Even I could bake them, but they'd end up charcoal rocks by the time he was done, and Mom would have to explain that ovens would continue cooking if there was no timer set.

Dad, for all he was his generation's Einstein, was remarkably simpleminded where regular shit came into play.

I guessed he was proof that no one was fucking perfect.

"It's nice to know you don't think the man was a complete lunatic," Daw sniped. "Just an arsehole who couldnae keep control of his car."

Black spots blossomed into being behind my eyes. "Look, if you're just going to give me shit, then go back to the hotel and I'll talk to you in the morning before you fly home."

Daw shook his head. "I'm tellin' ye, lad. Yer coming back with us."

"This is my job," I snarled. "You might not like it, but it's what I do. There's still shit I'm contractually obliged to complete.

"I'm not six years old anymore. I don't need you to kiss my boo-boos better; I need to do my goddamn job."

"There are only two races left in the season. You need surgery and rehab," Mom pointed out, her voice calmer than Daw's, like that would convince me.

I wasn't Dad.

She couldn't soothe me out of a fit of temper.

I didn't need to go home.

I needed to make sure John wasn't right.

The black spots ruptured, exploding behind my eyes so that I felt the nerve endings snag against each other like cheese against a grater.

'You only win because Sabre pays me to make sure you do.'

"You're in shock."

I blinked at her.

Shock? I wasn't in shock.

I stared at my feet, covered by blankets the nurses insisted I needed. *I didn't.* "I'm not, and rehab can wait."

"You keep saying that," she snapped, her temper making her voice turn shrill. "When are you going to let yourself heal?"

Her phone rang, sparing me from a lecture, and when she saw the name on the Caller ID, she glowered at me.

"You can deal with this." She shoved her phone at me.

I wasn't sure who I'd prefer.

Beau or Dad by this point.

Dad would tell me something math-related about the crash that would make my head ache harder than it already did.

He'd go into minute details because he'd have focused on the math rather than on the fact that I could have died. He'd do that to cope.

Angles and algorithms were my father's love language.

Beau would just...

I closed my eyes and reached for the phone. The slight movement jostled my bad shoulder, and I gritted my teeth to contain the grunt that would only confirm my parents were right.

I needed to go home.

But I had something to prove first.

"Hey," I said gruffly.

A soft breath sounded down the line.

Like always, it sent shivers along the length of my spine.

Beau and me... she was my ride or die. But like Dad and the rest of my family, she'd refused to come to my races anymore.

It was hard not to feel bitter about that. Hard not to feel fucking abandoned.

"I'm not dead," I told her, regretting saying that the moment the words left my goddamn lips.

Mom clucked her tongue. "He gets his charm from Devon."

If that wasn't an insult, I didn't know what was.

Scowling at her, only to get a scowl back in return, I mumbled, "I just dislocated my shoulder. Slight concussion."

Still no answer.

"I'll be fine for the next race."

She cut the call.

I stared at the cell phone with a frown, then Mom snatched it back and rasped, "I didn't know until this moment that I raised a fool."

The words slammed into me with more G-force than the collision with John.

"You only just realized that?" I tipped up my chin. "Now who's the slow learner?"

PART 2

THREE

BEAU

FOURTEEN MONTHS LATER

I looked good.

In fact, I looked better than good.

My curves were on display in a dress I'd bought a couple years back when I'd traveled with Jack on the circuit, but had ended up never wearing as it was risqué.

Beau Killian didn't do risqué.

She did jeans shorts and piercings and Ramones tees.

She didn't do dresses, certainly not ones that had a sweetheart neckline, that cupped her waist with corset-like boning, then flared out into a jaunty skirt that dashed around her calves.

No, Beau didn't wear things like that.

Not until tonight.

I'd taken it out of its box for the first time for the celebratory party, knowing that I could be my own lady in red, full-on Chris de Burgh-style.

I didn't need a man to rock this outfit.

Good thing too, seeing as the only man I wanted didn't want me.

"Why the long face, Buttercup?"

I didn't have to twist around to see my dad looking at me in the hall mirror. I was standing staring at myself like I was obsessed with my image, and we both knew that wasn't me.

"Thinking about changing my piercings," I lied.

I had a Monroe on my upper lip, dimples, and two sitting on my upper chest at collarbone height.

If I stopped to think about my appearance, I knew that I didn't look like I'd fit in at a swanky party up at the main house. Not that I'd been judged before by the people who lived there, but tonight, I just had a feeling there'd be judgy cretins around.

The vultures were in town.

Jack had won yet another championship, ergo they needed to sniff around him like the prize he was.

That meant there'd be a mixture of debutantes looking to tame a bad boy, socialites on the hunt for a rich boyfriend, and Z-list celebrities who'd scored an invitation to this party by sucking off someone they'd be ditching immediately.

This wasn't the first victory party I'd attended.

It would, however, be the last because I was done celebrating Jack's recklessness.

"You look smart," I told Dad softly, giving him a quick scan to make sure he was presentable—which he was.

In a tux, I knew if Mama were alive, she'd have been drooling over him.

Sixteen years without her and that was one of the only things that remained clear in my head—how she looked at him.

His lips curved. "Couldn't let the side down, could I?"

I scoffed. "What side? You'll fit in more than I do."

I didn't know why, but that had his head tipping to the side. "What's wrong, Beau?"

What was right?

I'd been feeling like I didn't fit in my own skin for the past year or so, and tonight it was worse than ever.

He stepped over to me and rested a hand on my shoulder. I

expected a pat, his usual attempt at comforting a daughter he didn't understand, except, he didn't.

He just stared at me in the mirror.

Dad was the archetypal Brit. Stiff upper lip. Cold and chilly at times of high emotion. Yet, he'd fallen for my very Polish mother. A woman who leaked emotions from every pore. And they said opposites didn't attract...

"You look like you're going to a funeral, not a party," Dad drawled.

The words stung.

Tonight was the end in more ways than he could understand.

"Could have been a funeral," I pointed out.

His expression turned thoughtful. "Jack did take risks this year."

"It's like he decided that he'd cheated death once and now he has to keep outrunning it."

"Outracing it," Dad corrected, making me grimace.

"Thank God for the HALO."

The HALO was an internal shield for drivers, and it exponentially increased the protection from high-intensity crashes.

He hummed his agreement. "I don't think he'd have walked away from Milan and Amsterdam without it."

I wished he weren't right about that.

"No. I was hoping the fact that no one was with him for the races would calm him down, but no joy."

He stared at me. "You still feel bad about that, don't you?"

"Of course I do," I whispered, my eyes meeting his in the mirror. "He's always there for me. But I can't watch him kill himself. I just... can't."

He patted my shoulder. "I know, Buttercup."

Because crying would destroy my makeup, I peered at the earring I was going to wear tonight and found myself smiling at the memory it triggered.

An ex had bought the tiny roses inside a small glass container à la *Beauty and the Beast*.

Shiloh had had the best taste in jewelry.

Slipping one of the roses into one ear, letting the lacy chain flutter down to my shoulder where the rose hung suspended, I murmured, "I think tonight's party is going to be yet another 'fuck you' to his parents."

Dad snorted. "Undeniably. Jack is a lost soul. That's why you two get along so well."

My brow puckered. "Gee, thanks, Dad."

"Hush. You know it as well as I do. He just found a way to channel it. You haven't yet."

Yet being the operative word.

My dad worked for Andrei Kirov, one of Jack's fathers. Andrei was supposedly retired and my dad worked under him, easing the workload while also managing the portfolio Andrei had spent a life-time building up.

Dad was smart and driven, focused and had a knack for making money. He'd *never* been a lost soul.

I felt as if he'd known his path since birth.

Me?

I'd gone to college for art but had dropped out, had tried again with a hospitality degree after Sascha, Jack's mom, had told me about hers and I'd figured it might suit me.

No dice.

So, I made coffee in the local cafe, and tried not to spill it on people when I served them, and considered it a good day if I came back with any tips at all.

Dad hugged me to him as I threaded the earring through my other earlobe. "You might have a good time."

"At the non-wake?"

His lips twitched. "Yeah, at the non-wake."

I grunted then patted my hair. As Dad helped me into my coat, I looped my arm around his as we headed out the door once I'd grabbed my purse.

It was freezing, and we weren't dressed for it, even with our coats, but it just made us walk faster as we crossed the stretch of lawn that separated our home from the family estate.

The Dubois country house ran into the hundreds upon hundreds of acres, some of that being an ancient forest that spooked me out, and twenty or so years ago, they'd started constructing properties for the members of staff whom the family needed to live on-site.

That was why we shared the same grounds as they did.

We lived in a very nice five-bedroom house that the two of us were rattling around in.

"You nervous about seeing him?" Dad asked me softly, out of breath because we were walking fast to outrun the cold.

"Yes. Things are weird now."

He patted my hand. "He broke records this year. Maybe he'll have calmed down some."

That was the rub.

"I like the Jack who's nuts though. I like that he doesn't fit into the mold he should. It's just—"

"You wish he didn't do things that could get himself killed in the process."

"About sums it up."

But that was what made Jack *Jack*.

It was complicated.

Love did that, didn't it?

Made everything complicated.

"You see that tree there?" I pointed to the right one, glad that it was faintly illuminated in the glow from the main house.

"I do."

"You know when we moved in, that same day, I met Jack."

"I didn't know that," he admitted.

"He'd climbed the damn thing, went all the way to the top and was standing there." I laughed, but it was mocking. "Not the lower branches for Jack, nope. Had to be the highest he could reach."

Dad paused, but it had nothing to do with being out of breath. "You thought he was going to jump?"

I nodded. "I screamed. He fell." A soft exhalation rattled from my lips. "I remember thinking I was going to see another dead body, and then he caught himself on one of the branches. I have no idea how he did it, but he did."

"You thought he was like your mother?"

"Yes. But Jack *isn't* like her. He isn't suicidal. He just lets death chase him."

"Isn't that two sides of the same coin?"

"Maybe. I try to find comfort in that when he's scaring the hell out of me."

"Why did you never tell me that story before?"

"I was sure we'd get into trouble: him for climbing the tree, me for being a big baby and screaming which made him fall."

Chuckling, he asked, "You've been covering his back ever since?"

I guessed, now that I thought about it, I had.

"He covers for me too. It's just in different ways," I reasoned.

"Not this year."

"No," I had to admit. "He's been upset with me. A lot longer than a year too."

"Since you stopped going to his races?"

"Yes."

"Does he know about your mother?" He sighed. "That seems a ridiculous question to me, considering how close you are, but I also know you're... never mind."

"He knows she died," I said flatly. "That she committed suicide."

Dad hummed because we both knew what I omitted from that particular tale.

Because of where the conversation had taken us, I was relieved when we made it to the house where a lot of very expensive cars were pulling up in the driveway.

From my job at the cafe, I recognized some of the local faces who'd been brought in to work as valets, and I also noticed the guards.

Though discreet, they stuck out like a sore thumb to me.

Brows high, I complained, "You didn't tell me Tin was coming."

Tin was Jack's elder brother. He'd married the heiress to the throne of Veronia five years ago, and whenever he came home, there was always a team of forty or so of the Guard Elect—the Veronian Secret Service—traipsing around the estate.

"Thought you'd have noticed the Men In Black hovering in the corners," Dad drawled as he tipped his chin at Crawley, the Dubois' butler.

At least, that was what I called him.

His official job title was manager, but in a house like this, as ancient as this pile of bricks was, he was a butler by any other name.

We needed no invitation, unlike the people lining up at the door, and just headed inside.

I passed women I knew from the circuit, ones who, beneath the coats, would be wearing next to nothing in an attempt to entice Jack.

I could have told them that he was a fuckboi. Fuck ya once, then fuck ya off. That was Jack. He only loved three things—his family, his cars, and me.

Just not how I needed him to love me.

"It's that hillbilly, Cassandra," one of the women whispered as we passed.

"The one who used to cling to Jackie? I totally recognize her."

I rolled my eyes at the nickname, rolled them double time at the insult.

To these inbred society bitches, I was a hillbilly because I had some ink and a few piercings that weren't solely in my ears. They needed to stop sniffing cocaine while they had some functioning brain cells left.

I cast Dad a look, checking to see if he'd heard and if he was insulted or embarrassed by what they'd said about me—jealous witches who wanted to be on Jack's arm. But he was neither. His cheeks were flushed and I saw why...

Loretta Hardy.

The new housekeeper.

I knew he had a crush on her, but he never made a move. Not in the six months she'd been here.

I squeezed his arm. "I hope you're going to ask her to dance tonight."

His cheeks turned impossibly red, making him look like a boiled tomato.

My lips twitched as he bumbled, "I don't know what you're talking about!"

Smile making an outright appearance, I jeered, "Yeah, okay, Dad. You tell yourself that."

He harrumphed. "I don't!"

"Kid yourself but not me. She likes you too."

His mouth rounded as he drew us to a halt before we could reach one of the servers who were standing by to take our coats.

"How do you know she does?"

"Why does it matter if you don't like her?" I countered, eyes gleaming with amusement.

Dad had been single since Mom's death. Sixteen years was a long time to be alone and grieving.

I didn't begrudge him happiness, and had often encouraged him to date, but no dice.

A part of me thought it was romantic that he still loved Mom enough that no one compared, but that was the artist in me.

And the artist was only forty percent of my nature.

The remaining sixty percent was pure pragmatist—it was why art college hadn't worked out.

Dying of starvation in a garret might seem *darling* to some, but not me.

Neither did dying with a heart that was still broken from your wife killing herself when you were in your thirties.

I squeezed his hand gently. "I think you should ask her to dance. You know you're good at it."

"Now you're just trying to make me feel better."

"I would tell you *not* to dance if I thought you sucked at it."

"Reassuring, love," he said absently, but his gaze had drifted and I had the feeling Loretta was back in the room. "She's working tonight."

I shrugged. "It's not like Sascha is a mean boss. I think she'll be allowed a break. Maybe she needs company?"

I watched him suck on the inside of his cheek, tugging it in and biting down on it. It was one of the few tells Dad had that revealed anything in his expression.

"You really think she likes me?"

Dad's nerves had me hugging him to my side. "I do. But if she doesn't, then where's the harm in asking her to dance?"

"She might accuse me of sexual harassment."

He was in a managerial position, so he wasn't wrong.

Pondering the delicate situation a second, I said, "Ask once, if she says no, back off. Do it in front of people and don't be creepy."

"Don't be creepy? What kind of tip is that?"

I grinned. "Don't look down her blouse and keep your eyes on hers. Don't stutter or shift on your feet."

He laughed a second, then his eyes darkened and he grumbled, "Do men do that to you?"

I arched a brow at him. "Ah, the joys of being a woman."

His scowl made a brief appearance. "At work?"

"It's life, Dad." I patted his arm gently. "Now, go. Ask her."

When he sucked in a breath like he was seeking courage, I gathered his coat to check it as he wandered away.

With our coats dealt with, I watched a second but then figured that was an odd thing to do, and instead, gave him some room to work his moves.

"Never thought I'd be giving my dad tips on dating," I muttered under my breath as I headed across the grand foyer and into a ballroom.

There was a dance floor that was already heaving at one end. The other housed dozens of tables dotted here and there with seated guests, drinking and eating amuse-bouches and hors d'oeuvres that staff whisked around on silver trays alongside flutes of champagne, an array of other wines, and juices too.

If this wasn't Jack's night, I'd probably be helping with the service, but it was a tradition that I come to the party.

What else was a tradition?

Me being a witness to him getting off with one of the guests.

Such fun.

Huffing under my breath, I snatched some champagne from a tray, asking, "How's it going?" to the server.

Bishop Rosen was a small town, almost a village, so everyone knew everyone.

I'd gone to school with Jude and didn't mind shooting the breeze even if, like I'd warned my dad against doing, the habit of checking out my tits first then my eyes was a problem.

Jude cast me a sheepish glance when I cleared my throat, but I merely smirked because my tits did look extraordinary tonight with the sweetheart neckline and the bones from the corset in the scarlet dress.

Before Jude could answer, however, a familiar voice snapped, "Her eyes aren't on her chest."

I twisted around in surprise at the anger in Jack's voice. "What the hell's crawled up your ass and died?"

Jack blinked at me, Jude was wise and scurried away, and I glowered at my best friend.

"Well?" I demanded when he didn't say a word.

"Nothing crawled up my ass. Your tits are not where your eyes are," Jack groused, his frown clear as he stared at me.

"Is that how you're going to greet me? I haven't seen you in three months."

"Whose fault is that?" he bit off, folding his arms across his chest.

"Yours," I retorted, folding my arms across my chest too.

"Mine?"

His splutter was so outraged that I fought a smile. "Yeah, yours? You got engine oil in your ears or something?"

"No, but you're talking so shrilly that only the bats in the belfry can hear you."

Hand snapping out, I prodded him in the chest with my finger. "Don't make out like I'm the one who went incommunicado with you. I told you you took an unnecessary risk at the Circuit Gilles Villeneuve.

"That entire race was a clusterfuck. If your head is so damn big that you can't take any criticism, then you can go and talk to another simpering bitch who'll take your shit and scoop it up like it's chocolate ice cream."

His scowl cleared and he laughed. His grin was like the sunshine peering through a miserably gray and gloomy sky.

I hated that it was.

I hated that it made my heart feel lighter.

His happiness shouldn't be so entrenched with my own.

I hadn't expected to see him so soon, or I'd have prepared myself, and because he'd pissed me off, I didn't get a chance to do much more than absorb him quickly.

Normally, I hid in the corners, found him and watched him work the room.

It was the exact thing I'd told my dad not to do—be weird—but watching Jack when he didn't know was the only time I had to get my response to him under control.

It wasn't that I started drooling or anything.

It was worse.

I wanted to touch him.

My hands craved to straighten his bowtie; my fingertips longed to rub over his sharp-as-glass cheekbones. I wanted to slip my fingers against his or have him swipe his thumb over my palm.

I craved those things with a visceral longing that went bone deep.

"Chocolate ice cream, Beau? Really?"

His reference to chocolate ice cream made me blink in consternation.

What was he talking about?

Oh. That some of the socialites here acted like his shit didn't stink. *Yeah.*

If anything, the way they treated him like he was the second coming made me harder on him than I'd ever been in my life.

Each year it grew worse until he was right—I *was* shrill with him.

His arm slipped around my shoulder, and I almost closed my eyes at how damn good he smelled.

I wanted to sink into him, melt into his bones, but instead of doing that, I slipped my arm around his waist like he expected me to because that was what we did.

Even when I gave him shit.

Feeling bad for always being rough on him, I peered up at him to mumble a greeting of, "Jackass."

Okay, I didn't feel *that* bad.

Someone had to keep his ego in check.

His lips curved. "Beau-Peep."

"I don't fit my horrible nickname. You do tonight."

"Just tonight?"

"Mostly always, but tonight for sure." I puffed out my cheeks on the brink of admitting that I'd missed him, but he squeezed my waist and pressed a kiss to my temple.

"Missed you too, brat."

I wanted to die.

There and then.

I could have died and I'd have been fine with that.

Sure, I'd accomplished nothing with my life, and to many, had probably wasted the opportunities I'd been granted, but I didn't care.

God could strike me down right this second and I was where I wanted to be.

Sometimes, I wondered how he didn't sense my feelings for him.

Other times, I feared he knew anyway and just ignored them.

Shoving my unrequited love aside, I demanded, "Admit it."

Though I caught him checking out one of the women who'd

called me a hillbilly back in the foyer, he didn't apologize, merely asked, "Admit what?"

I bit my lip as irritation filled me—of course, he'd want to fuck one of them.

Of. Fucking. Course.

"That you were a prick about the Canadian Grand Prix."

"It was irrelevant. I handled it well enough that I stood on the podium, didn't I?"

"Barely. You were damn lucky Ingelsen didn't crash into you on *L'Epingle*." I shoved out of his hold. "You're not even listening. Go and fuck one of those bitches if that's all you can think about when you haven't seen me in months."

Hurt and anger whipped at me, making more emotions than he was used to hearing from me drip into my tone.

"Beau!" he called as I strode away, but I noticed he didn't come after me.

Jerk.

I stormed deeper into the party, over toward the half of the room that had darker spots so no one would be able to see my angry tears.

Infuriated and hurt, I swallowed the flute of champagne in my hand whole then snagged another, slugging it back like it was cheap wine and not Dom Perignon from the estate's cellars.

That was when I drifted onto the dance floor now I had some liquid courage making the party a lot more fun.

I raised my arms in the air and slowly swayed to the music which was good enough that I knew Bethan, Jack's sister and one of my BFFs, had been pivotal in the DJ's selection.

Dancing and drinking were better than crying over Jack being a dick.

Jack was always a dick.

That was what Jack did.

Who he was.

I had no idea why I loved him.

None.

A hand slipped over my arm, making me tense as fingers tangled with mine.

I wanted so badly for the hand to belong to Jack, but I knew it didn't. I recognized her perfume as soon as she twirled me around in a spin.

I laughed, glad that it didn't trigger tears as Jack's other sister, Rosie, started dancing with me.

"Don't let the Jackass get you down," she shouted in my ear as we moved and twirled together.

Jack wasn't my only friend in the family. I'd been here so long that most of his fathers liked me as well, just not Devon who'd once sat on me because he hadn't noticed I was using one of the armchairs in the main living room.

"He's a prick!" I shouted.

And as luck would have it, the beat dropped, and my words seemed to echo around the dance floor.

The dance floor which I wished would open and swallow me whole.

Especially when I saw Jack looking at me across the way...

FOUR

BEAU

With Jack's gaze fixed firmly on me, Rosie saved me by laughing and hauling me deeper onto the dance floor. Deeper and deeper until we drifted off to the side and toward the door that led onto a private hallway.

She knitted her arms with mine then murmured, "I was waiting for you to show up. I got something for you."

Cheeks hot from the spectacle I'd just made of myself, I thanked God that my friend was incapable of being embarrassed and that she'd saved my life out there.

"What? I saw you this afternoon," I drawled.

Rosie was mischief incarnate though, so I didn't hold out much hope for whatever this gift might be.

"So? My life's busy, babe. Lots happens in the blink of an eye."

Rosie was a vet, and I'd seen her be called out on a job at three AM, only for her to return at six and then be called out again a half hour later—the perks of a practice in farm country.

She specialized in horses, but she treated all animals. Big and small.

Still, it was a Saturday, and I couldn't smell cow manure in the air around her.

Okay, that was being mean. But sometimes... it was there.

Just a whiff.

Was it a testament to how much I loved her like a sister that I'd grown used to it and didn't complain about it anymore?

Hiding a smile at the thought, I demanded, "What is it?"

"Don't be impatient," she grumbled as she dragged me deeper into the house.

There were ghost corridors like these peppered throughout the estate. Halls for the staff so that they could whisper through the rooms without disturbing their lofty lords and masters.

It was very *Downton Abbey.*

"Do you ever wonder what the staff saw when they were creeping through these corridors?"

She twisted back to blink at me. "No."

"Never?"

"How much champagne did you have?" When I scoffed, her grimace made an appearance. "We don't talk about these corridors."

"Why don't you? Are they haunted?" I teased with a chuckle.

"Because if you're unlucky, you see things you don't want to see."

I blinked. "So, they *are* haunted?"

"Yes, but no."

"Yes, but no?" I repeated.

She grimaced. "We've all caught Mom with one of the dads doing things no child should ever have to see because of sneaking around in these passages."

I snorted. "I think it's awesome that they still get it on."

"I never said it wasn't," she argued. "But when you're a teenager and you see your mom being spanked—"

My mouth gaped and I tugged her to a halt. "Your mom's into that?"

Rosie crinkled her nose. "Don't make me think about it."

"You brought it up, not me!"

She pulled a face. "I never asked what she was into. It's not something you talk about with your parents, is it?"

"I dunno. I think I'd have asked if I caught my mom and dad like that."

"That's because you're a free spirit."

I tilted my head to the side. "I am?"

All these compliments tonight. Free spirit, lost soul... which was it?

"Yes." She tugged on my arm. "You just don't think you are because you're not artsy-fartsy enough."

"What's that supposed to mean?" I complained even though my lips twitched.

Rosie never had been very good with her words.

"It means that you're not artsy-fartsy enough," she repeated.

"That's not an answer."

"I'm sorry, hon." Rosie sighed and slipped her arm around my shoulder. "I didn't mean to be vague."

"So why were you?" I sniped.

"Because I've been up for eighteen hours straight and I really need a nap?"

"No excuse," I sniffed. "You're always tired."

"But I haven't eaten either."

"Okay, I forgive you," was my immediate retort. Slyly, however, I asked, "Have you seen Bash today?"

Her eyes narrowed. "Yes."

I hid a smile. "That why you're in a bad mood too?"

She huffed.

"How about we don't talk about Bash and we leave the character assassination for another time?" I bribed, knowing full well she and Bash, her adopted brother, had a love/hate relationship.

"We won't talk about him," she said quickly. "I have a gift for you, remember? We'll talk about that instead."

Warily, remembering the time she'd given me a calf for Christmas, I asked, "What kind of gift?"

"He's in my living room."

"He?" I spluttered. "Is this a setup?"

"A blind date? What do you take me for? Mom?" she pshawed.

I had to smile. It was always strange hearing the very American-accented noun, 'Mom,' fall from the upper crust lips of my friend. But Sascha was North American, and all her kids called her that.

Humming, I mused, "I never did ask you how things went last night."

"Badly," was her grim retort. "I told Mom that if she ever set me up with anyone again, I'd move out."

I was pretty sure Sascha set Rosie up on bad dates just so that she could steer her into a relationship with Bash... I had no proof to confirm or deny that theory.

My brows rose at Rosie's declaration. "Fighting words."

"Yeah."

"Devon would never let her hear the end of it if you moved out."

She harrumphed. "Exactly."

Devon liked his children under the same roof as him.

I was pretty sure that if he could, he'd have them living in until they were in their fifties.

The thought had me tugging on her hand again. "How are Tin and Alice? I haven't had a chance to see them yet."

She rolled her eyes. "Because Tin hasn't let her out of their suite since they arrived."

"Why?"

A smirk creased her lips. "Mom is in 'grandma' mode so she's babysitting."

"Ohhhh."

"She's pregnant again. No wonder considering he never lets Alice up for air."

I winced. "Oh dear."

Rosie huffed. "He keeps knocking her up, and just when we get some peace around the place, she pops out another one."

Laughing, I said, "You make her sound like a dairy cow."

"The amount of times he breeds her, she might as well be."

I sniggered. "That's the future Queen of Veronia. Anyway, is it breeding when they've only had one kid? It's not like he's knocking her up every day.

"I know you prefer animal biology to human, but I think you might have gotten your wires crossed."

Rosie sniffed. "She should have better taste than to let my brother paw at her."

"I dunno, Tin's cute. And he's only gotten better since they started dressing him." 'They' being the royal household.

"Are you crushing on one of my brothers?"

As she gagged, I chuckled and shut up as she hauled me toward her private sitting room.

The fire was blazing in the hearth, and two Chesterfield armchairs were plunked in front of it, creating a definitely picturesque setting. There, like something from a Hallmark card, was a basket stuffed with blankets.

Immediately, I tensed and dragged my hand from hers. "Oh, no, Rosie! Not again! I told you no more fostering!"

"Just have a look, Beau," Rosie whined as she moved over to the armchair where the admittedly adorable Corgi was napping in front of the fire.

At her words, however, the pup peeped up at us, tail wagging before anything else as it scampered out of the basket toward us.

I groaned at the sight, already knowing she was going to sucker me into doing this again as she swept the little pup into her arms and cuddled it to her chest.

I had no idea what it was about the Dubois family, but all of them were magnetic.

At least, to me they were.

I wasn't sure if it was their nature, their confidence, or if it was just my curse that I'd be their sucker and that they could reel me in whenever they wanted.

I wasn't offended, not really, because I knew I was as much a part of the family as an outsider could be, but when she shuffled nearer to me, cooing at the dog, I huffed when I snatched the pup from her hold, muttering, "I told you no more."

It hurt so badly to let go of them.

I'd lost too much in my life, and I was sick to death of it.

"I was thinking that with this one, you could keep him."

"It's a he?"

There was a smile in her voice. "Yep. I'm trained to notice those kinds of things."

Amusement hit me and I grinned at her. "Smartass."

"You know it." She folded her arms across her chest. "His owner..." She sighed. "There was a road accident, and the pup's mom died."

I bit my lip and muttered, "Didn't the owners want the puppy?"

"They did."

"So, why does he need fostering?"

"Because I didn't like their setup. When I threatened to call the RSPCA on them over the accident, they handed him over to me with no argument."

I frowned at that, hearing the fishy undertones to the story. "What happened to make you call the charity in?"

"I got a weird vibe from the place. You know the Culpeppers over in Bishop Linden?"

"Yeah. The large farmhouse with the massive barn out back?"

"I'm pretty sure they're a puppy mill. They're licensed so it's not illegal, but I don't like it. Not on my turf."

Sadness filtered inside me. "Did you check out the barn?"

"I tried but they wouldn't let me go in. It was weird enough that when I saw him, I knew I wanted him out of the place.

"I can't save them all today, but I can work on figuring out what's going on."

"Don't get into any trouble, Rosie," I argued. "Just call in the RSPCA—"

"I have to have some kind of proof. That they let their dog get killed in a senseless accident is just a reason why they shouldn't be pet owners. It's not something I can report." Grimly, she tacked on, "Even if it should be."

"You saw their papers?"

"I did. But I just had a bad vibe, you know?"

Nodding, I cuddled the pup to my chest, cooing as he sleepily pawed at the two piercings on my décolletage. It hurt, but he was only batting them softly.

Nuzzling my face into his fur, I asked, "Does he have a name?"

"No. I was thinking you could name him."

Sighing, I shook my head. "I couldn't do that."

"Why not?"

"Because I'd make a terrible dog owner."

Rosie snorted. "Better than the ones he'd have had if it weren't for me stepping in. You can't be much worse. Plus, you're great with the fosters."

I felt like there was something she wasn't telling me about the story, and because I knew she'd seen some sights that gave her nightmares, I didn't prod because I had enough nightmares of my own.

"I work weird hours."

"You work shifts," Rosie drawled. "Nothing weird about them. He'll be fine for the time you're at work. Dogs cope," she mocked. "Come on, what other excuse are you going to give me?"

I frowned at her, but before I could answer, the door to the bedroom opened and we both turned around to face the intruder.

Seeing Jack, my scowl made a reappearance.

"Rosie is Beau still with you?" he asked before he came to a halt as he slapped on the light and saw me standing there.

Because he'd spoken first, I'd had the chance to brace myself, to shield my expression, but damn, the air around me felt turbocharged and I knew the pup sensed it too because he went from being sleepy to yapping.

I soothed him just as Jack asked, "Who's this?"

He wasn't surprised, and he was right not to be, because Rosie brought home a lot of animals.

There had always been many pets roaming around the place, but now, there were several packs of rehomed pups and kittens who had made the estate their home.

I wasn't the only one Rosie suckered into rehoming animals. Her dads each had a dog and a cat minimum. Devon had three that followed him around like he was the Pied Piper.

"I'm trying to convince Beau that she should adopt him," Rosie said cheerfully.

That was how she got you.

That cheerful nature belied an obstinacy worthy of a field marshal.

I had to thank God that she wasn't in a position of power. Rosie could very easily turn into Dr. Evil.

Jack's brows rose. "Beau doesn't want a pet."

"Says who?" I grumbled.

He frowned at me. "If you did, I'd have bought you a puppy—"

"You'd have bought one?" Rosie squawked. "How many times, Jack? You don't buy puppies—"

He rolled his eyes. "I meant I'd have consulted you first, sis," he replied quickly before she could take off on a diatribe. "Anyway, Mom wants you."

Rosie paused mid-argument. "Huh?"

"Mom wants you. Says there's a problem with Daisy."

"Shit. I bet it's her foot again."

Without a backwards glance, hyperfocus activated, Rosie disappeared via the other exit—one that led to a regular hallway and not the ones I called ghost passages.

Which meant Jack and I were left alone.

It wasn't like that was weird, but these past fourteen months had been strange.

We hadn't spent as much time together as we usually did.

I felt his eyes on me and the pup, and I drifted over to the fireplace, wanting the warmth from it to lick over my shoulders which were covered in goosebumps that had nothing to do with the chill in the air but everything to do with his presence.

I felt the constraints of my plan disintegrating now that I was around him.

The last couple of months with little contact had been close to impossible, and it made me realize I needed to grow up.

To move on with my life.

I couldn't do that when I was here, still living at home, pining for a man who'd only ever see me as a friend when I wanted to be so much more. A man who didn't realize how precious life was when he risked it so easily.

Aware that he hadn't said a word since his sister left, I felt his gaze on me and tried not to let it affect me.

Who was I kidding?

"Why were you looking for me, Jack?" I muttered to break the tension as I cuddled the pup, grateful he was here because it enabled me to split my attention instead of focusing solely on Jack.

I really needed to get over this crush.

Yesterday.

It wasn't like I hadn't tried to date other people. But everyone I'd tried out just wasn't Jack.

I hated that they weren't, and I hated myself for wanting him so damn much.

"I wanted to ask you something. It's been on my mind a while."

"What?" I snarked. "Fourteen months? Or just the last three where you didn't even pick up the damn phone?"

He growled under his breath. "You're as much to blame for that as I am, Beau. You're the one who stopped coming to my races—"

"Because I was tired of watching you almost kill yourself."

I didn't mean to, I really didn't. I never shouted. It wasn't in my nature.

But I yelled those words at him.

I yelled them so loud that the pup scrambled in my arms in fear and he nearly fell in an attempt to escape me.

Great start as a dog owner.

Snatching him up before he could hurt himself, I carefully tucked him into the bed, aware that he was probably petrified of me now.

I reached up to swipe a hand over my face, uncaring that the tears were already falling, and when I turned to look at him, I saw his shoulders were hunched, his hands in his pockets.

"I didn't try to kill myself, Beau," Jack denied gruffly.

"No? You did a damn good impression of it."

"How would you know? You didn't even—"

"I've watched every single goddamn race, you prick. Just because I couldn't stand to watch you die on the track when I was in the paddocks, didn't mean I couldn't check in with you."

Admittedly, I'd watched the races afterward.

Once I knew he'd survived.

But I'd been a secondhand witness to every reckless turn he'd taken and every foolish decision he'd made—just in the evening of the race and not the morning of.

"I thought you watched the highlights."

"Highlights? More like lowlights." I raised a hand and ticked them off on my fingers as I said, "Amsterdam, Milan, Beijing—they might have been your best speeds, but they haunt me, dammit.

"Each time, I almost had a heart attack watching you hurl yourself around those corners as if you had a date with the Grim Reaper."

"I don't want to die, Beau," he told me carefully, stepping closer with a cautiousness that didn't suit him because he threw himself into more dangerous scenarios every day he was working.

I wasn't scary. I wasn't dangerous.

But he approached me like I was a tigress.

Each step measured and wary.

The sight had me frowning at him, and I murmured, "You'd never tell from the way you are on the track."

He knew how I felt about these things. Knew that my mother's death—even if he didn't know I was the one who found her—made things hit me harder than it might someone else.

I sucked in a breath, trying to regulate my heartbeat. "Anyway, it's not like you've missed me. You barely called before the long hiatus."

"Only because you gave me shit every time I did."

"Shit? That was me caring, you prick. You forget I've watched as many of these races as you have, and we've even frickin' discussed strategy—" There was a reason his team had made me sign an NDA. "—I'm not some dumb fool out there who doesn't understand the danger you put yourself in when you take those risks.

"I see the real-life costs of the stunts you pull with the injuries you have. If you wanted an ass-kisser then—"

Jack raised a hand only to let it cascade down to his side. "I'm sorry, Beau."

"He's sorry," I scoffed at no one in particular, folding my arms across my chest. "What about? Sorries mean nothing, Jack. Not without a desire to change behind them—"

About to blast him, he stunned me by declaring, "How's this for a sorry? I'm quitting the team."

FIVE

JACK

God, I'd missed her.

Did she know how much?

I hated that she wasn't in the paddocks, listening in to the race as an unofficial part of the team and helping me strategize.

Hated that she was weird whenever I called her.

Hated that *she* never called me.

These past fourteen months had sucked.

They'd sucked dick.

But I'd had something to prove to myself, something to prove to the fucking world, and I had.

Every risk I'd taken, every move I'd made, every victory I'd scored was mine.

Hard earned. Hard won.

No risk, no reward.

"You quit the team?" she breathed.

The high pitch did something weird to my ears. It made me think about shit I shouldn't be thinking about where Beau was concerned.

I thought about Jude, and the jealousy that hit me made my heart pound.

There were very few women I actually respected, and that wasn't because I was a misogynist but because I hung around in a toxic environment where there were bunnies who'd do anything to be with a driver.

I'd taken advantage of that over the years, and I wasn't going to apologize for it. Not when the woman I really wanted was standing in front of me. Not when Beau was someone I could never have in that way.

And fuck, that hurt.

It was a raw wound in my soul.

"What are you scowling at?" she sniped at me.

I narrowed my eyes some more. "You're sparkling tonight, aren't you? Just a real joy to be around?"

She unfolded her arms from across her chest, and I noticed her hands balled into fists. "Didn't realize that was my job, Jack, to be your Moët and Chandon. You get enough of that when you're on the podium, don't you?"

When I didn't answer, she reached up and rubbed her eyes. I was pretty sure she was wondering why we were fighting.

Again.

That was all we seemed to damn well do on the rare occasions we *were* together now.

"Were you lying about quitting?"

"No."

"Sawyer said you got an offer to reup your contract?"

"I did." I studied her confusion, and though it wasn't something I should say, I couldn't stop myself from telling her, "You look beautiful tonight, Beau."

Her brow puckered. "What?"

"You look beautiful."

I shrugged to take away the awkwardness of the admission.

Not that it should have been awkward, but I was more likely to tell her that she had ketchup on her cheek than to compliment her on her beauty.

And she was.

Beautiful, that is.

I never wanted her to feel pressured around me. My feelings were mine, and she couldn't help that I wasn't the kind of person for her.

Still, she had an ethereal quality about her, like she was half-fairy and half-human.

I'd seen pictures of her mother, though, so I guessed I was semi-right.

Her mother had been a dancer, a famous one by all accounts. Beau had shared relatively few stories with me about her, but I'd seen the photos and knew she was incredibly tiny. Beau had some of her gracefulness, but she'd inherited her dad's height and some of his stockiness.

It was a pleasing combination, in all honesty.

I liked that she was smaller than me, but not so much smaller that I felt like I was talking to a little girl when we were walking together.

So many times I wished I could press my chin to the crown of her head, wrap my arms around her waist, and haul her against me.

Fuck.

The ache that triggered.

It was one of the reasons I'd put distance between us. Distance she'd helped sow by refusing to come to my races.

"I look beautiful?" she whispered, her surprise at my statement clear.

"Didn't you look in a mirror before you left the house?"

"I like the dress." She shrugged then reminded me, "Beauty's in the eye of the beholder."

I shook my head at her. "It's pretty damn sad that you don't see it in yourself."

She squinted at me, making her blue eyes sparkle like they were gemstones with the sun shining behind them.

She had a pointed chin that led to high cheekbones. Her eyes were wide set, her brow delicate as it arced into a widow's peak.

I loved that her hair gleamed auburn no matter the season or the weather. And in the firelight, it turned almost burgundy as it cascaded over her shoulders, sliding down to the middle of her back when she wasn't wearing it up.

When I was younger, I'd braided it for her.

God, I hadn't done that in so long.

Years.

Maybe eight or more?

I'd hated doing it back then, but she always did it wrong.

I'd fucking kill to have my hands on her hair now.

How couldn't she see how damn beautiful she was? Why didn't any of her girlfriends tell her that?

Curving my fingers and tightening them into a fist so that I didn't stalk over to her and tug on the chignon she wore to liberate the locks from their prison, I told her gruffly, "I didn't sign the contract to renew."

"Why not?"

Would she believe me?

And if she did, would she say anything to anyone?

I trusted her with my life, but this was... *I was ashamed.*

"I didn't want to work for them anymore."

There, that was an answer.

Well, it would have been to anyone else. But Beau *wasn't* anyone else. She knew almost everything about me.

If she'd been on the circuit with me, she'd have known the horrific truth, but her absence had made it easier to keep it a secret.

Oddly enough, I didn't like having secrets from her.

"You've been with them since the beginning," she pointed out, like I didn't already know.

I'd worked with Sabre since I'd graduated into Formula One, and not once had I realized that they'd been bribing other drivers on the team to make sure that I won.

By any means necessary.

It was one thing for a team to back a driver, to have their players duke it out on the track, but the way John had made it sound, I knew he'd gotten kickbacks.

Goddamn kickbacks to let me win.

How could I tell Beau that?

Every victory I'd celebrated, smug in my own success, proud of my achievements—all of them meant shit because I'd been handed them on a platter.

"Are you going to keep the dog?"

"What?" She shook her head at the change of topic. "Go back to what you were saying about Sabre. What aren't you telling me?"

So much.

There were so many things I wasn't telling her now.

My secrets had been building and building over the past year, until I felt like I was choking on them.

She'd always been my go-to person to share this kind of nonsense with, but ever since that race where John died, something had clicked in my head.

Something I'd been chasing to switch off.

"It doesn't matter, Beau-Peep," I said on a sigh when I couldn't get the words out.

She tilted her head to the side but surprised me by dropping it. "I don't know if I'll keep him. He probably doesn't want to be around me. I scared him when I yelled."

I grimaced. "I deserved it."

"Yes," was her annoyed retort. "You damn well did, but I didn't mean to scare him."

"Just me?"

She smirked at me. "You can take it, big boy."

I snorted at that then moved over to the Chesterfield closest to me and slumped onto it. The second I did, I had to hide the fact that I cringed.

Fuck.

My goddamn shoulder.

"Shouldn't you be getting back to your party?" Beau questioned, breaking into the haze of pain that surrounded me.

It took me a few seconds to answer, "If anyone can leave it behind it's the guest of honor. Plus, it's underway. They've no idea where anyone is, never mind me."

"I'm sure your mom misses you."

Well, that was because Mom had a superpower where her kids and husbands were concerned.

I wasn't sure if she'd grown eyes in the back of her head over the years, but whether they were there or not, she knew most of the stunts we pulled moments after they were through.

Thinking about her had a smile drifting onto my lips.

It was good to be back.

I hadn't returned since the accident aside from attending the British Grand Prix, but I hadn't come home. Mostly because everyone in the family always nagged me whenever I visited.

It was easier to focus on what I had to do when they were here and I was away from the UK.

Concerns about my safety were appreciated, but they didn't ease the shame and mortification that gnawed at me every day.

I'd proven myself now.

The humiliation of John's sneers had yet to fade.

Maybe they never would.

Letting my head flop back against the rest, I muttered, "Are you happy, Beau?"

I wasn't sure why I asked.

If it was because thinking about Mom and how happy she was to have her kids under the same roof again triggered the question, or if it was because I was *unhappy*.

A year of striving, of difficult calculations and tough training, and I still didn't feel the accomplishment I was hoping.

I'd won the championship.

I could do it on my own without any help from Sabre.

That didn't take away from the fact that John was dead.

It didn't resolve whatever was going on with Beau and me.

That didn't mean I knew what the next year held. I had plans, sure, but nothing was ever set in stone.

She was quiet a second, then she drifted over to me. The soft scent of her perfume lingered in the air—cotton and lily—and she perched her butt on the armrest.

I *ached* with the need to haul her onto my lap.

It was a craving worse than nicotine or heroin.

I clenched my fingers together to stop myself, but it hurt.

It fucking hurt.

"What's happiness?"

It took a second for me to realize that was her answer.

Okay, this was my prompt to wade out of my own self-pity because what in the hell kind of a reply was that?

"Only unhappy people would say that."

"Maybe," she confirmed. "I don't really know what I am. I'm not unhappy. But am I happy? I'm not sure. I'm happier knowing you've quit."

I rolled my eyes. "That was all it took? Gee, I should have guessed."

She kicked me with her foot. The point on her pump dug into my calf, but while it kind of hurt, it was the tip of the iceberg.

I'd been shoving aside a lot of injuries over the past two years, and they were creeping up on me.

I was barely twenty-three, but some mornings I hobbled around worse than my fathers did.

"I was wondering..."

"What were you wondering, Jack?" she asked quietly.

I rocked my head to the side, looking at her, wondering why I always felt as if we were alone in the world when she stared at me like she saw no one else, nothing else, and I rumbled, "Will you come to Veronia with me?"

Her shoulders straightened. "Huh?"

"Veronia? You know that tiny kingdom in Europe?" I teased, unable to help myself.

"I know where it is, Jackass." She kicked me with her shoe again. "I... why? I didn't think you liked it there."

My nose crinkled. "I don't hate it, it's just... weird."

"Weird?"

"Weird." I nodded my confirmation. "Tin's going to be the king someday. It's annoying."

"Because he'll literally be the boss of you? Can lop off your head if you piss him off?"

"Something like that," I drawled.

"He won't be king. He'll be Alice's consort, won't he?"

I shrugged. "Still powerful enough to be a pain in my ass."

Her smile packed the punch of a fifty-megawatt light. "You need that. It's good for you to realize the sun doesn't rise and set on you."

"Is that what you think, Beau? That I feel like that?" The question was more softly posed than I wanted, but I couldn't call the words back. Nor could I stop the next ones from falling from my lips: "Is that why you've been acting so strange with me recently? Because you really think I live up to my nickname?"

Silence fell between us, but then, slowly, she murmured, "You need to think hard and fast if you really want the answer to that question."

"Why wouldn't I?"

"Because you're not prepared for the truth."

I snorted. "Don't be dumb."

She shoved me. "I'm not being dumb. Don't say shit like that." Before I could do more than grumble, she retorted, "Why would you want me in Veronia with you if you think I've been strange around you?"

"You're always strange to a certain extent."

I didn't need to look into her eyes to know she was rolling them.

"You're such a charmer. I swear it's a good thing you race cars because otherwise you'd never get laid." She shook her head. "I'm going to London."

I blinked. "Huh?"

"I'm going to London," Beau repeated.

"For a weekend break?"

"No. Permanently. I decided I'm going to live there."

"Why?"

"Why not?"

"That's not an answer."

Jealousy began stirring inside me, its toxicity almost stealing my breath.

She heaved a sigh. "Because I want to? Because it's time I did something with my life?"

"Are you going to college?"

"No," she mumbled as she twisted away from me and stroked the nosy puppy who'd ambled closer to investigate the situation.

As she did, I got a perfect glimpse of her tits plumped up over the neckline of her dress, and I quickly looked away.

I hated when she wore dresses like this for that reason alone. I'd seen her in three since I'd known her.

Each one had become a regular feature in my spank-bank material.

"No?" I muttered after a couple seconds. "Then what's the game plan? You're just going to go and be a waitress there instead of here, only you'll have to pay rent?"

"You can be such a dick without even trying, Jack," she whispered after a couple of seconds. "Is that all I am to you? A waitress who lives off her dad?"

"Don't be ridiculous," I argued.

"Who's being ridiculous? That's exactly what you fucking said."

She leaped to her feet and swirled around, making that skirt twirl about her thighs and calves.

Everything in me itched to kiss her out of her funk, but that wasn't my job.

I was the best friend.

Fuck.

I thought about how to phrase what I was trying to say, but it wasn't that easy.

We never talked about the people we dated.

She bitched about the women I hung out with, mostly because she said they were too dumb to breathe—and she had a point. But that was the extent of our talks.

Still... London? I had a feeling there was someone involved in that decision.

Beau would never do that kind of thing on her own. She was too much of a homebody.

Unless her home had become someone.

That hurt.

That really *hurt*.

"That's a big move," I said cautiously, almost wheezing the words out.

"Not really. It's not that far away. Your mom said I could stay at your townhouse until I get myself settled in the city."

Note to self: kill Mom.

Didn't she remember how dangerous London was?

I cast her a look, and I couldn't stop myself from asking, from *torturing myself*: "Are you going there to be with a girlfriend?"

Her brow puckered. "My girlfriends are here. Your sisters, remember?"

"I get that you don't want to talk about this with other people, Beau, but I'm not other people," I reminded her gruffly, trying not to be hurt about her inability to share something so intrinsic as this with me.

For years, I'd told her *everything*. This shit with John was not the tip of the iceberg but most of it.

She twisted to look at me. "I know you're not other people, Jack, but what don't I want to talk about with you?"

I tugged on my collar. "You know, girlfriends."

"Huh?" She scowled at me. "I'm literally friends with you and the twins. I have acquaintances, I guess, but—"

"For God's sake, Beau," I snapped, watching as she jumped in surprise at my outburst. "I'm talking about your love life! It's been years now. I've been patient."

"Patient with what?" she snapped back, her temper stirred because I'd made her jump.

"The fact you haven't come out."

"Come out? Come out of where?"

Her bewilderment pissed me off. "The closet, dammit."

She blinked at me. "The closet?" She blinked again then tugged at her skirt, mouthing, 'closet' to herself. Then, she blurted, "You think I'm gay?"

"I don't think. I know," I spat, folding my arms across my chest. "I wish to fuck you weren't, but here we are. I know you're gay. I'm your best friend, and I should know shit like this. Maybe this is why you're constantly angry with me, because you feel bad for not sharing shit like this—"

"Shit like the fact that I'm gay?" she interrupted, wide-eyed.

"Yes."

I huffed, thinking about Shiloh and Jude and Penelope—God, I'd hated her the most—and all the others who hovered around her under the guise of being *girl friends* when they were actually girlfriends.

Those others who had the *right* to stare at her tits when I had zero rights.

"I'm hurt that you think I wouldn't accept that side of you. That you didn't feel like we could talk about this."

That wasn't a lie.

For all that I wished she were straight, she wasn't.

It was a shitty, crummy, screwed up, unfair fact of life but we were best friends.

I had her back.

Always.

Even if I couldn't get her *on* her back.

"Why would you wish I weren't gay?"

Her words were like a slap to the face.

Fuck.

I needed to backpedal.

But how?

Fuck.

Couldn't I have inherited at least one genius brain cell from my dads?

"It doesn't matter."

Great.

That'd work with a friend who sniffed out information better than a Doberman scented and mauled home invaders.

Way to go, Jackass.

Talk about living up to my nickname.

"It does, Jack. It matters." She tilted her head to the side. "Why do you wish that?"

Why wasn't she letting this drop?

I shot her a mutinous glance then stared fixedly at the fire.

She'd get the point eventually—this was not a conversation I wanted to have.

Then, she signed the death warrant on our friendship.

She pressed her hand to my leg, leaned into me, and demanded, "Jack! Tell me why you wish that!"

Stung and pissed off, agitated and jealous, I hissed, "Because I know that means we can never be anything more than best friends."

SIX

BEAU

His fury was delicious.

I'd seen him in a rage and had always wished he'd break that temper out on me, but as much as I was understanding what he was saying, I was also not understanding it.

"Jack," I told him softly.

"What?" he spat, angry and exasperated.

Hope flickered inside me.

I know that means we can never be anything more than best friends.

That meant he wanted more.

There was no misinterpreting that.

I reached out and grabbed his hand. "I'm not sure why you think this, but..." I hesitated. "I'm not gay."

He whipped around to look at me, his attention no longer on the fire in the hearth. "What?"

"I'm not gay," I said again.

"You are."

"I'm not."

He snapped, "You are. You can tell me, Beau. You can tell me anything."

"I'm not gay," I repeated. "I don't have anything to tell you."

"But... Jude."

The server?

I didn't see a correlation.

"What about her?"

"She was looking at your tits."

"I didn't look at hers," I reasoned as more of that foolish hope began to blossom inside me.

Had he been a jackass earlier because he was jealous?

A thrill buzzed through me.

Only his accusatory: "You like women," dampened it.

Temper slowly stirring even as my anticipation grew, I shrugged. "I do. Not as much as you," I drawled, meaning that in more ways than one. "But yes. I'm bi. Not gay. This isn't 2020. Do we have to come out of the closet now? Can't we just want and be with whomever we choose?"

"You never talk about guys, or men you want to date," he snarled, sounding angrier than before.

There was a very distinct reason for my never talking about other guys.

His accusative tone hadn't died, and though it was pissing me off, I felt like I was wading through quicksand to reach solid ground.

A solid ground that was very different terrain to what it had been before I'd dived headfirst into it.

But if this were a comedy of errors, then I'd take it to the bank, because if Jack's anger was anything to go by, he wanted me.

Maybe as much as I wanted him.

Jesus.

Could all these years of pining simply have been a misunderstanding?

It took a lot of guts to rasp, "The man I want to date doesn't want me."

"Is he blind? What the hell's wrong with him?"

My lips twitched, and his complete lack of insight into who I was talking about eased my nerves. "He thinks I'm gay."

For a second, Jack just looked at me.

Then his eyes narrowed.

Then he growled, "Me?"

That growl hit all the good spots, and I meant every single one.

I felt that in my core, and I almost shivered in response.

"Yes," I breathed, hope stirring inside me. "You."

His nostrils flared and he rasped, "You're not gay."

"I'm really not."

"You're bi."

"I am." I placed my hand on his knee again, but this time I squeezed.

He said again, "Jude—"

"She can want me, but that doesn't mean I want her." Hesitantly, I asked, "Does that change things? Knowing I'm not gay?"

His jaw worked, then, his voice raw, loaded with so much emotion and feeling that it set my nerves on fire, he whispered, "Beau, you need to get off this sofa if you're not prepared for me to kiss you."

I stared at him as an ache blossomed in my being that only he could ease.

"Why would I do that, Jack? When I've been waiting for you to kiss me since I was fifteen?"

That was when I'd realized why my braids always sucked— because I wanted his hands in my hair.

On me.

It was when I'd woken up from my grief because his family had drawn me into their circle, finally making me feel secure.

My words had a snarl escaping him, the sound angry, but when his hands cupped my face and he drew me to him, it was with a tenderness I'd come to expect from him.

From the times when he *had* braided my hair. Or how he always had tea in his room for me. Or when I'd been puking after drinking too much at one of his victory parties.

But this was different.

And it made me tremble.

Made the tiny hairs at the back of my neck stand on edge.

Made every nerve in my being jolt like I'd been shocked with electricity.

His fingers slid along my cheeks, not stopping until I felt each individual digit cupping my skull, until I was held firmly in his grasp.

Then his breath brushed my lips, making them tremble.

A part of me felt sure this was a dream.

After years of pining... of wishing... hoping... jealousy and fear and hurt... and he was about to kiss me.

His lips were two inches from mine.

One.

A half-inch.

A quarter-inch.

The lights flickered on.

"Jack, what the hell? It wasn't Daisy. It was Chester. Get it right —" A sharp screech sounded from the doorway, and I jerked back fast enough that I almost fell off the sofa. "Oh, my God! Were you about to kiss Beau?"

Jack's hands shot out to grab me, and his head swiveled around to glower at his sister all while he made sure I didn't fall on my ass.

If looks could kill, then she'd be dead.

Stone.

Cold.

Dead.

And I'd help bury the body.

My cheeks burned; perspiration prickled on my brow as I cringed so hard my muscles almost went into a cramp.

Then Jack made his move.

He dragged me into his side, his arm coming around me in a

possessive clutch that made my heart soar and had my vocal cords locking down as I choked on my relief.

In a tone that was cool enough to turn his sister into a block of ice, he declared, "Beau and I are an item now."

That declaration sent my system into overdrive.

More so than what our almost-kiss had done.

He'd claimed me.

We hadn't even kissed.

He'd thought I was gay three minutes ago.

But I was his now.

Typical Jackass, but thank the frickin' Lord for him.

Deciding to own it, my hand reached for his in a silent show of support.

Ever the detail-oriented drama queen, Rosie saw my hand, took note of where it was—on his lap—then staggered over to the other sofa and flopped onto it.

Her aghast stare flicked between the pair of us as she whispered, "But you're like brother and sister."

"No. We're not," Jack rumbled, and he moved slightly.

His leg shifting.

It caught my attention, and I knew why he'd moved.

He had a hard-on.

For me.

Sending Mama, Jesus, Yoda, and any other deity who was listening all my gratitude, I watched as Rosie's nose crinkled. "How long's this been going on?"

I heard the accusation. Knew it was aimed at me. Not that I really blamed her.

In her shoes, I'd have been pissed too, but even though she was directing the question at me, I let Jack handle this.

Why?

I guessed my vocal cords really were on hiatus.

I had a feeling they would be until Jack kissed me.

"Four minutes," Jack growled. "You interrupted us before it could reach five."

"You were going to kiss in my bedroom? That's skeevy."

She did look green around the gills.

Jack grabbed my hand and launched himself off the sofa. "If you think that's skeevy, then don't go anywhere near my bedroom for the next twenty-four hours."

My brows rose at that assertion, but I jolted when he dragged me up with him. I shot Rosie an apologetic glance over my shoulder, and for the first time in our friendship, when she looked *that* way, I didn't immediately rush to her side to comfort her.

Rosie and social cues didn't go hand in hand.

She was like her dad—Devon—in that sense. And when things were confusing, she got distressed.

Guilt started to swirl inside me as Jack hauled me down the hallway toward his rooms, and the second I was inside his private space, my voice made a reappearance.

Tugging on his hand, I told him uneasily, "She doesn't understand."

"She'll figure it out soon enough," he rasped, watching as I stayed close to the door.

I swallowed, and that was when I saw his gaze flicker like he'd noticed.

Which was when I realized that his eyes were on every move I made.

He tracked me.

Like a wolf would a doe in the ancient forest behind his manor house.

And I shouldn't have wanted to melt but I'd spent years craving this man, desperate to be at the center of his attention, wishing I had the right to act on how I felt for him, and now I could.

This, somehow, was happening.

Mouth dry, core burning, body quivering with what that look

represented, I didn't understand what he was talking about at first when he drawled, "She shouldn't pigeonhole people."

My brow furrowed. "Like you didn't."

"You never mentioned a single man you even crushed on, Beau. If you had, tonight wouldn't be the first time we kissed."

Biting my lip, I stared at him, saw the heat in his gaze, the edgy vibe to him that told me the anticipation was killing him, and selfish though it was to forget about poor Rosie, I just drowned in the buzz surrounding him.

I'd only ever seen Jack look this way before a race.

A race.

That meant he was as excited about this as he was about getting into his cars, and no one and nothing got between Jack and his Sabre.

"You really want me?" I whispered, resting my weight against the door to his room.

It was either that or crumble to dust in front of him.

"I've wanted you for as long as I've known you, Beau."

Hearing the yearning in his voice, I swallowed. "Why didn't you tell me?"

"Because when you got here, you were still grieving your mother. I kept telling myself that I'd wait, that you were hurting..."

I blinked, hating that he was right. I *had* been grieving. All those years on, I'd been mourning what I'd lost and what I'd found. I'd been fucked up when I got here. Really fucked up.

He sucked in a breath then blurted out, "Then I saw you kissing Penelope and I knew I was destined to always be the 'best friend.'" His jaw worked. "I'm the one who should be insecure here, Beau. Not you."

"I'm not insecure," I argued, and because his temper had made itself known, mine was stirred too.

Any nerves faded as I launched myself away from the door and stalked over to him.

He remained in place, as coolly confident as ever.

So goddamn *secure* in himself, in who he was, in what he was, that he was annoying.

But hot.

So damn hot.

I pressed my hands to his shoulders and murmured, "We're going to cause a stir."

His lips curved. "Beau, you and I do that wherever we go."

And that was when he grabbed me around the waist and dragged me into him. The second our chests brushed against each other, his mouth dropped to mine and there was no more anticipation because this was happening.

This.

Was.

Happening.

Eyes closing, I moaned the instant our lips collided.

Sensation hit me like a slap to the face.

It was everything I'd dreamed it would be and so much more.

I'd kissed. I'd had sex. I knew what was what.

But just the brush of his mouth against mine twisted my insides into one big knot that only he could untangle.

I reached up and ran my hands through his hair, but even that wasn't enough.

Shucking up the skirt of my dress, I climbed him, knowing full well that he'd support me, that he could take my weight.

And he did.

His hands went to my thighs and he dragged his fingers along the outer length of them. Each tip branded me with his fingerprint, and I could think of no better marks than those on my body.

His tongue slid against mine as he angled his head, diving deeper, devouring me, savoring me.

With each thrust, sensation rippled through me, heading straight for my core.

Whimpering against his lips, I cupped his chin and tightened my hold on him.

Slowly, the dynamic shifted.

I didn't just take. I gave.

The battle commenced as our tongues tangled, our panting breaths becoming a part of the soundtrack to a kiss that I'd been dreaming about for as long as I understood that *this* was what mouths existed for.

Not to eat.

Not to drink.

My mouth was made to be kissed by his.

His hands clenched down on my ass, his fingers curving downwards, pressing into my core.

My panties were in the goddamn way.

The idea of him touching me there was enough to make me shudder against him and I pulled back, lips red raw, and whispered, "I need you to touch me, Jack."

I loved this man.

I'd loved him as a best friend.

I looked forward to loving him as more than that.

But when he shuddered in return at my words?

I dove headfirst into whatever was about to happen.

That I could affect him so much made me want to cry with joy and relief.

His words seemed to be torn from him as he rumbled, "If you need to stop, you have to tell me now, Beau."

My lashes fluttered as his mouth dropped to my throat.

Lingering kisses, soft sucks.

Each one a brand.

A signature.

His way of leaving his imprint behind on flesh that had only ever wanted the feel of him against it.

"Which part of 'I need you to touch me,' did you—" I whimpered when he nipped me. "—misunderstand?"

His tongue traced a shape on my earlobe. "I'm making sure you want this."

I groaned, "I don't just want this, Jack. I *need* this."

And I did.

I really, really did.

A growl escaped him at my answer, and he twisted us around, his hands clenching down on my butt, his mouth back on mine as he walked us toward his bed.

With an ease I knew came from a lot of hours spent in the gym *and* experience—yes, that was jealousy talking—he rolled into a seated position on the mattress.

As he did, I widened my legs so I could straddle him better, and the second my pussy collided with his hard-on, we moaned into each other's lips.

I ground into him, my softness to his hardness, and squirmed on his lap. As I did, he pulled back and rasped, "I need you to be naked."

A stunned breath gusted from me. "That means I get to see you naked too."

He laughed, his eyes sparkling with it, and he drawled, "That's how this works, babe."

I cupped his cheek again and breathed, "You're going to be mine, Jack—"

The door barged open.

"For fuck's sake!" Jack snarled, head twisting to the side as Bethan, the other twin, shrieked, "Leave her alone, you jerk!"

My mouth gaped as she rushed over and started dragging me off Jack.

When she nearly dislocated my arm, I cried out, "Bethan! I want to be here! Also, OUCH. Fuck!"

"Of course you don't want to be there! You're gay!"

Jack's temper almost erupted, but then she ended with those two words, and he barked with laughter. "See? I wasn't the only one who thought that." His hands tightened on my ass as he sniped at his sister. "She isn't gay, Bethan."

"She is."

"She isn't," Jack argued.

"She fucking is, Jack, you piece of shit. How could you force her—"

"Force?" he ground out.

"I'm not gay," I confirmed, wading in before they could start fighting.

"She's on top of me, Bethan," Jack pointed out. "If Beau didn't want to be here, she'd tell me."

His sister blinked. "But... all the girlfriends?"

Blowing out a breath to get my fringe off my sticky forehead, I muttered, "I don't get many crushes on guys." His fingers bit into my butt cheeks and I yelped. "No crushes. Just... Jack."

Bethan's eyes rounded. "Just Jack?"

Sheepishly, I nodded. "And I hate labels. I never saw the need to..." I shrugged. "I just thought you accepted me as I was."

Guilt dampened the anger in her eyes. "Oh, honey, we do—"

"Is Tin about to come in here?" Jack grated out, interrupting her. "How about Mom? The dads? How about the entire party comes in to break us up? We could tell the whole world you're Jacksexual, Beau. That'd shut them up."

I should have smacked him for that, but instead, I groaned with laughter.

"Jacksexual?"

Unamused, Bethan growled, "Rosie was worried that Beau was drunk or something. She didn't know what to do."

"Naturally, *you* did." Jack grunted. "Cockblocked. Well, not again." He reached up, tapped my chin, and murmured, "Want to come to London with me tonight?"

My mouth dropped open a second before a smile creased my jaw.

Go to my favorite city in the world with my favorite man in the world?

Instead of all alone?

Instead of trying to start afresh because I couldn't get over a guy I hadn't even been with?

There was only one answer I could give:

"Yes."

SEVEN

Beth and Rosie worriedly watched us from the front steps as I opened the door for Beau, then rounded the car, and climbed behind the wheel.

They stood there, shivering, monitoring the situation, and while their concern was genuine for their friend, I had to admit to being peeved.

What did they think I was?

Bethan had barged into my room like she thought I was raping Beau, and Rosie acted as if it were alien for us to be together.

Didn't they see we were meant to be?

My family had come up with the nickname Beau-Peep when we were nineteen, not me.

Why?

Because where Beau-Peep went, Jack followed like a not-so-little-fucking lamb.

I grunted under my breath as I set off, and like she knew why, Beau murmured, "They're just looking out for me."

It was a testament to how close she was to them, I guessed. My base was wherever I lay my head; my sisters' was at the house. Ever since Beau had stopped coming on the circuit with me, she'd stayed here too and that meant their friendship had grown.

Ours, however, had deteriorated.

Fuck me, I was an idiot.

"I'd never hurt you. They should know that."

Although the last year didn't do much for my rep...

But I was not a fucking rapist, and the way they'd acted had my temper raging once more.

"Maybe they were trying to save me from myself."

Her words cut the wind from my sails and had me snagging my hand in hers. "I won't let you."

She snorted. "You won't let me save me from myself?"

"No. I'm going to ruin you. For all men and women."

Her laughter reduced some of the tension bracketing my mouth. "You already ruined me for men, and you haven't done anything yet."

I huffed because it was the women who concerned me the most.

They were the biggest source of my jealousy.

Because Beau might never have said a word about her 'friend-ships,' but those bitches sure as hell had.

I'd heard everything.

Everything.

They'd felt threatened by how close we were and had staked their claim.

Because I wasn't as big a jackass as she thought, I kept my lips zipped as I raced us across our estate and toward the houses where staff lived.

She'd told me she had a bag packed, so we were going to collect it. I had ten tons of crap at the house in Kensington anyway, so I didn't need to bring anything with me.

Pulling up outside the property that was already decorated for Christmas with enough string lights to fully illuminate the arched doorway, and a grand wreath made from pinecones and fern leaves around the knocker, I knew the outside would be the only signs of festivity in the house.

No way would her Christmas tree be up yet.

I climbed out first, opened her door for her, and walked her down the path.

I slipped my hand to the small of her back like I'd been wanting to do for nearly ten years, and as my fingers touched her there, her head whipped around to look at me.

"Jack?" she whispered, her eyes big and round in her beautiful face.

The way she said my name had lust arrowing straight down to my dick.

Tonight, at some point, I needed to hear her speak it like that when I was inside her.

I licked my lips at the prospect. "Beau."

My fingertips burrowed against her coat.

Like bare flesh was caressing bare flesh, she shuddered. "Dad won't be back for a while."

Christ.

"You sure? I don't think my dick can stand being that close to heaven only for us to be disturbed again."

Her laughter was soft, amused. "I don't think my pussy can stand it either."

I groaned, hauled her against me, loving how she settled her arms on my shoulders like they should always have been there.

This was Beau.

My brain couldn't get my head around it even if my body totally could.

This was the woman who'd nursed me through the flu when we were in Beijing for a race, who'd picked out the orange skittles of every bag she'd eaten around me because she knew they were my favorite.

This was the woman who had held my hand at my grandmother

Jacinta's funeral and who'd snuggled beside me and had read while I stared into space when my daw, Sawyer, had another cancer scare.

But she was so much more than that too.

I had the affectionate memories, the tender ones, but this was a new phase.

A new dawn.

I reached down and pushed my forehead into hers. "I was dreading that party."

She shivered so I squirreled her deeper into my arms to warm her up. "Why?"

"Because I needed to talk with you."

"And you dreaded it?" She snorted. "Charming."

"You'd been so..." I sighed, rocked my lips down and pressed them to hers in a soft peck. "Hostile. I knew we had to clear the air, and I was concerned."

"Concerned?"

"I thought you didn't want to be friends with me anymore."

She was silent a second. "You were right. I didn't." Before my heart could drop through my stomach, she whispered, "I wanted this. I didn't want to be *just* friends with you anymore. I've dreamed of this. And I know that's dumb—"

"Not dumb," I countered, deciding that it wasn't wise to tell her that every chick I'd banged for the last five years I'd imposed her face on them.

Yeah, definitely wise to keep my mouth shut.

"*Dumb*," she insisted.

One of her hands moved to the back of my neck and she urged me down.

Around us, the air was frigid. The temperature had really dropped, and I was pretty certain that it was going to snow, but wherever our bodies met, heat arced between us.

Her breath caressed my lips, and for the longest time, we just stood like that, acceptance and need coalescing and growing, morphing and changing, until she formed the bridge.

Up on tiptoes she went, and we kissed.

A shaky sigh escaped her, but I didn't feel shaky. I felt on edge, I felt *demanding*.

I wanted her.

Fuck, I'd wanted her for so goddamn long.

The wanting had lasted forever, but here, I had relief in my grasp.

I swept her up, arching her back against my arm so that I could swoop her into my embrace.

Carrying her, I walked us down the path to the doorway.

Blindly, her hand drifted behind her to find the door, and it opened because no one locked their doors on the estate—and I thanked God for that because I couldn't break our kiss if you'd paid me.

As I walked into the warmth of the house, I twisted her around and pressed her against the door, encouraging her legs to part and cup my hips.

Heaven.

I could die now.

Seriously.

Her lips ate at mine, feasted on them, and as I pushed her into the door, I encouraged one of her legs to droop down to the ground by unhitching it from my hip.

With the freedom that gave me, I slipped one hand up her leg, letting the fabric fall by the wayside as I moved it higher and higher, not stopping until my fingers played with the hem of her panties.

A deep moan whispered from her as I maneuvered between us, rocking the digits over to the crotch and sliding my pointer finger down the central line of her slit.

I pulled back just so I could whisper, "You know how long I've wanted you?"

"How long?" she breathed, her eyes dazed and her head arching back against the door in a pose of pure desire as I teased her pussy.

The words turned broken as I finally let my finger slide beneath the fabric to the slick folds beneath.

"Since we were fourteen. When I saw you in the yard the day you moved in.

"You were like a sprite floating around the courtyard. I noticed you before you noticed me. I was in that damn tree so I could watch you…" My mouth pecked at hers. "You were so unhappy, so sad, and I wanted nothing more than to make you smile."

I nipped her bottom lip, encouraging her tongue out to play as I dug beneath her panties and found home.

"Oh, Christ," she groaned as I explored her wetness, dragging my fingertips through it, coating them in her juices as I found her clit.

A soft wail escaped her until I quieted her by joining our mouths once more, and I rubbed her clit until she was panting, her kiss growing frantic, her nails digging into my skull as pleasure neared.

I knew when she was about to come.

I pulled back specifically so that I could watch her orgasm.

A sight that I'd been sure would forever be denied to me, I savored.

I reveled.

It was beautiful.

She was beautiful.

Her brow puckered, her eyes clenched, and her jaw tightened as it cascaded through her.

She clung to me, nails still digging in deep, her body undulating against mine, as she called out brokenly, making two syllables out of one, "Jack."

That was when I knew for certain—she would always be mine.

I just had to hold onto her and never let her fucking go.

I pressed my mouth to hers, slowly sampling her pleasure-slack lips, then I crooned, "Beau."

Her eyes popped open, and she watched me move my hand away from her pussy, raise it to my lips, and suck my index finger in deep.

As I cleaned it, her pupils dilated, and she rasped, "I need you."

I hummed as I sucked her flavor into me. "What do you want me to do about it?" I taunted, watching the heat in her eyes start to simmer.

She unhitched her other leg, and in a move that was pure Beau, she shoved me away then snatched a hold of my hand, dragging me into the living room just off the front hall.

Unclasping our fingers, she headed over to the fireplace where the logs were banked, more embers than anything else, and with the glow behind her, kicked off her shoes, dragged off her coat, and tossed it on the nearby armchair.

Her movements were utilitarian.

This was not a strip show.

But my dick hardened as she unfastened her zipper and slipped out of the dress.

No bra.

Just markings from the bones from a corset on her waist and chest.

I wanted to kiss each stripe.

And dear God... were her nipples pierced?

She lowered her panties.

Then she was standing there, bold as brass, looking at me.

Naked.

Unashamed.

Totally confident.

My mouth was dry.

My dick pounded.

And my mind exploded with possibilities.

She let me look my fill, her self-assured stance something that I hadn't anticipated as I explored her curves with my eyes.

"You're never allowed to wear clothes around me again."

A laugh escaped her at my command, and she reached up and taunted me by using her finger to tease the tip of her nipple. "Not sure your sisters or parents would survive that."

I sniffed. "They shouldn't look at what's mine anyway."

Her eyes widened at that. "Yours?"

That damnable finger I was jealous of started trailing around the circle of her areola, tugging on her nipple in a way that made my mouth water.

"Mine," I ground out the confirmation, dragging off my coat at my declaration of intent as she caressed herself.

I shrugged out of my suit jacket then unknotted my bowtie enough to tug it away and throw it on the floor. I pulled at my shirt and finally slipped out of my pants after I toed off my shoes.

I didn't stalk toward her. Instead, I sat on the sofa and murmured, "You going to tell me I'm not as much yours as you're mine?"

Her nostrils flared.

I grabbed my dick and jacked it a few times. Her gaze followed the movement as her tongue peeped out to circle her lips.

"That this doesn't belong to you like your pussy belongs to me?"

Her hand faltered, and for a second, she hovered, then she tipped up her chin. "Are you clean?"

I blinked.

Fuck.

We hadn't had *the* conversation.

"Yeah, I'm clean. Never had unprotected sex before."

She narrowed her eyes at me. "No blowjobs?"

"Only with condoms. Beau, do you think I wanted a surprise baby? I made sure I put a knot in those goddamn things when I was done."

She squinted at me then murmured, "I'm protected."

"You only had girlfriends," I pointed out, which made me huff over where the sexy times had derailed. "This is the unsexiest conversation we've ever had."

That was a record, as well.

Because very little was off the table where we were concerned.

"Remember when I got my period at the after-party in Monaco?"

"Yes?"

"I wasn't about to let that happen again. I have an implant."

My nostrils flared. "So... we can do this raw?"

She shuddered, nodded, and like we hadn't just had an insensitive conversation, she rushed at me with a desperation I felt.

To be inside Beau, *naked.* Jesus, I'd fucking die when I got the tip in her.

Straddling me, she rested her ass on my thighs and whispered, "You mean it?"

"What?"

"About us belonging to each other?"

Possessiveness roared through me and made my voice sound like gravel as I told her, "I do."

And I did.

"Wanted you for too long to dick around." I reached up and cupped her breast. "Wanted these in my hands for years. Wanted the taste of your cunt on my lips since forever—"

"Jack!" she chided, and I knew her cheeks would be burning.

Smiling, I leaned forward. "Your cunt belongs to me, that pretty pussy is mine—"

She kissed me to shut me up.

Like I knew she would.

Laughing into her kiss, I hauled her into me with my free hand, not stopping until she was pressed up against me.

When her slickness enveloped my cock, I could feel my control start to break, and as she rocked her hips, coating me in her wetness, I hissed under my breath.

Beau pushed my dick flat against my belly and then rubbed up against it as she loomed over me, her hair spilling around us both, perfuming the air with 'Snow Fairy' and drugging me with her scent.

As I groaned, she whispered, "Your dick is mine."

"It is," I agreed immediately because I heard her shy hesitation and didn't want her to feel like that around me.

My Beau was *never* shy with me.

"I want it inside me."

Her voice was a little stronger.

"Nowhere else it wants to be."

She nipped the butt of my chin, then she angled higher on my lap, grabbed my dick, and she brought me home.

Her wet heat surrounded me, velvet tissues caving into the insistent thrust as I sank in deep.

She shuddered against me as we joined together, and when her butt was back to resting on my lap, a soft laugh escaped her.

I grabbed the back of her neck and married our foreheads to each other. "Now isn't a laughing matter."

This time, her laughter sounded more dazed. "Thirty minutes ago, you thought I was gay."

"You don't feel gay now," I rumbled.

She gulped, arched her hips. "How do I feel?"

"Like heaven," I whispered, feasting on her mouth as my hands went to her hips to encourage her to move.

With the backlight of the fire surrounding her, and encompassed in its halo, she looked like an angel.

My angel.

Unforgettable.

Memorable.

I knew this moment would be stamped in my memory banks for as long as I lived.

And then the time for romantic thoughts drifted away as she started to rock harder into me, faster. Angling high on her knees until I was almost pulled free of her, she sank all the way down.

I let my tongue find the piercings on her clavicle as one hand explored her tit, hissing when I found the two tiny studs either side of her nipple. The other aimed for her clit, discovered it, and rubbed it, just so I could feel the clutch and play of her inner muscles.

That was when I took over.

I had no choice but to do so.

Thrusting from beneath, moving faster, harder, deeper, we were both meeting each other in the middle, driving the pleasure home, flinging us both into the unknown while tucked up in each other's embrace.

And that, of course, rammed it home like nothing else could—if I'd died on the track from the stunts I'd pulled over the years, I'd never have experienced this.

Before the grounding thought could settle in, the ecstasy hit me worse than any G-Force speeds ever could.

Better than an adrenaline spike from a Grand Prix win.

This, I realized, was what I'd been chasing all these fucking years.

This.

EIGHT

BEAU

"Does everyone think I'm gay?"

Jack's attention shifted from the road and quickly darted over to me. "Yes."

I frowned at the dark roads that were lit up with the lights of his 'super' car. "Dad can't—"

He shrugged. "Don't know about your dad. It's not something I've ever talked about with him."

"I'd have loved to be a fly on the wall for that conversation," I said with a laugh, grinning when he huffed.

"I wish I had. Maybe he'd have put me out of my misery sooner."

A soft smile danced on my lips as I thought about what had just happened in my front room.

We'd done it.

I had actually done the deed with Jack Dubois.

I thought about how his tongue had tasted my smile earlier as he woke me up, his hands exploring my back, touching me like he couldn't get enough of the feel of me, asking if I still wanted to go to London.

That was where we were headed now.

Huh.

That reminded me...

"Why were you mad about me going to London?"

"Thought you were moving in with someone. Why else would you be leaving everything you love behind?"

I shot him a glare he couldn't see in the dark. "Women can move to the city if they want. What is this? 1920?"

"Think you'll find women moved to the city before that." He laughed. "I'm not saying you *couldn't* do it; I'm saying *you* wouldn't do it without a good reason."

"What kind of logic is that?"

"You like home too much," he said simply.

My brow furrowed. "You make me sound boring."

"You're putting words in my mouth."

From experience, I knew why Jack was so calm—he'd just gotten laid. And I'd been feeling the after-effects of post-coital glow too.

So why was I sniping at him?

Because it was a force of habit?

Or because that was what we did?

I reached up and rubbed my bottom lip, trying to understand why I was feeling riled up.

His hand landed on my lap.

His fingers curved into my inner thigh.

They squeezed.

And I started breathing again.

The confidence in that one move made my heart pound.

The sense of ownership was *thrilling*.

"Stop overthinking this," Jack said easily.

"Stop knowing me so well."

"Impossible." Another squeeze. "Do you have work lined up in London?"

"No. I just thought I'd get a job in a cafe or something."

"How long did you intend on staying at the townhouse?"

"Just until I got a job and arranged for alternative accommodation."

"Were you going to live in a studio?"

I could hear the frown in his voice. "Maybe." I turned away to look at the road.

"What the hell were you thinking?"

"That I had to get away. That I had to do something with my life," I whispered.

"You've done plenty," he argued.

"Not enough. I don't want to look back and think I wasted my youth." Then, I threw caution to the wind and told him, "I needed distance from you. I wanted space and maybe the chance of finding someone without your specter hovering over things and messing my love life up."

He was silent a second, then, as smooth as silk, he told me, "I'll haunt you for the rest of your life."

My lips twitched. "Good to know."

"I won't be friendly."

"No Casper?" I pouted. "No fair."

"I'm talking poltergeists. Anyone who sniffs around you, I'll bring out the whole third act: throwing shit across the room, always moving their food one inch away from their reach, giving them wedgies." Another squeeze. "Beau, you're not wasting your life. You've visited all five continents. I know because I was there. You've done things most people wouldn't dream of—"

"Those were your dreams," I said. "Not mine. You're right about me being a homebody. I didn't even want to travel." Then, I choked out the embarrassing admission, "I just didn't want to be parted from you."

He turned to cast me a quick glance, making no comment other than to question, "What are your dreams?"

I couldn't get even more embarrassed though because his fingers made small, soothing circles on my inner thigh.

Who knew there was something better than a hug for mortification?

It made it easier to say, "That's the problem. I don't really know."

Up ahead, traffic started to grow because we were approaching London. He switched lanes a few times, always staying under the speed limit.

Having a man like Jack in a traffic jam was always amusing. A bit like giving a tiger a hamster's wheel to exercise in.

He was quiet for so long that I thought he was just going to drop our conversation, but then he murmured, "Okay, so we need to figure out what your dreams are."

I shot him a look from the corner of my eye and snuggled deeper into the turtleneck I'd changed into before I left the house. The car was warm enough to make me sleepy. It wasn't even eleven but it had been a long day.

Unexpected.

Full of happy surprises.

Weird ones too.

But still a *long* one.

"How do we figure out what my dreams are?" I asked, oddly touched that he'd been thinking about my predicament as he drove and hadn't just been thinking that I was a whining moron.

"I'm not sure." He drummed his fingers against the wheel as we veered into busier lanes of traffic. "How about we grab a college prospectus and see if there are any degrees you want to take?"

That wasn't a bad idea, but...

"You know I hate school."

He snorted. "You and me both, babe."

Inside, I squirmed.

Babe.

It was beyond ridiculous to get hot under the collar because he called me something I'd heard him label a hundred other women he'd fucked on the circuit.

Right?!

Mad at myself for being turned on, I tuned in at the last minute when he queried, "You wanna do something artsy? You love painting, don't you?"

My nose crinkled. "No. Well, I love painting but I don't want to study it."

"Music?"

"You know I have a crappy ear." I heaved a sigh. "I've been through this myself, and I don't really know what I'm good at."

"That's easy."

I blinked. "It is?" He sounded so confident, *too* confident. "What am I good at?"

"Strategy."

Grunting, I mumbled, "That's not exactly useful."

"Ha. It is for me." He tapped my thigh. "Take it back. Strategy is how you win shit. When you stopped traveling with me on the circuit, I lost points without your insight."

"Shut up. You totally didn't."

"I totally did." He cleared his throat. "Okay, so, I will admit that some of those points were lost because I missed you—"

"You did?" I whispered.

His grunt was agitated. "Bet your ass I did. I was homesick."

"Homesick for me?" I breathed.

He reached for my hand. "You *are* my home, Beau. Haven't you figured that out yet?"

I told myself it was only because we were stuck in traffic. That if we'd been moving, I wouldn't have done something so irresponsible because, where cars were concerned, we didn't need two irresponsible people in the front seats.

But we *were* stuck in traffic.

And I had to kiss him.

I just had to.

I unfastened the seat belt and grabbed him by the ears, tugging him and tilting him so that I could reach his mouth.

For a second, I just dived right in.

His flavor sank into me, seeping into every lost part of me that had been pining for him for years like the pathetic bitch I was. Pining for a man who'd been mine as long as I'd been his.

A stupid misunderstanding.

It wasn't even miscommunication.

It was...

I didn't even know.

At that moment, I didn't care.

I was just happy that was over with.

His lips tugged at mine, biting and nipping, claiming and marking.

I groaned long and low as one hand cupped my breast through my sweater, and I sagged as I cupped his dick, feeling him thick and hard in my hand.

Horns hooted behind me, and I jerked in surprise, pulling back to find that there was a good hundred feet of open space in front of us.

"Shit," Jack hissed before he took off.

Of course, I saw the flash of a speed camera.

Oops.

NINE

JACK

As we pulled up outside the townhouse that had been my second home as a kid and the light in the dash flickered on, I studied her mouth in the hazy illumination.

Her lips were still pink, red, the line around them blurred.

I'd done that.

Me.

My gaze dropped down to the studs on her clavicle, but my mind was thinking about *other* piercings, and I rumbled, "If I'd known your nipples were pierced before..." I shook my head when words failed me.

"What would you have done?" Beau taunted.

"Sobbed."

She laughed, twisted in her seat, and rasped, "You wouldn't."

"I would." I grunted. "You know you've got it bad for someone when you imagine them with another beautiful woman and aren't turned on but depressed."

"There's a lot to unpack there."

"Every guy likes some lesbian action." My nose crinkled at the bridge. "Unless you're me. And you're you." My eyes narrowed on her. "I don't like the thought of you fucking anyone else."

She sniffed. "Lucky for you that I wasn't the manwhore that you are."

I grimaced. "I had a lot of anger and resentment issues."

"What about?"

"Your girlfriends used to rub my nose in your relationships."

Tensing, she asked, "You don't mean literally, do you?"

Almost snorting at that, I retorted, "No, they didn't bring me your used panties and shove my face in them."

"Ew," she mewled. "Gross!"

My smirk died as I told her, "I've always been jealous of you, and that you never told me about them, that they were always the ones shoving your relationship status in my face, just made it worse."

I watched as she bit her lip a second before the light in the dash faded and died.

"I'm sorry, Jack. You know I don't like labels. I just never thought about defining myself in that way. The relationships were all super casual."

She was about to get *very* comfortable with labels.

Whether she liked it or not.

"All of them? Not one was serious?"

"No. Not one."

I almost wished I could shove two fingers in the face of Penelope, her first girlfriend, but that would have made me look childish.

In fact, screw it.

If she'd have walked down the street this second, I'd have stuck my goddamn tongue out.

"If I'd known," she continued, her hand clutching mine, "I'd have made them apologize."

"It wouldn't have mattered. Just knowing you were with them was enough to piss me off. It wasn't your fault. My feelings were something I had to deal with."

"So you fucked anything in a short skirt?"

I wasn't going to apologize for my coping mechanisms. "Yeah."

Beau was quiet a second, and I thought she was about to work her wiles on me to make me apologize for being a manwhore, but instead, she questioned, "Do I look like a lesbian?"

"A hot one."

"Is that supposed to be comforting?" she grumbled.

"What do gay people even look like?" I peered at the neighbors' house, seeing lights on. "Micah and Devlin don't look gay, but I—" My mouth twisted into a laugh.

"What?"

"Nothing."

She grabbed my arm, smiling, "What? What were you going to say?"

"I saw them fucking once."

Her eyes rounded and she turned to peer at the townhouse beside ours. It was owned by a lord who spent most of his time in New York. She'd been here often enough that she knew them too.

"You saw Micah and Devlin having sex?" she whispered.

"They can't hear," I retorted before I whispered back, "I wish I'd told you that before. From that blush alone, I'd have known you weren't gay."

A choked laugh escaped her, but it ended on a soft huff. "I wish you'd told me too."

"I thought you didn't like other men," I sniped.

"I don't. But Micah and Devlin..." She shrugged. "They're just... Micah and Devlin."

Even I had to admit they were hot. And I didn't have a gay bone in my body.

Her hand reached out and she trailed her fingers along my jaw. "Is this really happening?"

"It is," I said firmly, snagging her hand in mine and tangling our fingers together. I raised her knuckles to my mouth and kissed them, savoring the fact that I could do that.

That I could touch her in this way, that I could kiss her and hold her and call her terms of endearment.

It seemed impossible, so I understood why she sounded so pensive, but our whole world had just changed in the space of three hours.

"This is the best night of my life."

I groaned. "Why did you have to say that?" She tensed. "You know how competitive I am." She chuckled, but I saw her tension immediately dissipate. "Now I'm going to have to beat this. Buy you tickets to outer space or something just to one-up it."

"Don't be a jackass, Jackass."

My lips twitched. "But I do it so well."

"Oh, that you do." She turned to peer over at our neighbors' place. "I wonder if they're fucking now."

I snorted. "Doubt it. You know Devlin's mother lives there most of the time on her own now that her husband died."

"Next time," she said, "you see them, you tell me."

I scoffed, "I'll tie you to the bed first."

She arched a brow. "Didn't know you were kinky."

My lips curved. "You ain't seen nothing yet."

Her giggle set my soul on fire as she shoved open the door and clambered out onto the side of the street.

"Damn, it's cold." She shivered. "Hurry up."

Climbing out of the car, I headed to the trunk and grabbed her bags then flicked the alarm on my Sabre coupé—I'd need to trade this in now I was no longer associated with them—and rounded it to reach her side.

"Gimme the keys," she said, teeth chattering as she darted up the path to let us into the house.

The place was cold, but I knew from experience it wouldn't take long to heat up.

As I dropped her stuff on the floor by the door, I did my usual— looked at the wall of family achievements.

It was dumb, but it had taken so long for anything of mine to appear on there that it was always the first thing I looked at.

I wasn't like my siblings. Hadn't gone to college, hadn't *wanted* to. My mind was more mechanical.

In another life, I might have been an engineer or something like that, but now, I was just happy tinkering with cars.

The wall housed my parents' achievements as well as my brother and sisters'.

There were two Nobel prizes, a Pulitzer Prize, an OBE for my father, Sean, and an MBE for *Papa*, Andrei.

Tin, Rosie, and Bethan's degree certificates were up there, their graduation photos. But a shelf had been installed for my trophies—that was when *Vati*'s Academy Award had made an appearance on here too.

My F1 Drivers' Championship trophies were large silver vessels with a gold strand entwined around them with every victor's name since Farina's etched on there.

Some of them might not have been won fairly, but the last one sure as hell had.

A hand tugged at mine. "You okay?"

I shot her a sheepish smile. "It took me a long time to get on there."

"You're basking in your glory?"

"Stupid, huh?"

She turned to look at the wall. "It's a lot to live up to."

God, understatement.

I nodded. "I never felt like I quite fit in."

"I can understand that," she reasoned slowly. "Dad's always been so put together. So self-aware. I've never been like that. And then hanging around you three, it's easy to feel like the charity case."

My mouth gaped. "You can't be serious."

"We can't all win awards and work for The Hague and save every animal under the sun..." Her lips twisted. "*Or* save economies and write award-winning books or fix the world—"

I squeezed her fingers. "You underestimate yourself."

Her smile was sly. "And you don't?"

"Touché." I had to grin, even if it was sheepish. "Are you okay with sleeping in my room?"

She blinked at me. "Jack."

I blinked back. "Beau."

"Do you know how long I've wanted to sleep in your bedroom?"

Because those words were music to my ears, I tugged her over to me and hugged her close to my chest.

Unable to stop myself, I dropped a kiss to her lips. "How long?"

"Since I knew that your dick was the Klondike."

"Klondike?" I snorted. "I mean, babe, it's big. Dunno if it's *that* big."

The twinkle in her eyes made me happy.

Just that twinkle.

Christ, how had I lived without her for the last couple years? Never mind the past fourteen months where we'd barely communicated.

"Well, I don't really have much comparison to gauge with," she said blithely. "But it was plenty big."

Curious, I asked, "You haven't slept with many guys?" I cringed. "I know we shouldn't talk about this but..."

She shrugged. "Told you. You were the only one I was interested in."

I cleared my throat. "So you were a virgin."

"Nope," she said with a snort, and that twinkle turned heated. "You're just the first person to bear a non-silicone penis."

"Do you see why people thought you were gay?" I clucked my tongue. "In fact, I'm going to blame this on you for the rest of our lives—"

"What are you blaming on me?" she grumbled.

"If you'd have just let on that you batted for both teams, I'd have snagged your cock cherry before now."

"My cock cherry?" A laugh escaped her. "We have to tell Rosie that. She'll love it."

"She'll gag."

"Exactly." She beamed at me. "Think there's any food in the kitchen?"

"You hungry?"

"What gave it away?"

"Sarcasm is the lowest form of wit."

"To me, it's the highest." She tugged on my hands. "Well? Food? Rosie dragged me away before I could eat anything, and I've been nervous all day."

"Why?"

"Because I was going to see you again. And because I was dreading it."

"Charming," I retorted, throwing back her words at her. It was definitely her turn to confess... "Why were *you* dreading it?"

"Because I'd have seen some bitch drooling all over you."

"And you wanted to drool all over me?"

"Yep." She began dragging me toward the other end of the house. "Now I've stroked your ego, you have to feed me!"

"Can't we just order in?" I complained as we started to tread downstairs.

"Sure, we can. I want some tea first though."

Before I was born, the townhouse had undergone many renovations to accommodate all the kids, pets, and staff my parents had. What had once been a six-bedroom house with an attic and basement conversion had been redesigned.

Originally, four of the six bedrooms had been converted into offices, but with five kids, that had gone by the by.

The attic was no longer where Mom slept and had been converted into storage, but the basement, which had once been comprised of a dining room and kitchen, was now three times the size thanks to an extension at the back.

With a glass ceiling, on clear nights, you could see the stars.

Below, two further basement floors had been constructed, so everyone had their own space. Tin, Bash, Rosie, Bethan, and I were all above ground, whereas the folks were below it with their own pool to boot.

Because Beau had been here many times, she immediately headed for the kitchen, while I moved over to the TV and switched it on. Hooking it to my phone, I set that on to charge, then as a playlist I liked started, I looked back at her and had the strangest feeling of rightness settle inside me.

We'd been alone here before.

But she'd slept in Rosie or Bethan's room, and I'd gone to my own, wishing that shit were different and we'd be going to *our* bedroom.

"You're staring."

It wasn't an accusation, more an amused remark.

I shrugged. "I like you there."

"In the kitchen?" She arched a brow. "I could have sworn I beat the chauvinism out of you a long time ago."

"You did," I said sheepishly. "I didn't mean in the kitchen. Just... *here*. You look right."

Her eyes softened. "Because we're together?"

"I didn't think it would happen and it feels good, you know?"

"I do know." With the kettle humming in the background, she moved over to me and slipped her arms over my shoulders. "Are you freaking out?"

"No. Are you?"

"No. I, well, I mean I guess it's moving fast. But that's kind of what you do, isn't it?"

Her teasing made me smile. "Where you're concerned, I've made a snail look like a Ferrari." I placed my hands on the small of her back, hugging her tight to me. "You might have to pinch me in the middle of the night."

"I can do that," she said with a laugh before she pressed her lips to mine.

I sighed into that kiss.

Breathed into it.

Felt reborn by it.

The connection between us as friends had always been super-charged, and I knew that my days of dicking around were gone. I'd never sell our friendship short by letting her down. It wasn't in my nature. I was like my dads in that regard.

As I gently stroked her tongue, not to entice or to incite but to savor, we stood there, embracing, swaying slightly to the music until the kettle started whistling on the stove.

Before she pulled away, she said, "This is right, Jack."

I nodded. "It is."

"Jack?"

"Yes?"

"I love you."

I didn't imagine that she'd tell me this with a boiling kettle in the background, but it didn't lessen the impact. Not one iota. Those words settled inside me like lead weights, grounding me.

Stabilizing me.

My throat felt choked as I managed to get out, "I love you too."

We stared into each other's eyes, long enough for the kettle to carry on goddamn raging, then she whispered against my lips, "Are you going to feed me now?"

I squeezed her ass, because I had the right to when I didn't have the right before, and muttered, "Anything to keep this bubble butt happy."

Snorting, she shoved me away, but I saw the smug smile on her lips as she retreated to the kitchen.

I didn't miss the extra sway to her hips she threw in with each step either.

But as I watched her go, I saw her peer at me over her shoulder on the way, and I knew she was making sure I hadn't moved.

That I was here.

That this was happening.

Wanting to reassure her, I told her, "You and me, Beau."

She swallowed. "You and me, Jack."

TEN

BEAU

Jack's bedroom was the biggest because it had once been Devon and Sawyer's office.

It had views over the small private garden out front, and over by the back, if you squinted, you could see Kensington High Street beyond the crescent-shaped avenue where the house was situated.

That meant Harrods was at hand, one of my favorite places in the world.

His bedroom was uber masculine and was done in grays and blacks with leathers and concrete touches that should have been cold but were sleek and elegant instead.

The bed was ensconced inside a leather stand that made it take up twice as much room. The headboard reminded me of a sofa, with two large leather cushions that made watching TV in bed beyond comfortable.

I'd know now.

I'd watched Netflix on it last night because, in the footboard, the TV slid out of a compartment.

It also twisted around so that he could watch it on the two low leather club chairs behind the bed which had a coffee table between them.

To one side, there was a dresser which was littered with just a few of his many awards. Even his nightstands were decorated with them, never mind his bookshelves which lined the back wall.

As I peered around it in the middle of the night, a space I'd dreamed about seeing from this angle, with Jack curved against me, I had no alternative but to pinch him.

Hard.

He jerked in surprise because he'd been dozing, his breathing heavy in my ears. I hadn't realized he had jet lag until he'd gotten into bed and had fallen asleep during an episode of *South Park*.

"What was that for?" he muttered sleepily.

"You told me to pinch you," I reminded him. "And it was better to pinch you than to pinch me."

A breath gusted from his lips as he squeezed me. "You're a sadist, not a masochist. Good to know," he mumbled into my throat, making me smile.

"I'm here, Jack. I'm in bed with you," I whispered, but he'd fallen back asleep.

I didn't disturb him. Just stayed staring at nothing for a while, trying to take it all in.

The silence was comforting because it meant I could hear his breathing, and because he was using me as a teddy bear, I was warm and comfortable. Relaxed and content in a way that I hadn't been for years.

It shouldn't have taken me as long as it did to drift back to sleep, but I was enjoying myself and continued doing so until the next morning when I heard banging on the door.

Jack was out like a light beside me, and I groaned under my breath as the morning glare blared in from the windows we hadn't covered with the shutters.

Squinting, I slapped my hand over my eyes as the noise from the front door echoed through the house, only growing worse once the bell pealed up the stairs.

Disentangling myself from Jack didn't work, and he grumbled and grunted, tightening his arms around me, mumbling, "Don't go yet, Isabeau. Don't leave me yet."

My throat clutched at his words.

He never used my full name so I knew he was dreaming.

Dreaming about me leaving him.

"Jack, if I never had to leave you, that would be a day too soon," I breathed, voice hitching.

Twisting in his hold was difficult, but I managed to, and when I pressed a kiss to his lips, the sounds of the door banging and the bell pealing faded as I felt him stir.

His dick too.

Humming under my breath, I whispered against his mouth, "I need you to let me get out of bed."

"S'all that noise?" he slurred sleepily, but he obeyed.

"The door."

"Doors don't make noise."

My lips curved as I clambered out of bed and rushed over to the window, picking up his discarded shirt along the way and dragging it over my head.

Once I was covered, I opened it and peered over the ledge to look down at the street, shivering as the cold blasted me in the face.

"Sascha?" I called out in surprise.

It wasn't just Sascha, however.

It was the *whole* family.

Dad. Sascha. Devon, Sawyer, Andrei, Kurt, and Sean. Tin. Alice. Her guards. Rosie. Bethan. Only Bash was missing.

"What are you all doing here?" I sputtered.

"Saving you from yourself!" Rosie declared. "Come and let us in."

My brow furrowed. "Saving me from myself?"

"It's cold out here," Devon groused. "Come and open the door."

I shook my head. "Why do I need saving from myself?"

"Sweetheart, it's okay to be gay," Dad informed me kindly.

"It really is," Rosie confirmed.

Oh.

My.

God.

"I'm *bisexual,*" I shrieked. "How many times?! Bethan, I told you—"

"You're clearly in denial," Bethan disregarded. "Jack's turned your head."

My mouth rounded. "You have to be shitting me. You think Jackass turned my head?"

"I heard that," Jack rumbled, yawning as he appeared beside me at the window. He rested his forearms on the ledge and peered over.

I probably shouldn't have been looking at his happy trail, but who was I kidding?

Jack was naked.

Naked.

And beside me.

Damn straight he had *all* my attention.

"Bethan, you just couldn't keep your nose out, could you?" he sniped.

"Jack, come and let us in," Sean demanded, a warning in his voice.

"This is why I left the keys in the door," Jack said, shaking his head. "I knew you'd end up coming here."

I shot him a look. "You did?"

He shrugged. "Had a suspicion when I saw Rosie and Bethan freezing their butts off on the front step as they watched us drive off. They looked like I was taking you to the gallows."

"She's denying who she is for some reason. We're being supportive."

"You're being intrusive," Jack countered. "Trust me, I know Beau isn't gay now."

"Ew," Rosie groaned.

Tin shouted, "Jack, let us in so we can clear this up and we can all fuck off again."

Alice snorted, but Sascha grumbled, "Tin! The neighbors!"

Lights had already started flashing at windows as the neighbors took photos of what was happening in their posh enclave.

I wasn't sure whether the photos were going to be forwarded to the police or shared to social media—knowing this place, it was the former rather than the latter.

"Why is it when Tin swept Alice off her feet, he got a clap on the back and a hoorah, whereas when I make Beau mine, she gets an intervention?" he demanded.

That seemed to stun most of the group down below into silence.

Which was when Bash climbed out of the car.

I hadn't seen him until then.

"I told them this was a wasted trip, Jack," he hollered up at us.

Jack gave his brother a nod. "Bash, my man. Didn't see you last night."

"Came in after the fireworks," he drawled with a laugh.

"Fireworks," Jack scoffed under his breath, shaking his head. "Beau, tell them you're bisexual."

"I already did."

"Tell them again." Then, in my ear, he said dryly, "Or you *could* tell them that you're actually Jacksexual... the choice is yours."

Both amused *and* mortified—not an easy cocktail of emotions considering—and with my cheeks burning red hot, to them—and a small part of Kensington—I called out, "I'm bi and I've been in love with Jack for a very long time."

"That's why I'm not letting you in," Jack stated. "You can all go back to Surrey and think about how unfair this is."

"I told you he liked her," Devon said gruffly, elbowing Sascha. "You didn't listen."

"I did listen," Jack's mom countered. "But seeing as Beau's only ever been interested in women, I didn't think there was much point in discussing it."

"She's a one-man woman," Jack informed them, making me shove him in the side. His happiness spilled over in a joyful laugh that did things to my insides. Something that was only compounded when he hooked his arm over my shoulder. "Well, aren't you?"

"Yes," I muttered.

"Say it louder so they'll go home," he directed with a wicked gleam in his eyes.

"I'll get you back for this," I retorted.

"Please do. We've already established you're a sadist," he teased.

I had to chuckle. "You're incorrigible," I chided, but to our family by the door, I shouted, "I fell in love with him when I was a teenager. No guy ever compared." Then, back to him, I groused, "Your ego is already massive."

"It's like Everest now."

"I'll bet."

Sawyer grumbled, "I refuse tae leave wi'out having a cup of tea first."

"He means a whisky," Jack whispered in my ear.

"You think I haven't figured out your fathers' various codes over the years?"

"Go to a pub," Jack shouted. "I'm not letting you in."

"This is our bloody house," Andrei shouted.

"Oooh, he's pissed. He sounds really Russian."

"Now, Jack, there's no need for this," Sascha said, apparently realizing that diplomacy was required.

"There's every need. Until you think about how you always believe everything I do is reckless—"

"You *are* a risk-taker," Devon pointed out. "Statistically, your mother's well within her rights to be concerned."

"Have I ever taken risks with Beau?" he argued, and for some reason, that made me squirm against his side.

"No," Devon concurred.

"Well, then. I'd never do anything to harm her. I love her. I've always loved her. This..." He wafted a hand between us. "This is something that makes us both happy. You should be happy for us too, and you should feel horrible for misjudging me."

Kurt heaved a sigh. "What a waste of a bloody journey."

"It isn't," Sascha denied. "We can head to Fortnum & Masons. You always like going there."

Kurt perked up and nodded. "Yes. We can." He tilted back his head to look up at me and declared, "Jack, you think this is an intervention now? If you mess Beau around, we will return with pitchforks and flaming torches."

"I'm not Dracula," he muttered.

My lips twitched. "You've kidnapped me to your lair, though, haven't you?"

He snickered. "True."

Sascha nodded. "He's right, Jack. You hurt her and we'll be back."

"I'm shaking in my shoes."

"You bloody well should be," Andrei retorted, his displeasure clear.

"I'll ring you tonight, and I expect you to answer," Sascha intoned, her warning clear.

Jack shrugged. "I'll answer."

"Same goes, Beau," my dad called out.

"Will do, Dad."

His face was unusually stern, and I realized I'd genuinely scared him. Guilt hit me, but I didn't understand why.

I was with Jack.

Not some stranger.

Jack was too tired to be outright angry, but I got where he was coming from.

Last night, Bethan had charged in like he was a rapist, and Rosie had looked like she was going to cry when I'd left to go to his room.

Knowing we'd have to have a conversation about this, but because they'd traveled such a long way for me, because I mattered to them, I told them, "All of you, thank you. You don't know what it means to me to know you care this much."

"Beau, child, you're one of the family. Silly girl." Sascha tutted then waved her hand and said, "Come on, before we freeze to death."

As they clambered into their cars, waving at us in farewell, it was Jack's siblings who remained lingering behind. Bash close to hand.

"Don't fuck this up," Tin grumbled up at Jack before he helped Alice into the limo that came complete with little Veronian flags flying on the fender and ducked into it himself.

"Part of my job is to castrate bigger dicks than yours," Rosie hollered. "Be warned, Jack."

Bethan agreed, "And I'll help hold you down."

They nodded at the same time, doing that freaky twin stuff that came out occasionally.

"Shining Sisters, get your butts into the car and stop threatening my manhood," he retorted.

My lips almost twitched, but I knew they hated being compared to the twins in *The Shining*, so deciding to spare the emotionally-invested neighborhood from an argument worthy of a movie, I told them, "I'll call you later. Thank you..." *For what?* "...for caring enough to organize the troops."

Bethan shot me a worried look but blew me a kiss. "Speak later."

Rosie called out, "There's a basket by the door for you."

"What's in it?" I laughed. "A care package?"

She shrugged. "Your things."

Before I could ask her what that constituted of, Bash shepherded her toward the car, but when he touched Rosie's shoulder, she flinched like he'd hit her. Bash's expression was grim as he looked up at Jack who shook his head and waved at him.

"What was that about?" I demanded as the cavalcade of vehicles began drifting away from the curb.

"With our folks—"

"No. With Bash and Rosie." I pressed my hand to his chest. *Because I could.* "I know they don't get along, but Rosie flinched!"

"Rosie's weird with him. You know that," he pointed out, his gaze on the cars as they drove around the crescent and into traffic. "Can't believe they braved the commute for an intervention. If it wasn't for you and because they love you, I'd be pissed."

Though I was concerned about what I'd just seen, my heart warmed at that. "I didn't realize I mattered that much to them."

"Since when do you have such shitty low self-esteem?" He squinted at me. "It must have happened when you refused to come on the circuit with me."

I heard the agitation behind that and grumbled, "I only refused because you were doing dangerous stuff." Before he could say a word, I continued, "And now you know that I love you too, that I want to be with you, can you understand how much it hurt me to see you put yourself in danger that way?"

Those beautiful lips of his firmed, but his eyes were soft. "I'll let you have that one because you're pretty."

Snorting, I told him, "You're all heart."

He plucked at the tee I was wearing. "I like seeing you in my stuff."

Inside, my heart went boom. I felt shy, bashful, and happy all at the same time. "I like wearing it."

Should it have come as that much of a shock that I liked being on the receiving end of Jack's sweeter side? Probably not. But we'd never had that dynamic before, and I wanted more of it.

All of it.

"I especially like seeing you naked."

He chuckled as he chucked me under the chin. "Well, there's plenty more where that came from."

"Good." If I sounded eager, so be it. "I'd best go and get that basket."

He yawned and said, "Don't worry about it. I'll go get it."

"Maybe it *is* a care package."

"If my mom had packed it, sure, but not Rosie." His eyes gleamed. "Bet?"

Humming, I nodded. "I bet it's full of condoms."

He laughed. "Good one. Rosie packs for every eventuality, but this time, I think it's the puppy."

"Oh shit! I forgot about the puppy!" Aghast, I whispered, "I'd make a terrible dog mom."

"Nah. You've had lots of dogs over the years."

He wasn't wrong, but I still felt guilty.

Slinging an arm around my shoulder, he murmured, "Hey, last night was crazy. I think you're being tough on yourself."

Warmth bubbled inside me. How he touched me, comforted me... it wasn't new. I called him Jackass because he had a big ego and his sisters and I liked to bring him down a notch, but he was kind. Sweet.

I hadn't forgotten that.

But this was different.

I was standing in his tee shirt, our bodies still warm from the bed we'd slept in together, after having just argued with his folks and mine in the street...

We were together.

Together together.

And it was bloody fantastic.

I turned into him, letting my hand settle on his abs, before I said, "Last night *was* crazy."

"In the best way, right?" His fingers tweaked my chin. "No regrets?"

I blinked up at him. "None."

He beamed a relieved grin at me that told me, without words, he had zero regrets too.

"Want a coffee?"

Well, I hadn't expected him to ask that. Not after my admission.

"Tea, please." I patted his chest and decided to go for gold: "Are you going to give me a good morning kiss?"

Desire gleamed in his eyes. "A new perk. Interesting."

I laughed. "Wouldn't call it a perk."

"I would," he said wickedly as his hands dropped to my ass.

He tugged me against him, squeezing my cheeks as he did so, then he rocked his mouth against mine.

Just a soft peck.

A gentle connection, but it packed a hell of a lot of punch for all that.

"Good morning, Beau-Peep," he breathed.

I breathed back, "Morning, Jackass."

"I need a new nickname," he complained, but there was no heat to it.

Well, aside from the fact he had a hard-on.

And it was pressed into my stomach.

"Something doesn't mind being called Jackass," I whispered, arching against him just so I could watch his eyelids flutter to half-mast.

His fingers kneaded my ass, and he muttered, "Remind me that there could be a sleeping puppy on the front stoop or—"

I yelped, because I'd forgotten too, and I squeezed him in a hug a second before I untangled myself from his hold and took off.

As I flew down the stairs, I heard him descending at a more leisurely pace. When I unlocked the door, seeing that he was right and he'd left the key in the lock, I turned it and saw a wiggling basket on the front step.

"Either condoms come with legs," Jack declared, "or I win the bet."

"We never agreed on terms," I said absentmindedly as I dropped to my knees to unfasten the small leather latch. The second I did, a head bopped the lid and I came face to face with the little pup I'd met last night.

A squeak escaped him, and he wagged his tail so hard that it shook the box.

"I'm not the only one who's excited to see you," Jack teased, making me grin as I dealt with a barrage of puppy kisses.

I had to admit, though, I was glad the pup was happy to see me. I figured I'd scared him last night, but he appeared to have forgotten that.

Did he remember me? Or was he just glad to be free?

I really hoped it was the former as I slipped my hands around his wiggling form and heaved him against my chest.

Jack shuffled forward and grabbed the basket before he drawled, "Enjoying the show?"

His sardonic comment had me blinking in surprise, then aghast, I looked around the door and saw a man peering at us from the sidewalk.

Glancing up at Jack, I realized that along the way, he'd dragged on a pair of boxers—thank God.

Jack's comment had the stranger huffing and striding off.

"Who is he?" I whispered as Jack muttered under his breath and closed the door.

"Neighbor from across the street. Has a stick up his ass."

"You think everyone has a stick up their ass," I complained.

He grinned. "I don't think you do. That being said... I'd be willing to stick something up your ass."

"You said that in front of a baby."

"He can't hear," Jack scoffed.

"He can." The pup started licking my chin. "Anyway, my butt has an exit-only visa."

"Well, that didn't lower the tone," was his amused retort. "How do I get an entrance visa?"

"You'd probably have to bribe me with Grey Goose." I laughed when the pup gently nipped my chin. "Okay, that's gotta be his name now."

"Grey Goose?" Jack questioned dubiously.

"Yeah. Goose for short."

"He isn't gray."

"So? You're not a Jackass. Although you do bray sometimes when you laugh."

"That's not the name on my birth certificate," he grumbled.

"Goose, tell Jack to hush."

Goose yipped.

Huffing, Jack stooped down to peer into the basket. "Rosie's thought of everything as usual."

"She has?" I peered into the confines and laughed when I came across a bag of dog food, a pouch of puppy treats, a water bowl, a lead and a tiny harness, a small sweater, and a box of condoms. "I guess that means we both win the bet," I said with a snicker.

ELEVEN

JACK

Rosie, as always, managed to put kinks in my plans.

But Goose *was* cute.

Even if he had accidents *everywhere*, he made Beau smile which more than made up for the fact I'd stood in one 'accident' earlier.

When I came down to the kitchen after I worked out a couple hours since the family intervention, I found her on a video call with my sisters and Goose on her lap.

I'd always known I was in over my head with Beau, but it was rammed home to me when I was jealous of a goddamn puppy.

Jealous, too, of my sisters.

"You're back at Bishop Rosen already?" I questioned by way of a greeting as I strode over to the sofa in front of the TV and plunked myself down beside Beau.

Maybe I was living up to my nickname, but I planted my hand firmly on Beau's thigh. It was possessive and stupid, but my family had pissed me off this morning.

Beau was mine.

Always had been. Always would be.

We'd been friends *first*.

And now, we were more.

What was so complicated about that?

If anything, it was ridiculous that it had taken so long for us to get together.

Bethan spotted the move first and rolled her eyes. "Yes, we're back in Surrey. No, we're not back in the Stone Ages, Jack. You don't have to throw Beau over your shoulder—"

"No, he did that last night, didn't he?" Rosie chimed in, burying her face in Chester's fur—Mom's Pomeranian who was more bum fluff than dog.

"Hardly," Beau countered, laughing when Goose scampered over to sit on my lap.

A wheeze escaped me when he trampled my dick beneath paws that were like pinheads. Goose yelped when I hauled him higher up my chest then squirmed so he could drool over as much of my face as possible.

Rosie snorted. "At least someone approves of you, Jack."

"Hey, I approve," Beau defended. "And I liked that Jack swept me away last night! Don't discourage the sweeping."

Bethan's nose crinkled as she took in the pair of us. "Mom wants to talk to you both."

"Of course she does," I grumbled, leaning forward to snag some coffee from Beau's cup.

Was I ridiculous that I made sure to drink from where she'd been sipping?

Sure.

Did I own it?

Yes.

I had a lot of years to make up for.

A lot.

"I'm grateful for everyone's concern, but it isn't necessary," Beau reasoned.

"It is. You're—"

"Don't you dare say it, Rosie," I warned grimly. "She isn't gay."

Beau's fingers bridged mine on her lap. "Seems like everyone's believed that for a long time, Jack. I guess this was bound to come as a surprise."

"I can handle that, but the accusation they're throwing at me, I can't. Last night, Bethan, you came into my room like I was an attacker."

I saw some hectic color pop onto her cheeks. "Rosie gave me the wrong impression."

"So you both thought I was forcing myself on her? And let me guess, that's what you told the family?"

Bethan scowled at me. "No. We didn't tell them that. But we were shocked."

"Dad found us on the front step and wanted to know what was happening."

My brows lifted because it wasn't like Dad—Devon—to want to know anything. He just seemed to know it all without having to learn dick.

"He wasn't surprised, of course," Bethan said with a sigh then, much as I'd done, complained, "I'm not sure how he always knows everything."

"Learns it by osmosis, I guess," Rosie mocked, her fingers tangling with Chester's mane. "I think he was more concerned about us not wearing coats."

"True," Bethan confirmed. "It *was* freezing last night. I think the F1 Championship should end in the summer. At least that way we don't freeze our asses off when we go to your parties, Jack."

I taunted, "I'll just have a word with the director, shall I?"

While she grinned, Bethan said, "Dad told us to wait until the morning to tell the family—" I owed him big time. *Thank you, Dad.* "—and that we shouldn't always believe what we see with our own eyes."

Rosie frowned. "Know-it-all. He and Tin are so alike."

"Why?" I asked.

"Tin said the same thing. Apparently, everyone thought you were gay apart from Tin and Dad, Beau."

There was definitely an accusation in her voice.

Beau's cheeks heated, and because that pissed me off, I drawled, "Beau doesn't have to explain herself to anyone."

Not even me.

She squeezed my fingers. "It's okay, Jack."

"It isn't. You want to be here with me, don't you?"

I asked the question, and ridiculously enough, found myself feeling breathless, waiting on her to answer.

Her gaze was somber, like she felt my uncertainty. "Do you know why we call you Jackass?"

"Because I am one?" I joked, wondering where she was going with this.

"Well, yeah, but because you turn into one when you're with people. With us, not so much." She cupped my chin. "You weren't with us these last couple years. You were turning more and more into a jackass because you were surrounded by people who sucked your dick or kissed your ass..."

"So, turning straight hasn't unsharpened her tongue," I heard Bethan comment.

I didn't roll my eyes, though, because Beau's expression was deadly serious. "Your confidence is one thing I love about you. Your strength and ability to walk into any room and feel like you own it—it's annoying sometimes, and it's my, Rosie, and Bethan's jobs to keep you on the straight and narrow, but you never have to feel insecure with me.

"I love you, Jack. I've loved you for almost as long as I've known you. I've wanted to be with you for almost all that time, and being here, having this, even if it only lasts a week, is better than having nothing at all."

My heart stopped slamming against my ribcage, and I whispered, "I want more than a week with you, Beau. Seven days isn't enough."

"Are we seriously watching them woo each other?" Rosie complained.

"Yes, you are," I groused, my gaze firmly on Beau's. "But you could always end the call if you weren't Nosey Rosie." I didn't need to look at her to know that she flipped me the bird. "Anyway, she hasn't turned straight. She's still Beau. She's still bi. She just likes me too." I cast a glance at them. "Shame on you both for thinking that anyway. Invalidating bisexuals is just as bad as homophobia. Thought you'd have known that, Bethan," I sniped.

She narrowed her eyes at me but stunned me by saying, "You're right."

My brows rose. "Beau? Is that a pig I see flying over the garden?"

Bethan stuck out her tongue at me. "You have to see why this would come as a shock, surely? Weren't you surprised too?"

"Mostly I was just relieved. Beau's my..." I blew out a breath and decided to throw it all out on the line. They were my sisters. It wasn't the world's press. "...my happy place. I've missed her, and I want her with me."

Rosie tipped her head to the side in contemplation. "She won't go with you to races if you keep on doing stupid stuff."

"I won't. I was even going to stop coming to your victory parties," Beau agreed, and this time, though she didn't mean to, I felt the prick of her nails against my hand.

The involuntary reaction filled me with heat.

Not only did I love that she cared, but I wanted to feel the tips of those nails digging into my skull as she forced my face deeper against her pussy.

Slicing into my back as she gripped me hard and I fucked her deep.

Carving divots into my ass as she grinded into me as much as I did her.

Now was *not* the time to get an erection. Not with my sisters on camera and Goose ambling over to the corner where Beau had Ubered in some puppy pads from the nearby store.

"I've left Sabre," I told Rosie and Bethan. And if my voice sounded deep, well, fuck, I couldn't help it.

I had years of fantasies to drive me crazy. Years of need to burn off on the woman who'd owned my heart since the first day we met.

"Dad told us," Bethan said which had me rolling my eyes.

"How the fuck does he know that?"

Rosie shrugged. "How does he know anything?"

"He's tapped into Google or BBC News, I think. That hasn't even leaked to the press yet."

"Why not?"

"Because they're trying to counteroffer me," I answered Beau.

She pursed her lips. "Are you trying to up your contract?"

I shook my head. "No. It would be a good way of getting as much out of them as possible though."

"It would. You sure that's not your game?"

"No. It isn't." I hesitated. "I know you all think I'm reckless, but this year, I had something to prove."

Rosie blinked at me. "What on earth did you have to prove to anyone? You're the reigning world champion, Jack. All you do is win. What's to prove?"

My jaw tightened. "You don't understand."

"No," Beau agreed. I felt the prick of her nails again. "We don't. So explain it to us."

I shot her a glance, and while I was being harried into this, I was relieved that my boner had died a death.

"John was being paid by Sabre to lose."

Beau frowned. "You were teammates; they always favor one over the other. Like Hamilton and Alonso. Alonso was the golden boy until Hamilton was."

"I know that, but John told me he got kickbacks for doing stupid shit that would help me win. Remember Montreal two years back?"

Beau frowned. "Yeah? When Harald and Núñez braked too late and turned onto the runoff area?"

"That was John."

"Don't be silly," Beau countered. "That's a notorious spot for that kind of stunt."

"John said he was the reason they braked late, and Harald, that year, was up my ass on the leaderboard for most of it," I told her stubbornly. "Because of stupid shit, he never recouped those lost points."

Silence fell, and I knew the ramifications of what I was saying were hitting home.

"Why did he tell you any of this?" Bethan demanded.

I cast her a glance. "Because he wasn't going to do it anymore. He was tired of toeing the line, especially when I was stupid and ungrateful and didn't deserve to win. His words."

Beau sniffed. "I'd tell you if you didn't deserve to win. You pull crazy stunts, and the audience loves you for it, Jumping Jack, but strategically, you're damn smart."

Was it stupid that I choked up at that?

Her defense of me felt good.

So good.

"When did this argument happen?" Rosie asked carefully, her hands fondling Chester's ears. He panted happily away, his leg jiggling of its own volition as she'd found his happy spot.

"The morning he died," I admitted gruffly.

Beau stilled. "You argued the morning he died?"

"Yeah."

She hissed under her breath. "That's why you—" She spat something in Polish, a feat seeing as Polish only ever came out when she was truly pissed. Then, vibrating with rage, she spat, "Why didn't you tell me?"

I swallowed. "I was ashamed."

Beau jumped to her feet and started striding back and forth in front of the TV. Like the audience at Wimbledon watching the ball volley across the net, we followed her movements.

She started grumbling something else in Polish.

"Wow, you've really pissed her off, Jack," Rosie pointed out. "I've heard her speak Polish like three times since I've known her—"

Before she could finish, Beau growled, "You never have to be ashamed with me, Jack."

"This was different," I muttered. "You say you love me for my confidence, but all of that was built on a lie—"

"Bullshit." She snapped her fingers. "Núñez in Montreal that last year, remember his car had that new brake system? His team called it 'revolutionary' but there were three occasions where he lost control of the car. Remember?"

"Kind of."

"They said that it was user error. That was why he switched teams. Remember that?"

"I guess."

She grunted. "As for Harald, he always takes hairpin curves too fast. It's his thing. Give me more stats that John used against you to make you believe you didn't deserve to be sitting at no. 1, because from where I was sitting, you raced almost always at a high distinction.

"Sometimes, you didn't, and sometimes, you did unnecessarily stupid shit, but you always belonged on the podium. So give me some more so-called stats."

"The Dunlop Curve in Japan. Three years ago. Jamie Svensson."

Her eyes narrowed, but not on me. Like she was flipping through her mental filing system.

"The year he crashed into the barriers?"

I nodded, impressed even though I knew what she was like with race statistics.

"You remember that?" Rosie complained.

"She remembers most of my races. It's what makes her so good at strategy," I said absentmindedly.

"You know how difficult the S curves are there," Beau was saying. "He touched the grass. I remember that. And all it takes is a millimeter of your front wheel to touch the curb and you're going straight to the barrier or onto the gravel.

"Jamie almost always hits the gravel there. What did John say to make you believe he was behind it?"

"Said that he was up his ass for most of the race and that he 'encouraged' Jamie onto the gravel."

"That sounds like bullshit to me," Bethan muttered.

"Me too," Rosie agreed.

"Me goddamn three," Beau snapped as she slammed her hands onto her hips. "Let me guess, every race you two competed in together, he took ownership of a mistake that put you in the running for the podium?"

"Not all of them," I argued.

"No, just important races." She clucked her tongue. "John would never have had the guts to try to force people off the track. He was too cautious. That's why he never won.

"Now, I believe that Sabre gave him kickbacks, but to cheat? No. They didn't need to do that.

"Before John came along, you were the champ, and after, you were too. He was bolstering up his ego to take you on. To rattle you so that he could take you in the race."

I gritted my teeth. "All he ended up doing was taking his life."

Her mouth tightened. "And almost bringing you along for the ride. Why didn't you come to me with this? I'd have cleared it up in a few minutes, and we wouldn't have had to watch you flying around the tracks this season like you were an overgrown Tinkerbell on acid."

Bethan snorted. "Good one, Beau."

I flipped my sister the bird, but I couldn't deny that Beau's belief in me settled something deep inside.

It wasn't just Beau—the woman I loved. It wasn't just Beau—my friend. It was nothing more and nothing less than what I'd told her last night—Beau had a head for this kind of stuff.

This shit she was remembering now was shit she always remembered.

It was why I'd taken a hit when she left me to come back home.

I worked well when she was there because she was a calming

presence, sure. But also because her brain and mine, together, were a match made in F1 heaven.

"I just don't understand why you'd believe him," Rosie groused.

I cleared my throat. "Because my best bud wasn't with me anymore, and everything was harder without her."

Beau's mouth gaped a second. "Don't blame me for you being crazy on the track."

I had to admit, I smirked at her outrage. "I'm not blaming you. I'm just saying... you're my level. It was harder without you, and I was having to work twice as much to get the same results as when you were there. He hit me on the raw."

"On the raw?" she repeated, just as she started to tap her toe against the floor. "Jack, were you or were you not the person who smuggled me out of the Monaco after-party when I got my period and I was wearing white pants?"

"Yikes," Bethan whispered.

"I was," I agreed.

"Did you or did you not dive into the pool at that after-party in Madrid when I fell in? And then you made it look like we were having fun?"

I blinked. "I did."

"Were you or were you not the guy who hid me behind him when Harald doused me in champagne and made my shirt see-through? On purpose because he's a creep."

"What a jerk," Rosie agreed.

"Are you always so accident-prone, Beau?" Bethan questioned kindly.

I shot her a glare. "She isn't accident-prone. Stuff just happens around her. You're getting on my nerves, Bethan, blaming Beau for shit she can't help.

"I'm sure she asked to get her period in front of the world, and Harald *wanted* to see her tits, that's why he sprayed her with Moët. That's not her fault either.

"As for the pool, I saw that bitch Claudia elbow you in the side—"

"You did?" Beau gasped.

"I did," I said grimly. "Why do you think I stopped dating her?"

"You never said!"

"I didn't think I had to," I muttered, on edge. "We have each other's backs, don't we?"

Her tone turned soft. "We do."

"Well, then, what changed?" Rosie asked quietly, her gaze intent on the pair of us.

"Nothing changed," I denied.

"It did," Bethan countered. "You pulled apart. Beau came home and stayed at home even though she was really unhappy here. And you did become a deranged Tinkerbell on the track, Jack. Beau's right about that."

Beau plunked her ass on the coffee table, her back to the girls, as she turned all that powerful focus on me. She broke me by pressing a hand to her heart like it was aching.

"Unrequited love hurts," she whispered, her tone pained.

I stared at her, stared at the pain reflecting back at me, and felt comforted by it. Not because I was cruel, but because I hadn't been alone.

It *did* hurt.

Knowing the person you loved wasn't ever going to be yours...

"Why did you never tell me how you felt?" I whispered, aware I sounded like I was wheezing. "You know why I felt like I couldn't say anything..."

She bit her lip, bowed her head, then mumbled, "You're the golden boy. Why would you want me?"

"Did you hear her, Rosie? She was mumbling. Beau, stop mumbling. We can't hear you!"

I glared at Bethan. "Why are you even listening to this?"

"So that we can act as a go-between for you and Mom," she said smartly, promptly, *too* promptly and too damn smartly for my liking.

Because she was right.

If Bethan passed this on, Mom would let us have some peace and might let us sort things out for ourselves without trying to wade into the mix.

I hissed at her, glowering when she hissed back, but Rosie said, "I think she was saying she wasn't good enough for Jack, but I must be wrong. He's not good enough for her."

"Gee, thanks, Rosie," I grumbled, but I turned to Beau, reached for her hands, and murmured, "Beau, she could have been nicer about it, but Rosie's right. I'm the one who's not good enough for you.

"Don't you see that you live up to your name? That you're beautiful? Inside and out? *I'm* the lucky one. Don't you get that?

"You're the one who makes my world make any goddamn sense. Even before, as a friend, you were my balance. My equilibrium. How couldn't you see that?"

"Because I was a hanger on. You have many of them."

"A hanger on?" I repeated, and I'd admit, I was starting to get mad now. "A hanger on?" I said again.

"Think he got stuck on repeat," Rosie whispered, but I ignored her.

"You compare yourself to my agent and manager and all the other fuckers in my goddamn entourage... is that what I'm hearing?"

She stared up at me with agony in her eyes. "No. They have more use than me. They have jobs. I just..."

"You just what?" I asked carefully.

"I'm a scrounger."

"A what?!"

If Goose jumped then peed himself at my roar of outrage, well, I couldn't help it.

"Jack! Don't shout at her!" Rosie growled which, in turn, made Chester start yipping on her knee.

"I bloody well will shout at her if she dares talk crap like that about herself." I sucked in a breath, trying to stay calm. "The rest of those motherfuckers can go to hell. You're the only person I want in my entourage, for fuck's sake!"

She swallowed, but her gaze was fastened on mine. "You mean that?"

"Of course I fucking mean it."

"Stop swearing," Bethan chided. "It makes everything sweet you're saying sound horrible."

"Fuck off, Bethan. In fact, both of you, go away."

I found the remote and switched off the TV, leaving us alone, with no audience, pretty much what I should have done the second I came down here.

"That was mean," she chided, but I saw the tiniest of gleams in her eyes.

I knew I'd amused her.

Good.

An amused Beau I could handle.

A distressed one? One who didn't realize she made *me goddamn happy?* Was it any wonder my blood pressure was surging?

"Tough," I retorted, then I leaned forward and I snagged her hands in mine. "Beau, baby, the second you left, there was no fun in it anymore."

"Hush," she chided, starting to tug on her hands to make me let go of her.

Not. Going. To. Happen.

"I won't hush. It wasn't fun. It became serious. A job. Then that shit with John happened, and it just made things worse." My brow furrowed. "I've clearly failed you."

Her eyes rounded. "What?"

"If you don't know how important you are to me, then I've failed you."

She swallowed. "I've failed you too because you don't know how important you are to me either."

I shook my head. "You could only ever fail me if you did one thing."

"What is it?" she breathed.

"You could stop loving me. And not like this, but like we were before this. As friends."

For a moment, she said nothing, then she surged off the coffee table.

For a split second, I thought she was going to rush away and leave me or something, but that was before she elbowed me in the eye as she hurled herself at me.

I yelped as the bone collided with my face, and she jolted back, her knee going straight between my legs, but the damage she did was a hell of a lot worse than what Goose had done.

For a second, I thought I was about to become a mezzo soprano for the rest of my life, but one moment she had pressure on me, the next my dick was liberated.

This time, I really *was* goddamn wheezing.

Beau sure as hell had the habit of taking my breath away...

TWELVE

The second my elbow collided with Jack's gorgeous face, our yelps mingled.

When I scrambled to get off him, I nearly castrated him—and that would have been a huge shame because his dick was *delicious*—and when, after that wonderful declaration of his, he was sitting there, shielding his eye like he'd been in a fight, I burst into tears.

He scrunched up his face then, as was his way, said, "Baby, I'm the one who should be crying."

A sniffly laugh escaped me, but I groaned in horror as I clambered to his side, being careful not to hit him with anything, just huddling closer to him while he cupped his dick with one hand and carefully prodded his cheek with the other.

"Let it be known that you can handle yourself in any dangerous situation," he drawled softly, teasing me out of my tears.

"I'm so sorry, Jack," I whispered.

"Sorry enough to negotiate a new nickname?"

He said it so slickly that I peered at him through narrowed eyes. "You want to negotiate?"

"Away from Jackass? Yes. It's worth a bruised cock for that."

"Is it really bruised?"

"Want to look?" he retorted.

His tone was snappish enough that I didn't think I was being played.

Only Jack would turn a situation like this around to his own advantage.

If I was the queen of strategy—at least, according to him—then he was definitely the king.

"What nickname do you want to be called? And is this just between us or Rosie and Bethan too?"

His lips twitched. "Cumlord. Think they'll have a problem calling me that."

"You jackass." I shoved him in the side as he snickered at me. "What's the real nickname?"

His amused smirk disappeared and was slowly replaced with a softer, more embarrassed smile. I braced myself for it because while he'd been teasing before, he wasn't now...

"Honey."

"Honey?"

He nodded. "Or love. Babe. Sweetheart. Sweetness. Just... not Jackass."

It was such a simple request, but it represented so much.

"Jack?"

He cast me a wary glance.

"I'm sorry I elbowed you in the eye and kneeled on your dick."

"I appreciate the apology, though I do expect you to kiss it better later."

"Your eye? Sure." I smirked back at him, but much as his had, my wry amusement died too. "I won't call you Jackass again. Unless you really deserve it," I tacked on. A little worriedly, I asked, "How's your dick..." I paused, cleared my throat, blew out a breath, sucked one in, then added, "...sweetheart?"

"All the better for hearing that." He raised an arm. "Stay still before you figure out a way to decapitate me with the coffee cup," he rasped, curving it about my shoulder and drawing us back into a seated position.

"Can this work between us?" I asked him softly, *hopefully*.

"I'm not the kind of man who gives up on the woman he wants, Beau. You've never seen me like that because I've never wanted anyone like I want you.

"It's going to be a learning curve, but we'll get there. Together. Won't we?"

I shot him a soft smile. "We will." I believed it. I believed him. Licking my lips, I whispered "Together."

And it felt right.

So right.

Beau: *Daddy? I'm sorry if I worried you.*

Dad: *You and I don't live in each other's pockets, Buttercup. I didn't even know you weren't home until Sascha came knocking on the door.*

Beau: *I'm sorry if I embarrassed you. <3*

Dad: *I wasn't embarrassed. I've caught Sascha in far too many compromising situations to be embarrassed around her anymore.*

Beau: *You have? O.O*

Dad: *Yes. But I signed a very comprehensive NDA, so I won't be giving you or anyone else any details about that!!*

Beau: *Understood lol.*

Dad: *I was concerned for you. I knew you were planning on leaving for London, but I was worried about what the twins were saying about Jack and you and wanted to make sure you were okay.*

Dad: *I'm not really sure how to ask this, but, there's only one way I suppose—you're not gay?*

Beau: *No. TBH, I knew we'd deal with this better over text. That's why I didn't call you. I'm not gay. I'm bi. Not gay.*

Dad: *Just like you told half of Kensington this morning.*

Beau: *Yeah. It's a wonder it's not all over SM.*

Dad: *SM?*

Beau: *Social media.*

Dad: *Ah. Yes, that is fortunate. I didn't realize you had feelings for Jack. I suppose it makes sense—you used to fret over him something fierce.*

Beau: *I love him.*

Dad: *I can see that now. Well, I'll be frank and say I don't mind if you want to marry an alien so long as he treats you well and you're happy.*

Beau: *Lol, thank you, Dad. You've been checking out my bookshelf.*

Dad: *Maybe. I didn't realize blue aliens were even a thing.*

Beau: *They are in the land of romance. Anyway, I think I'd pick

Jack even over blue aliens. Which, trust me, comes as a massive surprise even to me.

Dad: I'll bet. If you love him, and if he makes you happy, then I can ask for nothing more.

Beau: Thanks, Daddy.

Dad: Tell him I'll smash the windscreen on that fancy Sabre of his if he hurts you. I'd threaten to beat him but I fear I wasn't the best at fighting even when I was in my twenties, never mind now.

Beau: LMAO. I'll tell him, but don't destroy the Sabre. He's leaving the team.

Dad: Your influence?

Beau: No. He told me last night. Before everything went down. Speaking of... how did it go with Loretta?

Dad: Struck out.

Beau: Shame. Try again?

Dad: Maybe. I think I'm too old for her.

Beau: Doubt it. You just need to try again. Talk to her. Charm her.

Dad: Not sure in my position I can do that, love. We'll see.

Beau: Try again, Dad. Mama would want you to.

Dad: Would she? She was very jealous. I think she'd like the idea of me pining away for her until the end of time.

Beau: I probably shouldn't say this...

Dad: You can tell me anything.

Beau: I love you, Dad. I loved her. But she was selfish. She was selfish to let it be me who found her. It was selfish that she chose that way to end it and that it put me in danger of finding her body. And if that's how you feel, that she WOULD be happy for you to pine away forever, then it confirms she WAS selfish.

Beau: I don't want you to be stuck on a woman who didn't fight hard enough for us both.

Dad: That's not how depression works.

Beau: Adult Beau knows that. The kid who found her mom swinging from a tree in the back yard DOESN'T.

Dad: *Every day since then, I've wished I'd been the one to find her and not you.*

Beau: *I wish neither of us had.*

Dad: *She fought for us, sweetheart. You might not think so, but she did. She was lost. For a long time.*

Beau: *I know. But that doesn't mean you have to spend the rest of your life wishing she hadn't cut hers short.*

Dad: *Ouch.*

Beau: *Sorry, Dad. I think I've been bitter for a very long time about this.*

Dad: *I can understand. You should never have seen what you did.*

Beau: *I miss her.*

Dad: *Me too.*

Beau: *We can never have those days back, but we can make something new for ourselves. Maybe this with Jack won't work out, maybe it will. Maybe you'll get it on with the new housekeeper or maybe you won't, but you have to try, Daddy.*

Beau: *Promise me you will?*

Dad: *I'll try.*

Beau: *You mean it?*

Dad: *I do. I love you, Beau. When did you get so sensible?*

Beau: *I'm not sensible lol. But I DO love you, and I want what's best for you. And I know that means being happy. I don't think you are right now. I don't think I've been for a long time. I'd like for us both to have that.*

Dad: *Me too. xx*

Beau: *xx*

THIRTEEN

BEAU

TWO DAYS LATER

I peered around the garage, watching as Jack climbed in and out of the luxury sports' cars housed within this expensive four-story forecourt that was an ode to every boy's hopes and wet dreams.

While I was bored, it amused me that he knew more about the engines than the bitch who was currently trying to stroke his ego... and other things.

I leaned back against the wall, Goose at my side on his purple harness and dressed smartly in his hoodie that was pure Rosie—it said, 'Just Woof It' and he looked like he was about to start running track with Usain Bolt.

Though I might have looked casual, appearances could be deceiving.

This wasn't my first brush with jealousy where he was concerned, but this was the first time I had a right to feel that way.

It was both validating and exhausting.

Goose whined, and I squatted down beside him, glad to stop tracking the saleswoman who had legs as long as her entire body.

"She can't help that she's beautiful," I told Goose. "She's prob-

ably really nice and needs the commission for a great Christmas...
Right?"

He licked my face, and I appreciated the gesture so I scooped him
into my arms.

"What do you think? Should I go over there?" I asked, well aware
that she was looking at me.

Was she wondering who I was?

Did she think I was Jack's PA?

I was hovering.

Like the scrounger I'd called myself two days back.

But I wasn't a scrounger. He'd told me that himself and wore the
battle scar in the form of a bruised dick for his pains.

"I didn't even know you could bruise a cock," I muttered to
Goose, but he was no help.

I didn't know that much about penises. By choice and design.
Still, the bruise had been bad enough that I'd refused to have sex
until it healed.

Jeez, I hoped the big, black mark had faded by tonight. The one
on his eye had, so it couldn't be much longer, could it?

I watched the saleswoman bend down, leaning over so that she
could talk to him through the open window of the car. He was behind
the wheel, his arm on the window ledge.

When she brushed her tits against it, jerking back with an embarrassed, affected laugh as she shot me a glance, I narrowed my eyes.

I'd seen way slicker stunts than that in my time, and that was my
catalyst.

Surging forward, Goose in my arms, I strolled toward the car. As
I did, I saw that Jack was peering at the dashboard, while the saleswoman simpered at his side.

The second he noticed my approach, though, his eyes lit up.

And it had nothing to do with the stereo in the new Bugatti
model.

It had everything to do with the joy he found in being with me.

The happiness I found in that was kind of crazy. I knew the smile I shot back at him probably made me look deranged, but I didn't care.

This felt good.

Like it was meant to be.

Something the past two days had only cemented.

We'd done nothing major, mostly just hung out and reconnected, but after fourteen months apart, that was *everything.*

We caught up on Netflix, and he worked out. I baked bad cookies, and we took Goose out for walks before Jack ended up carrying him against his chest—cue ovary meltdown. We spent hours in cafés, and at the end of the day, we slept together...

It really had been bliss.

Today, life had intruded because he'd had Sabre pick up his car, which was why we were here, but I refused to let it spoil things.

I needed to stop feeling like a scrounger and start feeling like I was his girlfriend.

If that made me straighten my shoulders and stride over to him with more confidence, then so be it.

"Beau," he declared, shoving open the driver's door. The saleswoman jolted back on her heels in surprise. "Oh, sorry, didn't realize you were so close," he said absently, not even shooting her a look as he rounded the car to open the passenger door for me.

I knew it made me a bitch that I found that funny, but I hid it as I walked toward him.

"You can't let the dog in there," the woman called out, panic in her voice.

I blinked at her then handed Goose to Jack.

He accepted the bundle of fluff and said, "I want to see how you look in the passenger seat."

I snorted. "Why?"

"I need to see if it's a fit."

Laughing, I shook my head. "It isn't a dress."

"A car is the perfect accessory," he chided, bopping me on the nose with his fingertip. "And that you don't already know that I think like that is concerning."

"I know you think that way," I retorted. "I just didn't know that I had to match too."

"Well, you're different."

He said it so matter-of-factly that I gaped at him. "Huh?"

"No one else has had to match before. But you do."

Snickering, I told him, "You're crazy."

"About you," he murmured with a wink. "Now, sit that pretty ass down and let me see if it suits you."

"So, you like the car, but if I don't suit it then you won't buy it?"

"Nah." He shrugged. "It's gotta fit you too."

Though I rolled my eyes, I was kind of touched as well. Sure, he was weird, but fuck, I wasn't exactly ordinary.

I didn't think anyone who existed in his family's orbit was ordinary.

You couldn't be.

Sascha Dubois lived to the beat of her own drum, and Jack's fathers more than made up the orchestra around her.

Sitting down in the crazily expensive car, I tucked myself into the bucket seat and watched him stare at me.

The saleswoman shuffled over to him, and satisfaction choked me as Goose, the friendliest pooch I'd ever met, who greeted every single person and dog on our walks, who yipped happily at *everyone*, growled at her.

"Good boy," I mumbled under my breath.

Jack moved away from her, and I heard him say, "Huh, that's weird. He likes everyone."

Appreciating that I had a pup who was an ally, and determining that he deserved some chicken as a treat later, I popped my head through the open window and asked, "Well? Do I suit it?"

He pursed his lips. "Mind trying the Aston Martin?"

"I don't mind," I countered, even more pleased when he moved to open the door for me again.

I climbed out then asked, "Which one?"

Reaching out, he touched my hair. "I think we need to go vintage. You're not a super car kind of woman. You're retro." He laughed. "There's probably something Oedipal about the fact you're like Mom."

My nose crinkled. "Ew."

He smirked. "Mom doesn't have piercings. Plus, she doesn't speak Polish when she's pissed," he pointed out. "You really never speak it around my sisters?"

"They don't piss me off like you do."

His shoulders straightened and he actually preened. "I'm going to take that as a compliment."

"You do that," I said dryly. "Which Aston Martin?"

"The DB6," he replied, pointing to a navy, low-slung, two-door coupé that was pure sixties.

"Not your speed, is it?"

"Sloane told me it's been completely refurbed with a V12 engine."

"Surprised you're not drooling."

"Oh, I'm saving my drool for you later."

My nose crinkled again and he snorted at my grossed-out look.

As he wandered into a long-drawn-out explanation of all the new fixtures and fittings, I was left thinking that *of course* she was called Sloane.

Preppy, London. Naturally she had a name to suit.

I didn't hang around for him to open the door this time, just plunked my butt on the leather seat and waited for him to stare at me from in front of the car.

As Goose licked his chin, I'd admit, watching him walk back and forth, catching glimpses of me from different angles, I fell a bit more in love with him.

The car was *nice.*

Perfectly restored, a small fit, low to the ground, with that bullet shape that would make it like a whippet on the roads, it was, I'd admit, a beaut.

He'd told me it had a twelve-cylinder engine and a five-speed gearbox, but mostly, I liked the fact it had a tiny backseat where Goose could sit.

Of course, four hundred thousand for a minuscule car with a backseat was a lot of money, but Jack was rich.

His family was rich.

Hell, they all crapped pound coins.

After watching him peer at me from several angles, oddly nervous, I asked, "What do you think? Do I suit it?"

A frown puckered his brow. "You got that the wrong way around."

"Got what the wrong way around?"

He wagged his finger. "You've done it three times now."

"Done what three times now?" I groused. As far as I knew, I'd only done as he asked—tried out cars as if they were dresses.

"You don't have to suit the car, Beau," he reasoned calmly. "It has to suit you. There's a difference."

Oh.

Well.

There went my heart turning to mush.

He didn't let me comment, though, which somehow made it all the more powerful. His brain was clearly on horsepower and chassis, not on this, but even in the middle of a forecourt, where he was amid his favorite things in the world, he thought about me.

Fuck.

If I didn't love him already, that was me *done*.

So, no, he didn't let me comment, just pursed his lips, paused a second to duck down so he could stare at something on one of the tires, then turned to face Sloane, declaring, "I'll take it."

Sloane shot me a look then quickly headed into her spiel, and I zoned out, looking around a car that apparently suited me as much as I suited it.

There had to be a compliment in there.

It wasn't that I looked like a retro old-fogy. It was that I was worth four hundred K.

Jack ignored Sloane, strode over to the car window, and plunked Goose on my lap.

"He'll scratch the leather," I warned.

He shrugged. "No point in keeping it pristine. Where's the fun in that?"

I hid a smile. "No fun," I agreed.

"Think if I pay cash, she'll shut up?" he asked wistfully.

"Who?"

"Sloane. She talks. A lot."

"You noticed?"

"Her yapping more than Goose? I did," was his grim retort. "You might as well stay here. I'll be ten minutes." He leaned through the window. "You look hot in here, by the way."

I felt wheels of color emblazon themselves onto my cheeks. "I do?"

"Yeah. We need to have sex in here. Baptize it, you know?"

"Not sure that's how baptism works."

"Nope? Then no wonder religious people have sticks lodged up their asses."

Snorting, I told him, "Anyway, you can't have sex yet. Your dick's still bruised."

He rolled his eyes. "Bruised but not broken."

He'd been telling me that since Dick Day, but I wasn't taking any chances. No matter if he whined.

"That should be a hashtag." Tongue-in-cheek, I told him, "I could make that go viral, I'm sure."

"If you do that, Tiffany will be after your blood."

I huffed under my breath at the reminder of Tiffany, who was on his 'team.'

Another hottie that I'd been jealous of along the way.

"What is it, sweetheart?"

His soft voice had me staring up at him and shooting him a glum smile. "Nothing. Just being stupid."

"Not possible. You're too smart to be stupid."

"Were you always this sweet and I didn't notice?" I questioned.

"I was sweet within the parameters that you allowed. Just like you."

"What do you mean?"

His bunched shoulders hitched up as he said, "Hugs, but no kisses. You'd get me coffee, but you'd have the barista write Jackass on it instead of just Jack like this morning."

"It's been three days," I pointed out, but I knew where he was coming from.

"Exactly. Not a lot can happen in three days, but the little things stand out." He shot me a gentle smile. "It's nice, isn't it?"

I licked my lips. "Very."

"So, what's not so nice for you?"

Tucking a lock of hair behind my ears, I murmured, "It's crazy."

"See my earlier response—you're too sane to be crazy. I'm the crazy one."

"Well, I won't argue there. On the road, at any rate." Embarrassed, I told him, "I'm jealous."

"Of whom?" he asked in confusion.

"Who?" I huffed. "*Sloane*. She keeps brushing her tits against your arm and laughing at everything you say. Jack, I love you, but you're not that funny."

He snickered. "Thanks. I think. But you'd laugh at everything I said if you were looking to earn twenty percent commission on a four-hundred-grand sale. Just before Christmas too."

"True," I conceded.

"Anyway, she's gay. I'm the one who should be jealous."

"What?" I frowned. "Shut up. She keeps rubbing her tits against you."

He sniffed. "She jerked back like I was an electric fence and I'd shocked her."

"You noticed."

"'Course I did. She made me jump."

"Nothing to do with her tits, I suppose."

"Nothing. Prefer your tits. They belong to you."

"You're a two-tit-man now, are you?" I retorted scornfully.

"For as long as you'll let me be. Which is going to be forever."

My brow furrowed. "Stop it."

"Stop what?"

"Being sweet."

His eyes gleamed, then he stunned the hell out of me. So smoothly it could have been a move, but I knew it wasn't because I'd seen most of Jack's moves over the years, he slipped his hand behind my nape. His fingers dug in, and with a soft amount of pressure, he dragged me forward so that his breath brushed my lips.

It should have been awkward.

Me, twisted the way I was, him, holding me like I was his captive.

Instead, it was hot.

All of a sudden, I had every ounce of his attention.

And my body sat up and took notice.

Slick—that was the move. So slick it was delicious.

"What kind of family was I raised in, Beau?" he rumbled softly, the words deep and growly. Enough that I shivered in his hold.

"An unorthodox one," I whispered, absently aware that Goose had scampered over to the driver's seat to sit there.

"Unorthodox not only because I have five fathers, but because those five fathers worship my mother. That's the oddity. Not that she has five men. But that each one *adores* her."

I had to concede he was right, but I defended, "My dad adored my mother. That's why he hasn't dated since she passed."

He conceded that with a nod. "True. It's rare. But we both come from that kind of background. After I've spent years wishing you were mine, do you really think I'd be so much of a goddamn fool that I'd be interested in a piece of fluff when I have you?"

"She's hot," I said miserably.

"And you're not?"

I bit my lip. "Not like her." I huffed again. "This is pathetic. I'm pathetic. It's your fault for being so gorgeous, and for all the women wanting you. I'm used to seeing that and always used to feeling like I don't measure up."

He rasped, "Don't you know that you're beautiful?"

"Well, I mean, I don't think about it every day," I grumbled, "but I know I'm attractive. Sure. I wouldn't make a baby cry if I surprised them."

Jack shook his head. "You have to remember that I fucked all those women because I didn't know the one woman I wanted in my bed wanted me back.

"Your jealousy is tied to the fact that you wanted me for as long as I wanted you but you couldn't have me because you thought I didn't see *you*. That I preferred them over you.

"When, really, I was just settling for them, Isabeau," he rumbled, and holy crap, how he said my full name had me squirming in my seat. "I couldn't have you, so I had them. I didn't think I could ever have you, so I took them.

"I didn't worship *them* like I want to worship you." His mouth hovered over mine, making me realize he'd moved nearer to me, so much so there was barely an inch between us. "Do you want me to worship you, Beau?"

Nodding, nervously I licked my lips, and because we were so close, it meant my tongue flickered over his too.

He growled beneath his breath, and I whimpered as he took my mouth in a kiss so all-encompassing that he branded me with his truth.

He was right, after all.

I was jealous because I'd felt like I was lacking.

Like I wasn't hot enough for him.

When, really, that wasn't the case at all.

His tongue surged into my mouth, tangling with mine, and because he'd quenched my jealousy with his reasoning, and because he'd done it in a way that hadn't belittled my emotions, I was left with no other alternative than to fight fire with fire because that was what he brought out in me.

He always had.

He made me *live*.

He made me *fight*.

And I'd missed that.

I'd missed *him* so much.

My hands reached up, and like we were dancing, like we were born to dance together, they didn't collide with his.

Nope.

They slipped around his neck, and I dragged him into me, wishing there wasn't a car door sticking into my tits and a saleswoman watching us.

I explored his mouth, savoring his taste, glorying in the possessive flavor that filled my senses, but more than that, I mimicked what we'd be doing later.

Bruised dick or not.

His fingers tightened around my nape as he pulled back, pressed our foreheads together, and rasped, "If you think I'm ever going to be so much of a fool that I'll let you go, you're mistaken."

I pushed against him. "I don't want you to let go."

"I won't. You can try to break free of me, Beau, but I told you back in Rosie's bedroom. You had one chance to get off that sofa. The second I kissed you was the second I made you mine. You're going nowhere.

"You can fight this, you can fight me, you can fight the fucking world, but we'll do it together. From now on. Do you understand me?"

I'd never realized that those were words I'd needed to hear, but having heard them, I recognized that they were my love language.

His arrogant stance should have pissed me off, but it didn't.

If anything, it had me repeating, "Don't let go, Jack. Don't let go."

"I won't," he ground out. "I won't."

And I clung to that. Clung to him. Clung to the possibility of forever.

Maybe that wasn't something he could promise, but if anyone could, I knew it was my Jackass.

Oops.

I meant *sweetheart*.

Damn, that was going to be a tough habit to break.

FOURTEEN

JACK

We drove away in the Aston Martin.

Her hand was on my lap. My fingers entwined with hers.

I swore it still felt like a fucking dream, but if it were, I never wanted to goddamn wake up from it.

Time slipped through our grasp with the beat of our hearts, but it didn't matter how hard they pulsed with our excitement, it didn't stir London traffic.

It said a lot that both of us remained silent. That we didn't tease each other or argue.

This was the next phase, and I was glad we'd graduated to this place where heady excitement stole the words from our lips and kept our bodies humming along like we were a part of a song that only we could hear.

By the time we made it back to Kensington, the desire between us should have dulled itself down. The last time I'd kissed her had been a good ninety minutes ago, after all.

But she squeezed my fingers as if silently wishing my hand farewell before she climbed out of the car, Goose yipping playfully as he pissed against the gatepost.

I followed her down the path and up the stairs to the front door, and as she unlocked it, Goose rushed in, sliding all over the floor, and she let him dart off once I closed the door.

Locking it behind me, I turned around, and she was there.

In my face.

Right where I wanted her.

Her arms were around my shoulders, her legs clasping my body after she hurled herself at me.

As her mouth collided with mine, I realized that this was home.

This townhouse had been my whole life, but that was nothing to this.

Nothing to a kiss I wanted to drown in.

The woman made my heart fucking ache with a need that ran so deep it didn't just give me blue goddamn balls.

She ravaged my mouth, nipping and biting like her hunger made her wild, and I was there for it.

Every step of the fucking way.

My hands explored the expanse of her back as I turned her and pressed her into the front door.

My tongue thrust against hers, feasting on her, lusting after every taste of her she was willing to give me.

All the while, my fingers shaped her thighs, exploring the strong length through the jeans she wore.

I ground my dick against her denim-covered softness, moaning with her when that hit the fucking spot as if we were naked.

With a grunt, I pulled back and nipped at the pad of her chin before I rumbled, "I want to fuck you."

"Do," she whimpered. "You won't hear me complain."

I growled under my breath then dove onto her lips once more, grinding my cock into her again, torturing us both as she arched her back and wriggled her hips for maximum sensation.

Knowing I'd go nuts if I wasn't inside her soon, I encouraged her to stand, carefully lowering one leg, then the other, before rasping, "You're only allowed to wear skirts from now on."

"So you can fuck me against doors?"

"Yes," I rasped.

"That's a compromise I can live with," she retorted, her tone serious.

I almost laughed because there was no way in hell she'd ever change that much; Beau was not a girly girl. She might work the vintage look, but unlike my mom who was Rockabilly chic, Beau was darker. Edgier.

She wore skinny jeans and low-cut blouses that showed off her tits and wore little scarves knotted around her throat.

She'd had a Betty Page fringe for almost as long as I'd known her until she'd grown it out this year, and her tats and piercings were on display as much as her tiny waist and big bubble butt was in her slender skinny pants.

She reminded me of Sandy from Grease. Not the good girl, but the bad one. All sex appeal and snark.

Fuck, she revved my engines.

My hands went to her waistband, and I tugged at the buttons, uncaring if they popped, before I slipped my hand down her panties. The confines of her jeans meant that when I found gold, there was pressure, and she groaned, melting into me and using the door to keep her upright.

I rubbed my fingers along her slit, finding her wet and ready before I dove beneath the crotch and found her slickness for myself.

As I nipped on her bottom lip, I rumbled, "Tell me what you want, baby."

She blinked dazed eyes at me as she gave me a kiss that stole my breath away.

I pulled back though. "Words."

"I want you—" A sharp cry escaped her as I rubbed her clit. "—to worship—" She groaned as I thrust a finger into her. "—me."

That it took three tries to get that out of her pleased me.

I smirked to myself as I thrust my tongue against hers, mimicking what I was going to do to her later, then I rasped, "You know you're mine, don't you?"

She groaned again. "Yes."

I thrust another finger inside her and scissored them. "You know I'm never going to let you go?"

"I do," she whimpered.

I rewarded her by grinding my palm against her clit.

She shot up onto tiptoes and cried out my name.

My. Fucking. Name.

God, I didn't know if she knew I was being deadly serious or not. I wasn't messing around.

She was mine.

All mine.

No fucker else's.

And I wasn't afraid to stake my claim.

As she rocked against me, her mind focused on the hunt for pleasure, I nibbled on her bottom lip before I whispered, "Never gonna let you out of the house unless one part of you is covered in my cum, Beau—"

A shocked breath escaped her, and her eyes flared wide in surprise.

That was when she came.

She rocked against my hand, then her cries filled my ears as she screamed with her orgasm.

It took her a while to come back down because I carried on teasing her, and she moaned against my lips, "Only if your dick is coated in my pussy juices."

I snarled, uncaring that I sounded more like a fucking beast than a man. "Deal."

Another shaken breath escaped her, but she was the one who nipped at my chin, mimicking the move I'd made earlier.

I hissed at the sting then dragged down one side of her waistband, grateful when she helped with the other side.

My fingers stayed in the cosseting heat of her cunt, and I ground the heel of my wrist against her core every now and then as we worked to free her from her jeans.

I placed one booted foot against the crotch and shoved them down to the floor. That was when I had to be practical—my hand made a retreat as she toed out of her Converse sneaker then started wiggling around to free herself from one leg.

A guttural groan escaped her when she saw me unfasten my pants and jack off.

The moment one of her legs was liberated, apparently uncaring that the other was still encased in denim, Beau climbed me like a spider monkey.

When her long, slim thighs were back around my waist, I rasped, "Who do you belong to?"

Fire appeared in her eyes, an inferno I knew was blazing because of the pleasure she'd just experienced.

"You," she snapped. "Who do you belong to?"

"You," I bit off as my sopping wet fingers dug between us so I could caress her clit.

She squealed and arched against me, so I reached up and ordered, "Clean my hand. Get my knuckles wet."

Pressing a finger to her lips, she sucked it in deep, cleaning herself off one then the other I gave her, sucking on them in a way that made me look forward to her first blowjob.

My knuckles returned to her core once she was done, and as I brushed her clit with them, she cried out, but that was nothing to the second guttural groan she made that throbbed from her lips, which drove me crazy, as I thrust my way home.

As I fucked her against the door, her head arched back, and I feasted on her throat, leaving behind bruises that had faded from the last time I'd had her.

Nipping and sucking and lathing the flesh, I tormented her as I rode her, finding my own pleasure, insisting that she find hers again too.

When her pussy clamped down around me, and she screamed

loud enough for anyone on the street to wonder what the hell was going on, I roared with triumph as her cunt waltzed around my cock, drawing my seed from me.

As pleasure whacked me full frontal, I shoved my face into her throat, needing this, needing *her,* more than she could possibly understand.

She was my baseline.

My fucking balance.

I needed her to know that. I had to show her that truth.

And then she reminded me of why I loved her so fucking much. Because even as she was panting so hard the words came out on a wheeze, she rasped, "Think we'll ever make it past the front door and into a bed?"

Smiling against her throat, I nipped her there, enough for her to squeak at the bite, before I rumbled, "Not if I can help it."

Rosie: *I'm starting to get really mad now.*

Beau: *Why? What's happened?*

Bethan: *She's being a drama queen.*

Beau: *As per usual.*

Rosie: *You're such bitches.*

Bethan: *We try, don't we, Beau?*

Beau: *Every morning we wake up. Lol. What happened in particular?*

Rosie: *Mom tried to set me up again.*

Bethan: *You're lucky she does. I think she reckons I'm a lost hope.*

Beau: *Hardly.*

Rosie: *We can switch places like we did when we were twelve.*

Bethan: *LMAO. I can't see that working now.*

Beau: *Your date wouldn't know. Anyway, since when do you WANT to date?*

Bethan: *I don't particularly.*

Beau: *Then what's the problem?*

Bethan: *No problem. Just the principle. Why's Mom going out of her way to set up Rosie but not me?*

Rosie: *Why aren't we pulling a Parent Trap switcharoo? This would solve everything.*

Bethan: *Because we're no longer twelve? And I don't want to date. I just don't see why YOU'RE the only one being set up. Anyway, there's no point in switching places. Dad always knows who's who.*

Rosie: *Dad knows everything.*

Bethan: *Yup.*

Beau: *You two are crazy.*

Rosie: *You're the one screwing Jackass. Now who's crazy?*

Bethan: *She has a point.*

Beau: *No. She doesn't. Jack isn't always a jackass.*

Rosie: *Just most of the time?*

Bethan: *At least half.*

Beau: *I agreed I'd stop calling him that.*

Rosie: *We didn't agree to those terms.*

Bethan: *No, we damn well didn't.*

Beau: *I said you'd back off, but I think he knows he'll need to negotiate with you.*

Bethan: *Should hope so.*

Rosie: *I still can't believe you're dating him.*

Beau: *I'm not dating him.*

Rosie: *You were doing a good impression of cozying up to him the other day!*

Beau: *Cozying up, dating... I love him, guys. That's different. It means more, right?*

Bethan: *Technically, no.*

Rosie: *Relationship status: complicated?*

Beau: *No. We're together. It's never been simpler.*

Beau: *He did hurt my heart the other day though.*

Rosie: *Why?*

Bethan: *What did the fucker do?*

Beau: *You two are really protective of me, aren't you?*

Rosie: *This comes as a surprise why?*

Bethan: *Yeah. DUH, Beau.*

Beau: *o.O ANYWAY, he didn't hurt me. Just my heart. He told me that my exes used to rub it in his face that we were dating.*

Rosie: *How did they know he was into you but we didn't?*

Bethan: *That's weird. Your fault, Beau, for not sharing with us.*

Beau: *I don't like labels. Anyway, it wasn't weird. What they did was CRUEL.*

Rosie: *Yeah, I hated your exes. You have bad taste in women. Just saying.*

Bethan: *Me too. Bitches all round.*

Rosie: *Huh. Maybe Jack IS a kinder evil.*

Bethan: *Lol. You might be right.*

Beau: *They were that bad?*

Rosie: *Yup. Penelope actually came onto me once.*

Bethan: *Oh, crap, I remember that!!*

Beau: *WHAT? Why the hell didn't you tell me?*

Rosie: ***shrugs** What was I supposed to tell you? You stopped dating her like a few days later. I figured she knew you were pulling away from her or something.*

Bethan: *I hated Shiloh but I gotta say she had really good taste in jewelry.*

Bethan: *Maybe you're onto something, Rosie. Jack IS better to handle. At least we can tell Mom if he pisses us off.*

Beau: *LOL. What are you? Five?*

Rosie: *You're never too old to rat your baby brother out to your mom.*

Bethan: *Agreed.*

Beau: *Ha.*

Rosie: *You really love him, huh?*

Beau: *I really do.*

Rosie: **sighs* I guess we'll have to put up with him then.*

Bethan: *I'm still calling him Jackass. Especially when he acts like one.*

Rosie: *Same.*

Beau: *You can argue over that with him.*

Bethan: *Don't you worry. We will.*

FIFTEEN

JACK

With my ass on the sofa, my hands in Beau's hair, I'd admit I was in heaven.

I was pretty sure the only way this could turn out better was if she ended up sucking me off, but it wasn't imperative for my happiness.

Which, if I'd been doubting how much I frickin' loved her, spoke volumes.

A holiday movie on in the background, two steaming mugs of hot chocolate close to hand, I split her wet hair into three locks and started braiding it.

Sitting between my legs, she'd pressed one arm over my knee and had her face smushed to my inner thigh as I worked.

Relaxed wasn't the word.

My shoulders hurt, my back too, and my right hip was aching like a bitch, but I was on cloud fucking nine.

"This always reminds me of Bash."

Lost in the strands of red gold in my hands, I blinked. "What does?"

I wasn't sure what mesmerized me about her hair, but it was like shining a laser light in front of a cat. Only, I didn't want to attack it, just jack off with it.

"This story."

It took me a second to figure out what she was talking about. Then, I grumbled, "You've watched it before? Why are we watching it again, then?"

She sniffed. "I'm a professional holiday movie watcher."

"Since when?"

"Since always, I just never watched them around you."

"Why not?"

Her shoulders hitched. "We all have our secrets."

"Not anymore."

From her profile, I saw her small smile. "Everyone has secrets."

"Nah. Not us. Not going to happen."

"Are we going to confess to each other every week?"

"Maybe we should." I smirked. "In the bedroom. Post-orgasm so we're really relaxed."

Laughing, Beau retorted, "I don't think I'd survive hearing your confessions."

"How dirty do you think my thoughts are?" I tugged on her hair. "Oh, wait. You don't have to answer that. Just lean back and you can feel my boner."

She snorted. "Stop lowering the tone of my Christmas movie."

I grinned to myself as I continued plaiting the strands of her hair together. "Okay, tell me why you think this reminds you of Bash?"

"He's an orphan and he moves in with his forever family for Christmas."

"Ha. Bash isn't an orphan, and he moved in with us in the summertime."

"Isn't he?" This time, she twisted around to stare up at me. "Really?"

"You didn't know?"

She shrugged. "Rosie never talks about him, and you know what Bethan is like."

"Close-mouthed? It's a good thing she isn't a criminal defense attorney."

"Yeah, she inherited too many of your father's smarts. She'd get the bad guys out all the time."

"Instead, she's holier-than-thou, that's for sure," I sniped.

"Only sometimes."

I scoffed but explained, "Bash's stepmom beat him something fierce. She got sent to jail when the police picked him up as he tried to hitchhike to Yorkshire where his birth mother was in prison."

She gasped. "That's so sad!"

"It was. He was messed up when Mom first brought him home from one of her charity housing projects."

"Did she foster him?

"I don't know. I guess so. We didn't really ask questions back then. Plus, I was only four when Bash showed up." I stared at the Christmas movie. "He was difficult. I remember that.

"Mom didn't often bring kids to stay with us because Rosie was a precocious brat and it used to get her upset, but when she talks about him, Mom always says that Bash called to her and she couldn't leave him behind at the group foster home."

"Rosie's a brat," she agreed, "and it's so weird because I don't think I've met anyone with a bigger heart."

I didn't argue because she was right.

"She's always been possessive of family," was all I ended up saying. What happened the other day, after all, was proof of that. Beau, to Rosie, *was* family. "Anyway, Bash came to stay and he never left.

"He was a fucking nightmare too. He used to steal shit all the time, and he refused to shower for weeks on end. At one point, he was more toxic than Chernobyl."

"Devon must have loved that."

Laughing, I asked, "You know how Jemima, Rock, and Harry followed him around?"

They were his dogs.

"Yeah?"

"Well, Bash was one of his pack for a while."

"Devon let him?"

"He did. Even though he stank."

She angled her head back to look at me which stilled my braiding. "He clearly became a part of the family on your end. I wonder why he wants to stick to the outside?"

"Because he can back off without getting hurt?"

I didn't understand Bash, but I didn't have to. He was who he was, and I usually appreciated his point of view on life. Still, it hurt that, to me, he was a brother, but to him, I was probably just Jack Dubois.

"That's sad."

"It is," I said with a soft sigh.

"I wonder why he never uses people's names?"

"Same reason. Little attachment. Means any connections can be broken off quickly."

She bit her lip. "Is it dumb that I hope the kid in the movie doesn't end up like Bash?"

"No. *But* there's one consolation—Bash has always been allowed to be himself. We never pigeonholed him. I think that helped him with his trauma." As I finished up the braid, I tugged on it gently. "Acceptance is precious, wouldn't you say?"

She nodded. "I guess. I just... He loves Rosie, doesn't he?"

I shrugged. "Who knows with Bash. If he does, I don't think it eats him up inside."

Beau turned fully to peer at me. "Like it did with you?"

"Like it did with me," I rasped, my gaze locked on hers.

Reaching up so she could cup my chin, she whispered, "And me."

SIXTEEN

BEAU

My arm tucked in Jack's, we headed down the stretch of market stalls. I tried to shop and simultaneously stop Goose from peeing on everything in sight.

It was cold, on the brink of snowing, even, but while my cheeks burned with the frigid air, happiness was like a warm glow in my soul.

The festive cheer was intoxicating, and the trees and decorations made my inner child grin with glee.

The scents of fried foods and sweet treats had my stomach rumbling, but that was only exacerbated by the fact that Jack hadn't let me up for food once since those meager sips of hot chocolate I'd had in front of the TV earlier in the day.

"Your smile gets any bigger, it'll light up the place better than that Christmas tree."

Chuckling, I squeezed his arm. "Stop being the Grinch."

"I'm not being the Grinch. I'm here, aren't I? When I very much wanted to stay in bed."

"We've been in bed all day," I retorted.

"What's wrong with all night?" He sniffed. "Anyway, it wasn't the whole day. We watched movies when I braided your hair, didn't we?"

"We did. You owe me the other half of the movie," I told him absentmindedly as I tugged him to a halt at one of the stalls. "Two mulled wines, please," I told the stallholder as I shoved Goose's leash at Jack before I dug around for some coins in my pocket.

Jack had other ideas—he had a twenty-pound note in his hand, and cash was exchanged before I could so much as blink.

Before she served us our drinks, he handed Goose back into my care then grabbed the cups.

I scowled at him. "That was my treat."

He shrugged. "Prefer you to buy something memorable. I wasn't being a chauvinist, just accepting that you earn a lot less than me and I don't want you to waste it on drinks."

"Drinks are fleeting." He sloshed them gently. "But hopefully, there'll be something here you can buy that'll make you think of this day forever."

Wow.

For a second, I was speechless.

Then, I rasped, "I like 'Boyfriend Jack.'"

Arching a brow at me as he took a sip of his wine, he asked, "What's 'Boyfriend Jack?'"

"Better than 'Best Friend Jack.'" I smiled at him. "You're cute. I never knew you had it in you."

He scoffed. "I've always been nice to you. I like you."

Grinning, I teased, "Are you blushing?"

"No," he grumbled. "And anyway, you wouldn't be able to tell seeing as it's dark out."

"I see all and hear all," I intoned.

"Yeah, yeah, you wish."

"Seriously though, you're very sweet. I mean, I always knew you were kind, but this level of sweet is like ice cream, and no woman can turn down a pint of that.

"I'm wondering why someone didn't snap you up." I let my gaze drift up and down. "Let's not forget that I've seen beneath the boxers, so I know the wrapping matches the goods."

"My dick isn't sweet."

"Says who?"

He snickered but informed me, "Maybe I didn't want to be snapped up, huh? I had a say in it, you know?"

"You sure? I'd have pinned you down."

"Really? You can still do that."

"I did this afternoon," I retorted.

"You can do it every day. It has to be better than an apple a day."

"What? That keeps the doctor away?"

"Exactly."

"Keeps your pipes clean?"

His nose crinkled, but he barked out a laugh before he could stop himself. "Crude, Beau, crude. I expect better of you."

"Why? I thought you'd like it if I was dirty."

"Not in a public place," he told me calmly. "That side of you is for my eyes only."

"What would happen if we were in a private place?" I taunted a little breathlessly.

"You'd know if you hadn't dragged me out here."

"I didn't drag you anywhere."

"You did."

"Didn't."

"Did!" he said with a sniff.

"Are we really arguing like toddlers in the middle of Chelsea?"

He grinned at me. "Bet your ass we are."

I laughed up at him. "You're crazy."

"Crazy for you." He nudged me in the side. "Want me to prove how sweet I am?"

"How would you do that?"

"Tomorrow, I'll put up the Christmas tree with you."

A mock-gasp escaped me and I slapped my hand to my chest.

"You? Jack Dubois, the Grinch himself, will put up the Christmas tree for little old me?"

He nodded piously. "Aren't you lucky that you're my girlfriend?"

"Oh, man. So lucky. I just have one question..."

"What?"

"Is your heart the only thing that grows three sizes?"

SEVENTEEN

I stared at the tree we'd bought today and the bags of decorations on the floor, then I stared dubiously at Goose and went back to staring at the tree once more.

"He'll tear it down," I predicted.

"He won't," Beau retorted. "He's a good boy."

"How many puppies have you been around?"

"Well, none. Rosie always has me foster older dogs."

I arched a brow. "We've had dozens of puppies. Mom always had a fancy pen around our trees.

"I'm going to assume that was for a reason and not because she liked to treat her Christmas trees as if they were prisoners."

She studied Goose, who didn't help matters by staring up at her like he was an angel and she was God.

"Would your mom have a pen here?"

"Maybe? In the attic? I can look."

"I guess there'll be old Christmas decorations too?"

"I mean, most of the good ones will probably be back home, but I'm sure there'll be some here."

"That sounds like a treasure hunt to me."

I snorted. "More like a chance to sneeze."

Christmas was a big thing in our house, and while I definitely wasn't the Grinch she accused me of being, I preferred leaving the decorating to Mom who had everything down pat.

Still, a promise was a promise, and I kind of liked the fact she thought I was sweet.

Especially after years of being called Jackass by her.

Beau, unaware of my thoughts, peered at the tree. "Think that it'll survive us heading up there?"

"We could take him with us."

"To get dusty?" Her nose crinkled. "I know, we'll put him in your room."

Goddamn Rosie.

She couldn't have gotten a house-trained puppy for Beau, could she?

Nope.

Inwardly rolling my eyes and determining to get my sister back at a later date, I nodded. "We'll leave him there."

Forty minutes later, Goose was hopefully snoozing in my bedroom and not chewing on anything he could get his teeth around, and we were in the attic.

Once upon a time, Mom's room had been the attic conversion, but now it was used for storage.

I turned on the light and came face to face with a lot of memories.

Smiling at the sight of some of the small cars Dad had bought me, I saw Beau noticed them and laughed. "Wonder who hauled them up the stairs?"

"Probably Daw. He'd have considered it a workout."

She whistled as she wandered through a couple decades worth of my family's history.

"It's so strange to think that your mom met and fell in love with your dads here, isn't it?"

"Strange?" I pondered the word. "I guess. I like that we're here now. I feel as if it's fitting."

She turned to cast me a look. "What do you mean?"

"I mean, you said it yourself. They fell in love here. This was the start of their happily-ever-after. I like that it's the start of ours too."

Beau blinked at me then stepped closer and slipped her arms around my waist.

Burrowing her face into my chest, she whispered, "I'm so lucky."

"I'm the lucky one," I rasped.

In a way, we were closer than a couple could ever be because of so many years spent together, not just as kids but as adults too, yet this was all new.

I just felt so fortunate because I'd never expected to have any of this with her, but here we were.

Like I'd told her the other day in the car showroom—I wasn't an idiot.

Adrenaline junkie, sure.

Addicted to bao buns, definitely.

Problems with authority, yup.

But an idiot? No.

I didn't intend on squandering another damn day.

Not a single fucking one.

"This is our first Christmas together." My hand slipped through her hair so I could cup the back of her head. "The first of many—"

"It is," she inserted before I could finish my sentence, which made me smile.

"Next year, I'm going to take you somewhere better than London."

Warmth lit up her eyes. "What did you tell me? That I'm your home? Jack, I don't need to be anywhere other than right here."

When she squeezed my waist, I pressed my forehead against hers and just breathed in the same air as her.

This woman... did she know she was the only person who could break me?

"I want to explore," she murmured a couple minutes later. "I wonder what your mom stored up here."

I cupped her ass and hauled her into me. "You might be okay with London but I want to take you somewhere tomorrow."

"What does that have to do with me wanting to explore the attic?" When I shrugged, she squinted up at me. "Where?"

"A surprise."

"I hate surprises."

"I know. But... once we locate the pen, I'll investigate this cesspit of dust *for you* if we visit the place I want to go without you asking any questions."

She arched a brow. "Is it a sex dungeon?"

A snort escaped me. "No. Neither is it a serial killer's lair."

"Pfft. I didn't think it was a serial killer's lair, but I could imagine you in leather and wielding a whip."

"Is that a fantasy of yours?" I joked.

"Maybe if I was the one with the whip," she sniped, but her eyes were gleaming. "Okay. I have to assume it's some boring F1 museum, but agreed—we'll go. No questions asked. But we explore first. We could find the pen along the way."

We shook hands on it, my thumb pressing between her knuckles and hers doing the same in our own not-so-secret handshake.

"Where do you want to start?"

"I want to see pictures of you as a baby."

"You've already seen them," I scoffed, well aware that Rosie and Bethan had taken great delight in embarrassing me by showing her photos of me toddling around in diapers years ago.

"I'm greedy. I want to see that and Rosie and Bethan and Tin. Ooh, do you think there'll be pictures of Alice?"

"Is this for future blackmail purposes?" I queried warily as she dove headfirst into the gamut of trunks and old crates and boxes that littered the space.

She grinned at me. "Now, Jack, would I ever be so nefarious?"

"Of course you would. Remember I'm the one who knows how good you are at strategy."

Laughter pealed from her, and it did my heart good to hear.

Shaking my head, I waded into the fray and inadvertently had a great time doing so.

A couple hours later, surrounded by boxes, the pen leaning against the door for me to carry downstairs once we were done, she'd found a Hermès scarf which she tied around her hair in a '50s' bandana-style, I'd found one of Sean's old Rolexes which was on my wrist, and even though we were trawling through ten tons of dust, she'd plunked on a pair of my mom's old high heels.

It was like dress-up. Adult-style.

We hadn't found a single Christmas decoration other than the pen that would keep Goose from attacking the tree.

"Oh my God!" she squeaked. "How fucking cute is this?"

She shoved a picture at me, and I chuckled when I saw Bethan and Rosie sitting around a small table clearly playing at serving tea, only their guests were Christel, Victoria, and Alice... actual princesses.

"You don't think those are real crowns, do you?" I joked.

"I do. Look at them! They don't look fake."

I squinted as I held up the picture to the light. "Jeez, that's awesome if they *are* real."

"We'll ask your mom. Put it on the pile."

By this point, we had a small stack of pictures that required further explanation from Mom.

One included Dad with a pair of shorts on his head instead of covering his actual ass—thankfully the important parts had been shielded by a newspaper, Daw standing up at a podium beside a US president, and *Vati* at what appeared to be the after-party of some kind of award ceremony. Only, he wasn't wearing a suit but Lederhosen.

That was a story I needed to know.

Hell, they all were.

Beau rifled through a trunk and pulled out a stack of folded papers that had been tied together with string.

I frowned at it and asked, "What are those?"

"Don't know until I open them."

It was a testament to the fact that Beau had been family for years that I didn't have any qualms about her opening private letters. Maybe my parents wouldn't like for us to be searching up here, but I didn't think they'd mind.

We were open by nature.

It was one reason why the kids had such a good relationship with the folks—there was no point in lying when your parents accepted you.

And even though I'd had a chip on my shoulder about them stopping traveling to my races... I knew they supported me.

They just didn't support me trying to kill myself on the track.

As she untucked one of the letters from the pouch, she read it and said, "It's in German."

I plucked it from her hand and scanned it quickly. As I did, my brows rose in surprise.

I half-imagined it was from Kurt to his parents, but it wasn't.

I translated:

"Darling Sascha,

It's been three weeks since we lost Camilla. Three weeks and I can feel you pulling away from us. We're losing you, sweetheart. I can see your grief crawling between us and it's tearing me apart.

But that is not your burden to bear. I write this letter to you, knowing you'll never read it, and I don't want you to. I write this here so that I can hold my tongue.

When I see you skipping meals, staring despondently into space, grief eating at you... it hurts my heart. It hurts all our hearts.

You're our world, darling.

I just wish you'd see that for yourself.

All my love,

Yours,

Kurt."

"Your mom lost a baby?" she asked quietly.

"Apparently."

"You didn't know?"

I shook my head as I scanned the note, finding comfort in the scatty nature of *Vati's* handwriting.

"This is from Sawyer." She cleared her throat before reading the letter aloud:

"*Wee, Sascha,*

I think this is a daft idea, but Kurt came up with it, and he keeps staring out of the window like the earth is about to fall from beneath our feet.

But I have faith in ye, lass. I ken yer goin' naewhere."

"He actually spells like he speaks," Beau mumbled, angling the paper and squinting at the handwriting.

"Yes. That's why *Papa* writes most of their reports."

"Why my *dad* writes them," she corrected dryly, making me smile.

"*I'd spank yer arse black and blue before I'd let ye leave us. And I'm nae talking about ye going back to the US either.*

I love ye, lass. Ye make my heart full.

Sawyer."

"She must have been depressed," Beau murmured. Her free hand clenched on her leg, though, as she leaned back against a box at her back.

I shot her a look. "Are you okay?"

"Yes." She blinked down at the paper in her hand. "It's stupid."

"Nothing's stupid between you and me."

Her lips curved. "Stop being sweet. You're going to be mad at me in a minute."

"Why? You're not reneging on our promise," I warned.

She sniffed. "It's not about that."

"What then?"

"You know my mama killed herself?"

I did.

I also knew it was something she hated talking about.

"I do," I said softly.

"I found her."

Her words were barely imperceptible.

"You found her body?" I demanded, totally aghast.

When she nodded, I gritted my teeth to stop myself from snapping at her. She was clearly still dealing with the aftereffects of finding her mom... and for her never to have shared that with me was almost beyond my comprehension.

For a moment, I dealt with hurt and anger before I swallowed both down, got over myself, and grated out, "You know you can tell me anything."

It sounded more accusatory than I'd intended, but hell, that I'd kept my tone low was a miracle in itself.

"I do, but this..." She shrugged, her fingers drifting over Daw's love letter to my mom. "I couldn't talk about it with anyone. Dad had me in therapy for years, but I never uttered a word. They knew I found her because..." She gulped. "Well, it doesn't matter."

"It damn well does," I retorted. "Why did they know?"

"Because I broke my arm climbing the tree, trying to get her down." She turned her face away, her right hand absently stroking her left arm where I assumed she'd broken it. "I don't want to talk about it." Her mouth tightened. "Do you think your mom ever read these?"

I stared at her, trying to find logic in what she was saying, but because her eyes were no longer gleaming with the joy she found in hunting for treasure amid our family memories, but were glinting with the onset of tears, I rasped, "I don't."

Her mom had hung herself in a tree and Beau had found her?

My hands balled into fists.

I knew her mother had died when she was six...

Jesus Christ.

"Why?"

I jolted at her question, and it took me a while to figure out what I was answering.

"Because Mom would never have left them to rot up here if she had."

"Why did they bundle them together like this?"

"Maybe they thought she'd find them years later."

"Like we have."

"Yes."

She licked her lips. "It's sweet."

I nodded, stared down at *Vati's* letter. "They gave up a lot to be together, but it never felt like that."

"What do you mean?"

Shrugging, I said, "No outside family. Only what we made for ourselves."

Once *Papa's* grandfather and Granddad, Mom's pop, had gone, then Jacinta and Hamish, Daw's parents, had left us too, that was it.

"We had no one too." Her brow furrowed. "You became our family."

"And you became ours. That's why everyone's so protective of you."

She straightened at that, and while their interference a few days ago had pissed me off, I was glad for it.

"You'll never be short of family now," I predicted. "Not with the way Tin and Alice are at it like rabbits."

Beau snorted. "You and Rosie are obsessed. They have one kid with another coming, and Noelie is sweet."

"The golden child. She'll reign hell over the new world," I intoned, mostly just to make her laugh.

"That poor kid."

"Poor kid? She's going to be Queen one day."

"Exactly, poor her. What a feat." She carefully folded up the letters. "We won't read anymore. I think we should give them to Sascha, though, don't you?"

I nodded. "I think she'd like them."

"You don't think it would remind her of sad times?"

"Maybe. But there's no sadness without joy and no joy without sadness."

"How very Buddhist of you."

"I'm a wise man," I taunted.

"A wise ass."

"I thought we graduated from always talking about my ass?"

She smirked as she bowed her head, her fingers taking great care to close the old letters along the original folds.

"Your ass has gone viral," she pointed out as she worked.

"It has." My butt had been the 'face' of an ad campaign. "You're never going to let me live that down, are you?"

Humor hit her eyes, chasing away the sorrow of moments before.

Just like I'd hoped.

She'd opened the door between us in a way I hadn't even known was locked until now...

Did she know what that meant?

I doubted that she did, but I was well aware of the ramifications, and I was grateful for it.

EIGHTEEN

As we headed out of London toward Dartford, I frowned but didn't really ask what we were doing. I'd promised I wouldn't complain—

"You sure it's not a car museum?"

Okay, so some complaints were necessary.

"Dammit, I took you to one when I was sixteen," he grumbled. "One time. You'd think I spent my whole life making you visit them."

"You knew how to show me a bad time," I mocked.

"I took you to plenty of other good places. We went to that silver museum, didn't we?"

"You mean the Guggenheim?" My brow furrowed. "Philistine."

"I prefer to think of myself as a hedonist."

"I wonder why." I grunted under my breath, then with hope lacing the words, asked, "Is this as good as the Guggenheim?"

"Maybe. Depends."

"On what?"

"If you give it a go."

"Give what a go?"

"Is this you not complaining or arguing even though you promised—"

"Yeah, yeah, yeah. I get it." Huffing, I plunked my hands into my pockets and muttered, "You'd think for four hundred K, there'd be a decent heater in here."

"Flick that button. It warms your seats," he directed.

"I don't want a hot ass."

"Too late," he retorted, tongue-in-cheek.

My lips twitched. "You just want in it."

"I can't argue with that," he agreed, a smile dancing about his lips. "But seriously, it's nice. Eases any aches you might have."

The statement drew a frown out of me. "How's your back?"

We hadn't talked about work since we'd come to London. Mostly, I guessed, we'd been having a vacation from life: playing house, getting to know Goose, and that was all without enjoying each other.

This was a snapshot of time away from reality, but reality didn't disappear for long.

I knew that, so did he, and I felt like we were both taking advantage of it.

"It's okay," he said easily.

But I knew him too well.

I also knew his rap sheet better than he probably did.

And, no, I wasn't talking criminally, but medically.

"Leave it, Beau," he said softly, his hand gently patting my knee.

I grumbled under my breath, knowing that he was touchy about his injuries, then watched as he drove us out of the city and toward the coast.

"I'll leave it," I said, "but when's your next physio appointment?"

He grunted. "A few days' time."

"You've skipped a few sessions."

"You're all the physio I need."

I scoffed, "I've seen you after physio. You look like you've been to war. Is that what happens in our bed?"

"Well, I prefer to make love not war."

"Yeah, but as much as I'm sure I'm good for your endorphins, not sure if I'll help that shoulder injury from last season."

He grunted. "I'll make Jensen come tomorrow."

"Good."

Now I'd gotten some of my own way, I sat back in my seat and just settled in for the ride.

It was a grim day, but deep inside, there was a warmth I couldn't and didn't want to escape from.

It was like his being here took away some of the bitter cold.

I knew that was impossible, but I couldn't help how I felt.

Things were still up in the air. I had no idea what I wanted to do with my life, no real direction, but this with Jack made me feel less like a boat without a rudder.

Life, after all, was long.

I had plenty of time to figure myself out, and in the interim, I could wait tables or do some temping.

If Jack needed to go to Veronia, like he'd mentioned the night of the party, I could get the same jobs there as I could here. I might spend every cent of that wage on splitting our living costs, but that was okay too.

Every now and then, a song would come on from the playlist he was playing, and I'd turn it up full blast so I could sing away to it.

Those were the moments that made me appreciate what we had.

He knew I couldn't sing.

He knew that I always puked if I drank tequila.

He also knew that with a hangover from hell, appeasing my beast consisted of feeding me bacon and eggs.

He knew I loved art and that I hated video games, even though I played them with him—and I always won.

He knew my quirks.

And he liked me for them.

I knew his.

And I liked him for them.

Of course, my pleasure in the moment, in him and *us* as a unit, waned when I saw *where* he was taking us.

"No way," I complained immediately when we started heading for a racetrack.

"It isn't what you think," he retorted.

"No?" So much for a vacation from fucking life. Exasperated and kind of hurt, I sniped, "This isn't you sneaking in some practice time?"

He sniffed. "This isn't an F1 track anymore."

"Then why are we here?"

"Because I wanted to test a theory."

"A theory?"

My brow puckered as we pulled up outside the track, but the second the cameras spotted us, the gates opened and Jack, seeming to know where we were going, drove along a short road before he reached another gate.

That was when we were on the frickin' track.

I didn't see a damn person between there and here, and as we started moving around the circuit, I demanded, "Why are you driving at a snail's pace? We're literally the only people here."

"I'm curious. Watch the road."

Pissed, I blinked at him, then folding my arms under my tits, I huffed and watched him as we drove around the track twice.

"This has the engine of a sports' car. The refurbed model packs more of a punch than any Italian stallion."

"You would say that. You don't like Italian cars."

He sniffed. "Are you watching?"

"I'm watching. I just don't know what I'm supposed to be looking for."

As we made it back to where we started, he stopped the engine and pulled off his seatbelt.

Frowning, I demanded, "Where are you going?"

"We're switching seats."

"Huh?"

"You're going to drive."

"What? Why?" Utterly confused, I muttered, "You know I don't like driving."

He shrugged. "Wanted to test a theory."

"You keep saying that."

"Yeah, and you promised not to whine if I went through thirty years of my family's shit up in the attic," he countered silkily. "Are you breaking a promise, Beau?"

I squinted at him. "That's a low blow."

He smirked. "I can go lower."

"I'll bet." I raised my chin. "In fact, I expect it."

"Tonight."

"Tonight," I confirmed.

"Not sure why you think it's a punishment," he drawled.

"Straight men always complain about oral."

He sniffed. "That's because they're dipshits."

"And you're not one? Our presence here says otherwise."

"Now, now, no mean names. Especially not when my tongue's gonna be buried deep in your pussy later on, Beau, and I can make you scream my *real* one."

Well, that made shit interesting.

I could feel the color crawl over my chest and up my throat.

Narrowing my eyes at him, I retorted, "Okay, I'll go around the track as many times as you get me off tonight."

His lips quirked. "Deal. But you're the one who'll be exhausted. Not me."

"Cocky."

"Something about me is," he agreed with a laugh as he shoved open the car door and climbed out.

My temper lessened when I saw the slight wince as he straightened up.

Goddamn him for skipping his physio.

I should have been on him about that. It wasn't like he wasn't used to me nagging him.

Grumbling under my breath, vowing that I'd give him a massage after he'd gone down on me because it wasn't often you saw Jack limping or wincing with pain, I climbed out of the car too.

As we rounded the fender, he called out, "How fast do F1 cars accelerate from 0-60 mph?"

I hummed. "Two and a half seconds?"

"Two point six." He tapped the roof. "This might look vintage, but it's sleek as fuck underneath. This hits 60 mph in five point six."

I whistled. "Really?"

"Yeah. When they pimped it, they meant business."

For a standard car, that *was* impressive.

Hopping behind the steering wheel, I moved the seat as he settled beside me then readjusted the mirrors.

"I hate driving," I pointed out again.

Just to be contrary.

"You can't hate it. You never do it," he retorted. "I always drive us everywhere."

"Duh. Because you're the driver."

"I'm a racing champion, not a chauffeur," he corrected, but he was grinning as he strapped on his belt.

As I did too, I murmured, "What do you want me to do?"

"Just drive around the circuit."

With an irritated sigh, I started the engine and rode around the track as he suggested.

While I drove, he fiddled with the radio, and some EDM started to throb through the speakers.

"Might not have great heating, but it has an epic sound system," he hollered over the beat.

Nodding, I concentrated on driving.

It was a full Grand Prix circuit, and I monitored the layout as I drifted down a slightly curved stretch with an off-camber. It plunged into a right-hand bend with a sharp gradient.

Experience told me that the curve might be a tough one, especially at high speed, but it'd be a great place to overtake a rival.

The next corner was a hairpin bend and was followed by an

uphill braking zone before the track curved around a spectator area, shifting downhill onto another off-camber bend which flowed into a stretch beside the pit lane.

After, the circuit cambered uphill, drifted into a turn, and onto the back straight.

With the wide expanse of space around me, no one else on the track, I was tempted to let my feet do the talking and to speed up, but I didn't.

After the straight, however, there was a deep elevation—a steep hill and a drop—which was made even more complicated as it merged into a crazy sharp bend.

There were a couple of loops, each one necessitating some heavy maneuvering because there was a dip and some blind curves. I cambered onto another bend before driving down a short straight. There was another uphill curve as we approached the pit straight, and then there was the start/finish line.

"There," I muttered. "Done."

He smiled at me. "Do it again. But faster."

"I'm not the one who likes speed," I countered, shooting him a frown.

"Give it a shot," he retorted, increasing the volume to the point where the bass boomed beneath my seat.

With a grumble, I stared at the circuit, but it was no longer just an expanse of tarmac broken up by token areas of woodland that were supposed to make it prettier.

There was no longer an empty stand at my side...

I'd been to enough races to know the air felt electric with expectation.

I'd hung around the drivers enough to experience the adrenaline rush by proxy. As if there were so much of it in their pheromones, I was breathing it in myself.

The music throbbed through my veins.

The day was light, the sun bleak but sharp enough to illuminate all the nuances of the curves, and as my hand tightened around the wheel, I carefully eased off the brake and stopped idling.

One hand on the gears, the other on the wheel, I went faster this time.

At top speeds, I figured the track would only take just over seventy or so seconds to complete.

The first time, I did it in around four minutes—I took note of the time on the dash.

The second, I did it in just three.

On that occasion, sweat prickled the back of my neck, and I could feel the pounding of my heart as it chimed at the same rhythm as the music.

But for all that I could sense my body was stressed, I felt calm.

My gaze was watchful; my palms were dry.

As I settled by the start line, I didn't need Jack to tell me to go again.

That time, I finished the lap in two minutes.

When I returned to the finish line, the adrenaline surge of before was no more.

It was an outright buzz.

As I idled the car at the line, I configured all the different things I'd learned along each lap, and this time, I put them into practice.

Did I take note of Jack watching me?

Maybe.

But I wasn't focused on him.

I was focused on the road.

I raced around hairpin bends, moved into the curves, throttled my way up the hills, and flew down the straights.

By the time I made it back to the finish line, I knew I was drenched with sweat, and it had nothing to do with my coat, sweater, and heavy-duty cotton tee, but I didn't care.

"Fuck," I rasped, my voice hoarse as if I'd been shouting when I'd been silent the whole time.

Jack thrust something into my line of sight, breaking my uninterrupted view of the racetrack.

I blinked when I saw it was the timer app on his phone.

"Eighty-nine seconds," he murmured. "Adam Carroll has the record on this track. Seventy-two. With an F1 car, Beau."

I licked my lips, stared at the figures, jumbled them around my head, and tried to figure out how to shave more seconds off my time.

That was when he launched himself at me.

It might have been out of the blue, but I knew why he did—*a celebration.*

I felt the same crazy high that he experienced whenever he was behind the wheel on a track like this, and he wanted to share it with me.

It was only once one of his hands went to my nape as he dragged me into him that I realized I wanted to share it too.

Our mouths collided in a firebomb of energy that sent shockwaves through the air, amping up the blast of adrenaline to my system to unforeseen heights.

His teeth tore at my lips; our tongues fucked the other. Passion and need were no longer crawling through my system, but raging inside us both.

A mutual rage.

One that had to bear fruit.

His hands cupped my head, holding me in place, but mine weren't trapped.

I reached for his cock, shaped it, then snarled into his kiss as I felt his thick length in my palm.

A hunger so powerful I'd never known anything like it consumed me.

It wasn't enough that our mouths were fucking; I needed him inside me.

I needed to feel *him*: his heat, his energy, his want and need for *me* burning itself off inside my body.

Freeing him from the cage of his fly, I delved between the tines to grab his cock.

He hissed against my lips, pulling back as his eyes glowered into mine.

"Don't fucking tease."

"Who's teasing?" I growled.

Letting go of him, my hands went to my own fly, and I tugged at the button, unfastening it before I arched my hips and worked my jeans down my legs, toeing off my Converse at the same time.

With my bottom half uncovered, I noticed he'd dragged the seat back, and though it was awkward as fuck, I launched myself at him.

I didn't give a damn that we were in the middle of a racetrack.

Didn't care that there might have been cameras zooming in on us as we fucked.

I felt alive.

Like he always made me feel.

I throbbed with vitality, vivacity.

It ran through my veins, turbocharging everything until I felt electric with wanton power.

I nearly got myself a stick shift as a butt plug, but when I clambered onto his lap and straddled him, he helped guide me onto his dick.

Wasn't he a gent?

The second his thick length pressed into me, the heat of him burning me up, I let loose a groan before I slammed our mouths together again.

I rocked against him, hard and fast, not slowing down, rocking and rocking so quickly that I wouldn't need to work out for at least three days because this had to beat a couple workouts in the gym.

His hands grabbed my ass, clutching and clenching at the soft curves as he angled me, encouraging me, giving me strength.

I knew he'd always do that.

Not just in this. As a friend, he'd been supportive, but as my man, I knew that would only grow too.

I looked forward to being Jack's partner.

I reveled in the knowledge that he was mine and I was fucking his.

His to hold.

Forever.

The thought triggered the detonation.

I went off like a light show, groaning against his lips as the pleasure hit me on all sides.

The only thing that made it better?

He came at the same time.

Our mutual explosions sent more of those shockwaves through the air, and because there was nowhere for them to go but the car, it felt as if they were absorbed back into us.

G-Forces couldn't feel this overwhelming as we dealt with the catastrophically delicious aftermath of that fast fuck, but there was no one I'd rather be devastated with than Jack.

NINETEEN

JACK

Upon our return to London, Mom called.

Ordinarily, I'd have told her to call back when I was at home, but I put her on speaker, deciding that it was the best way to save time.

I had plans when I got home, plans that involved being horizontal, and they didn't include talking to my mother.

Plus, she hadn't disturbed us since that first morning, and I figured that was because Rosie and Bethan had done Beau—not me—a solid and had eased Mom's concerns.

Anyway, Beau was still driving, having refused to relinquish control of the DB6, so I figured I might as well talk now so that I could get down to business again as soon as we got home.

Seven times she'd gone around the track... but *six* orgasms she was owed.

My boner was already aching just thinking about it and I'd only gotten off forty or so minutes ago.

"Sascha!" Beau chirped, sounding cheerful as hell.

I had to smile.

Going around the track combined with that explosive quickie had definitely put a spring in her step.

It'd put more than a spring in *my* step. Just call me Tigger.

Mom's voice sounded wary, a little shaken, as she asked, "Beau? Is that you?"

Wondering what was up, I said, "Beau's driving, Mom. We just finished up some errands. Everything okay?"

"I—" She was quiet a second. "I need you to not get mad."

"Get mad?" I repeated. "Why? What's happened?" I thought about what could make Mom lose her cool and demanded, "Daw's not had a heart attack, has he? *Vati* is okay?"

Kurt—*Vati*—and Sawyer—Daw—were the fathers with the health issues.

They were the ones that could make her lose her shit.

I straightened up in my seat as she whispered, "It's Rosie."

"Rosie?" Beau demanded, her hands tightening around the wheel as she pulled onto the shoulder of a road, clearly wanting to focus on the conversation and not the mass chaos of traffic up ahead. "Sascha, what's happened? Is she okay? Did she eat some nuts?"

Rosie had a peanut allergy.

Tension hit me because I'd never thought of that. I'd seen her deal with an allergic reaction twice, though, and just the memory had my heart skipping a beat.

"Mom? What is it? What happened? Did she eat peanuts?"

"Oh, she's so naughty," she declared, sniffling all the way. Beau and I shared a glance. "Why does she have to put herself in these situations? She's a vet! A country vet! Who the hell gets into so much trouble as a country vet—"

Beau tensed but warily tossed in, "The puppy mill?"

Mom sucked in a breath. "You know about that?"

"Rosie told me about it the night of the party. She said she was calling in the RSPCA. Did she?" She rubbed her brow. "I spoke to her yesterday, but she never mentioned it."

"You talked to her yesterday?" I muttered.

"I did. And Bethan. I talk to them every day," Beau replied, her surprise clear. "Why?"

I shrugged. I'd known they were close but hadn't realized they were *that* close.

"Doesn't matter," I countered, unsure if I liked the fact my sisters could weave me in a web that could tumble me out of Beau's good graces.

"Jack?"

Grimacing when I realized my mind was definitely not on the right track, I asked, "What?"

"I need you to keep your cool."

"When do I lose it?" I drawled.

Mom sucked in a breath. "The puppy mill... the owner... Rosie broke in and stole some puppies. H-He, oh, Jack, the owner beat her."

My eyes rounded, but just as the words hit, a wave of fury had me sinking beneath the tide.

"Rosie was beaten?" I repeated, my words so soft that it almost belied the welter of rage pummeling me.

"Y-Yes." Mom sucked in a breath. "She's—" A sob escaped her. "She's got a broken collarbone, a sprained arm, and her face... The bastard must have gone to town on her. It's a wonder she didn't lose any teeth."

Rage had me bunching my hands into fists then slamming them down against my thighs.

Then, Mom signed the death warrant on my temper when she continued, "Jack, Bash... he's been arrested."

For a second, the words didn't resonate. Then, they hit harder than the news Rosie had been beaten because I knew *why* Bash had been arrested.

"Did he kill him?"

"Bash?" Beau squeaked, her head whipping to the side to gape at me. "Did Bash kill someone? Why would you ask that?"

I shot her a look. "I know you think you know Bash, but you never really know Bash. Did he ever tell you about what he had to do to survive before Mom brought him home?"

At the time, none of us had been very happy to have a scrawny street urchin hanging around. I was well aware that sounded Dickensian, but it was the truth.

He'd been tiny, all bones and mouth. Pure Cockney mouth at that. He'd hated baths, thought Mom was trying to poison him when she fed him broccoli, and nothing in the house was free from being pickpocketed.

Mom being Mom hadn't minded. She'd just found where he placed his loot and had calmly returned the items he'd stolen back to their original positions.

Like a reverse Fagin.

Eventually, Bash had stopped biting the hand that fed him, had no longer tried to run back to London, and all the broccoli seemed to turbocharge him into the man he was today.

All six-feet-four, two-hundred-and-fifty pounds of him.

Beau's brow furrowed. "No. You know what he's like. He doesn't really talk."

I had to concede that. For a long while, we'd thought he was mute. He wasn't. He was just selective. Then, out had come the Cockney slang which had died a death over the years thanks to our school.

Clearing my throat, I murmured, "He loves Rosie. He'd do anything to protect her." I heard Mom start sobbing, and I feared the worst. "Is there proof?" I rasped, hoping to fuck there wasn't. Because Bash was family. Bash was... *Bash.*

"No. What there is is circumstantial. But he's still been arrested."

"Is *Papa* on it?" I demanded.

"Yes." She sniffled. "But Bash told him not to bother. They arrested him twenty minutes ago—"

"Wait, when did Rosie get attacked?"

"Last night," she whispered. "Rosie told us not to tell you."

"Since when do any of you do as you're told? I can't believe you didn't tell me!"

"Bethan didn't say a word last night," Beau stated grimly, apparently as pissed as I felt.

Which, of course, was when my unease about her being so close with my sisters faded.

Bash, Bethan, Rosie, and Tin were *her* family too.

She was angry.

Not on my behalf, but on theirs.

I snagged her hand and tightened mine around hers. She bridged her fingers with mine then rasped, "Bash... There's a body?"

"Yes. The owner..." Mom gulped. "He was beaten to death. They found him in his stable."

My nostrils flared as I stated, "Living up to his name."

"Stop it, Jack. He didn't really do it. It's just some—"

"What? A coincidence?" I sniped. "Mom, this is Bash. You know who you brought home. I know you do. I'm not saying you shouldn't have. I love Bash. He's my brother. But we all know what he is."

"You say that like he's an ax murderer," Mom growled, her defenses kicking into high gear.

"I didn't say that. I'm just saying that you know where he came from as well as I do."

Beau tugged on my hand and mouthed, "Where?"

I shook my head. "What's Papa doing? Is Tin getting involved?"

She sucked in a breath. "Tin's trying to make it so that Bash has diplomatic immunity."

"He can do that?" I queried, my voice higher pitched than usual.

"Apparently. Bash has... well, Bash has done some work for the Veronian government. I don't want to know, but it might work in our favor if they push ahead with this."

Rubbing my eyes, I muttered, "Is Rosie still in the hospital?"

"No. She came home a few hours ago," Mom admitted on a shaky breath.

I gritted my teeth, but it was Beau who slipped in, "We'll be back as soon as we stop at the house to grab Goose."

"You don't need to—"

"Yes," Beau insisted, "we do, Sascha."

"We do, Mom," I agreed.

"She doesn't want to be a bother," Mom whispered.

"Well, she should have thought about that before she turned into Rosie," I sniped.

Beau elbowed me in the side. "Take that back. Rosie is the kindest person in the world. She doesn't deserve this."

"Of course she doesn't, and of course, she's kind, but she could piss off a Buddhist monk when she gets fixated on something.

"You can't go around getting in people's faces, buzzing around them like you're a fly, without expecting to get whacked from time to time."

Beau scowled at me but to Mom, asked, "Is Rosie... Does she know... about Bash?"

"She's sleeping."

I plucked at my bottom lip. "She's going to be upset."

"Of course she is," Mom argued.

"No, I mean she's going to be distressed." Carefully, trying to ram home how devastated Rosie was about to be, I enunciated, "I think she has feelings for Bash."

"Don't be ridiculous, Jack. Rosie's..." She sighed. "You know she didn't like it when I brought Bash home."

"Be prepared—" Headache brewing, I rubbed my temple. "Just... maybe don't say anything to her. If *Papa* and Tin are both working on angles to get him out, then she doesn't need to know."

With *Papa* working behind the scenes, and Tin working on a legal front, I couldn't see Bash spending the night in jail.

"You should have seen him, Jack," Mom whispered. "When the police came, he kissed me on the cheek and said, 'Don't worry, Mother Hen. I'm going where I was born to be.'"

Beau sucked in a breath then rasped, "Oh, fuck."

When Mom started crying, I couldn't blame her. I nearly had a goddamn tear in my eye too.

Suddenly exhausted, I scrubbed my hand over my face and considered the situation. "*Papa* and Tin won't allow that to be his fate, Mom. Just... have faith. We'll be there as soon as we can, okay?"

"O-Okay."

It broke me to hear her crying, so I asked, "Is Bethan there?"

"Y-Yes."

"Go and sit with her and Rosie. Please? For my sake?"

"I will. Jack? I love you, son."

"I love you too, Mom. Please, don't worry. Everything will be okay."

"Y-You don't know that."

Something popped into my head. "If Bash had already done the dirty work," I murmured, "why were you concerned about my temper?"

"The puppy farm is owned by two men. Please, promise you won't do anything crazy."

"I won't," I promised easily.

"Jack," she warned, just as Beau tugged on my hand.

"I won't," I repeated—and I meant it. Later, when Bash was home and safe, I'd shake his hand though. "We'll be there as soon as traffic allows. Give Rosie a kiss from us, Mom."

Disconnecting the call, I turned to Beau and demanded, "You want to get some points on your license for speeding?"

"You're the one who needs the clean license," she reasoned.

"What I need is to get home."

Her mouth tightened, and she stared at me for so long that I almost barked at her to hurry the hell up, but that was when she pulled off the shoulder.

Of course, that was also when there was the faintest gap in traffic, so I knew she hadn't been wasting time by gawking at me, just waiting to make her move.

As she drove, my mind raced, and because I couldn't settle, I started to phone *Papa*.

"Jack?" Beau rasped, breaking into my train of thought so I cut the call. "You... you won't do anything stupid, will you?"

"I'm a race car driver," I said simply. "What can I do?"

"I don't know," was her wary response. "That's what concerns me."

I spoke no word of a lie.

I was only a race car driver.

But *Papa*—Andrei—wasn't.

He had the Bratva at his back.

I knew he didn't believe in them, knew he didn't agree with the way they did their business, but I also knew *Papa* could be a hypocrite where they were concerned.

Rubbing my chin, I decided not to say anything until I was sitting with him.

After all, knowing how my fathers and brother worked, I wouldn't have to say a word.

A plan would already be underway.

No one hurt the women in our family.

Not unless they had a death wish.

TWENTY

BEAU

Jack wasn't restful by nature.

Unlike his siblings who were intensely curious and focused on accruing knowledge like it was Pokémon cards, Jack was always on the go.

I figured that was why we got along. I was a little like him and a little like his twin sisters.

It meant I blurred the lines between them, meant I could fit in.

It was why we worked as a group.

So seeing him *be* restful was unnerving.

He hadn't demanded that he take over behind the wheel, hadn't even climbed into the driver's seat after we stopped at the house in Kensington.

He was pensive.

With his mind clearly wandering, I let him drift because I was terrified he was plotting a second murder and I didn't want to lose him when I'd just found him.

Guilt speared me whenever Goose, who was strapped into the backseat, licked my elbow when I changed gears.

Goose was a reminder of Rosie's gung-ho nature.

I loved her. She was my best friend, a sister to me, but there was no denying that Jack had been right.

Rosie was a bull in a china shop. She didn't care that she rammed down everything that surrounded her. She just questioned why the bull had been placed in the china shop in the first place.

Animals, after all, required appropriate housing and husbandry. What other result was to be expected if one placed a bull in a china shop?

Because I could easily imagine her saying that, I tried not to laugh because I knew I'd end up crying.

She'd been beaten.

Bash had killed her attacker.

And Jack had said all that as if I should have expected it.

What the hell was going on?

Sighing, I rubbed my forehead as we finally made it to Surrey.

With reality definitely smacking us in the face, I raced toward the village, uncaring that speed cameras flashed a few times along the way.

"Bash—" I started a few minutes along the road to the Dubois estate.

"Bash is Bash," was all Jack said. "He is who he is."

"You were..."

He seemed to know what I was saying. "No. I wasn't surprised. Bash is Bash."

I frowned because I knew what he meant, but there was a big difference between being a nitpicker by nature and being a murderer.

"He'd never hurt you, Beau," Jack chided, and his tone was such that I felt even guiltier.

"I didn't think he would," I argued.

"You did." He rubbed his bottom lip. "Mom saved him. You know that."

"I do." There was no disputing that. "He was always like a shadow though, wasn't he?"

"Yeah. That describes him to a tee. Bethan, Rosie, Tin, and I all made a racket, but Bash was like a shadow."

"You included him," I argued. "Don't feel bad about that."

"No. You're right. We did try, but he was..." His tone morphed, becoming both tired and sad as he explained, "I guess he was broken long before Mom had a chance to fix him."

I thought about what he'd told Sascha and whispered, "I hate that he's in jail."

We both knew Sascha would have called again if she had news on that front.

"I don't like it either."

"I never realized he called your mom 'Mother Hen.'"

Jack shrugged. "Haven't you noticed? He doesn't call anyone anything. Doesn't even call 'Mom' Mom, and she's the nearest thing he's ever had to a real mother."

I pondered the American variant of Sascha's title a second. "Maybe he can't pronounce it?"

Jack's lips twitched. "You can say it."

"Only because I've been around you a long time. It's one of those words that's difficult to pronounce, isn't it? Like 'mall.'"

"Or how Americans can never understand Brits when they say, 'water?'"

I smiled. "Yeah."

It was getting dark by this point, and the lights in the massive mansion were blaring in almost every room as I made my way down to the courtyard where cars parked to the side of the building.

That every room was illuminated wasn't altogether surprising considering how many people lived under the one very large roof, but I knew it was more to do with the current family drama.

As I cut the engine, we stared up at the side of the house for a second, and that was when Jack snagged my hand and requested, "Don't leave?"

I blinked. "Why would I leave?"

"To go home. Stay. Please?"

Swallowing, I whispered, "There's nowhere else I want to be."

I couldn't see his smile, but I could sense his relief.

He sucked in a breath. "It's going to be chaotic."

"It is," I confirmed.

"We'll get through it."

He said that more for himself than for me, I thought, but it didn't stop me from telling him, "We will."

With a final squeeze of my fingers, he opened the door with his other hand then clambered out.

This time, I couldn't help but notice the awkward movement as he straightened up and determined that I'd be calling his physio for an emergency appointment whether Jack liked it or not.

Following him, I grabbed Goose, planted him on the ground, locked the car, pocketed the keys, and moved around to join Jack.

"All roads lead to Bishop Rosen," he intoned softly, staring up at the estate.

The village was named after the house which had been standing for hundreds of years, watching over the world as time drifted by.

I arched a brow at him. "You barely spend any time here."

"No," he conceded. "But that's only for now."

"You're the one who wants to go to Veronia."

He shrugged. "For a short while. This is home."

I didn't say anything. Couldn't. I agreed.

This *was* home.

"You don't agree?" he asked, clearly mistaking my silence.

"No, I do. This is home," I repeated.

"Then why did you want to go to London?"

"A change is as good as a rest, and I had to do something. You were wrapped up in that." I tugged on his hand. "If this is happening—"

"It is," he uttered under his breath.

"—then," I continued with a soft smile, "I have no need to run away."

"I'm sorry you felt like you had to."

He sounded too mournful for my liking, so I peered up at him and asked, "Hey, what's going on with you? I thought you'd be riding in there to rip Rosie a new one."

He was silent for a second, and I let him process his thoughts. It didn't matter that the wind chill was bitter, that Goose was pulling at his lead, ready to go on a walk after the long drive.

All that mattered was this small bubble we were standing in.

A sanctuary that belonged only to us and one I wouldn't rupture unnecessarily.

"Do you remember when *Vati* had a heart attack?"

Kurt had angina.

"Yeah. I remember."

"The whole family got together…" He rubbed his chin. "It feels weird. That's all."

"The whole family *is* here."

"No. *Papa* and Tin might still be working to get Bash free. And Bash, well, God only knows where he is."

I wasn't entirely sure if the village had a large enough police station, so he had a point on us not knowing where his adopted brother could be at this second.

"Rosie isn't ill, Jack. She's hurting, but she's not…"

"You can say it. At death's door?"

I sighed. "Yeah. But Kurt's fine, isn't he? Your mom force-feeds him chia seeds and turmeric root and only God knows what to make sure he's healthy, doesn't she?"

His laughter was soft, gentle, but I knew he heard my truth.

"It's like Sawyer. He's on every supplement known to man, and Sean's eating enough Stevia that he's going to turn into a leaf before anything happens with his diabetes."

"I know. I know they're all well. It's just life has a habit of stealing the people you love away from you." I felt his attention shift onto me. "You know that better than I do."

Silent a second, I rasped, "Yes, I do. But it wasn't life that took Mama, Jack. She did that."

"Life made her the way she was," he countered softly. "Who knows what goes through someone's mind when they're on the brink of making a decision like that? I just wish she'd had someone to speak with."

"She had my dad," I said gruffly, aware that I sounded bitter.

"You're mad at her," Jack intoned, his surprise clear.

Which, of course, put me on the defensive.

I almost jerked my hand from his and stalked off, but like he could predict that was my next move, he tugged a hold on me and said, "I told you already—you can tell me anything. No shame, no judgement. No reprisals or recriminations. That's how we work."

Mouth tight, heart hurting, I muttered, "I'm very mad at her."

"She didn't do it to hurt you."

"No? Well, regardless, it *did* fucking hurt me." My lips trembled from how hard I was pressing down on them. "Do we have to talk about this now?"

"I don't suppose we do," he countered, his tone gentle. "I just... family, you know?"

"Can't live with them, can't live without them," I rumbled in agreement.

"Yeah."

He took a step forward, and, together, we walked toward the house.

Like always before eight, the front door was open when he turned the handle, but the hall was surprisingly clear of people when we drifted inside.

It was cute how he steered me down the hall, like I didn't know where Rosie's room was, but I let him take the lead, finding it surreal that the last time I'd done this, we hadn't been together.

We'd been a pipe dream I'd never anticipated coming true.

Moving closer to him in thanks, Goose yipped as he struggled against the lead, and Jack muttered, "Let him loose. He'll find his way amid the packs."

"He might have an accident."

"So? We're all used to standing in dog shit in the middle of the night and having to clean it up."

My lips twitched but I leaned down and freed Goose. He surprised me by sticking near to me and not dancing away like I'd thought he would. Nor did he go chasing down the super long hallway that was lined with suits of armor and all kinds of things that would have made really great bathrooms.

He stuck close.

"He's loyal," Jack pointed out.

"Well, we'll see. You know your mom's like the dog whisperer."

"You ready for him to be a turncoat?"

"Sure am."

His half-smile died a death as we came to a halt in front of Rosie's door.

"She's going to be fine," I rasped, comforting him even though I was nervous as hell too.

He sucked in a breath, then without another word, knocked on the door and stormed in, dragging me with him.

This one, Bethan's, and Jack's were all rooms I was comfortable with, but I never saw it like this.

Because of its open-plan design, I saw there was a fire burning in the hearth, Bethan was napping on the Chesterfield, and there was a lamp glowing on the corner of her desk, but the shade was angled away so that it created a soft glow.

Sascha was seated beside Rosie's bedside, but at our arrival, she jerked to her feet and rushed over.

I let go of Jack's hand just in time for her to hug him, but she stunned me by including me in the hug.

As a trio, we all embraced, and she whispered, "Thank God you're here now."

The sense of inclusion went to my head like a pint of vodka, but I hugged her back and asked, "Any news on Bash?"

"No. Andrei isn't home yet. Tin came by earlier, but it was to pick Alice up."

"Why?" Jack questioned, pulling back to stare down at her.

"He needed her to sign off on something."

"Does it put her in a difficult position?"

"Probably, but you know Alice. She was born difficult."

Jack tutted. "You're too tough on her. Especially when she's doing Bash a massive favor by lying. Because I'm sure he *did* work for the Veronians, but that doesn't make him hold diplomatic immunity."

Sascha sighed. "I meant it as a compliment, Jack."

He grunted. "If you say so."

Before they could bicker, I said, "Bethan looks uncomfortable."

"She's been resting there most of the day after a long night at the hospital. She refuses to leave Rosie." Sascha gnawed on her lip. "This is such a mess."

"He'll be home before Christmas, Mom," Jack said softly. "You know *Papa* won't let you down."

"And Rosie might not be back on her feet, but she'll be more mobile by then," I pointed out.

"Beau? Is that you?"

Hearing the soft, croaky voice filled me with relief but also put me on edge. I twisted away from Sascha and Jack and rushed over to the bedside.

When I caught a glimpse of Rosie's battered face, I sucked in a breath, tried not to cry, and also tried not to get mad at her.

She was hurting.

She didn't need a lecture.

As I took a seat at her bedside, being careful not to jostle her, I bit my tongue hard enough that it was a wonder I didn't make it bleed.

Taking in her battered self, I queried gently, "Rosie, what the hell have you done now?"

She winced. "The police laughed at me when I reported the puppy farm. They didn't even visit the place because they called me in to help with the mother of a new litter! I had to do something."

So she'd waded in like she always did, thinking that she was immune to danger, and now, she was in bed, beaten and bruised, and Bash was in a goddamn jail cell.

I was quiet a second because it was either that or shout, and that was the last thing she needed. Instead, I wearily rubbed at my eyes.

"You're mad."

Capturing her good hand in mine, I gently clasped her fingers and murmured, "I'm furious."

Rosie pulled a face then grimaced when it tugged on the various cuts and swollen patches on her lips, chin, and nose. "Bethan's mad at me too."

"I'll bet she is."

"Mom is as well."

"I'm sure everyone's mad at you."

"Bash wasn't," she whispered, dropping her chin to her chest. "At least, he might be now. He hasn't come to visit me since I arrived back from the hospital."

Shit.

"I didn't think you'd want him to visit you. Last time I saw you together, you flinched when he touched your arm."

"Because he's Bash," she said gruffly.

"What does that mean?"

If I was short with her, then so be it.

The man had *murdered* for her.

He was in jail for her.

Her family was going to pull strings that should never have to be pulled for her.

But because he was Bash, she had to flinch when he touched her?

Rosie's eyes watered. "Don't be cross with me."

Guilt speared me, so I heaved a sigh and muttered, "I'm not cross with you."

"You are. I know I deserve it but please, just, get mad at me tomorrow. Not tonight."

"You do deserve it," I agreed with a huff. "But okay... What's going on with you and Bash though?"

I'd hung around the house plenty, and I knew him as well as anyone else on the estate, but I doubted Bash would go and kill for me.

Rosie peered at Jack and Sascha who were muttering under their breaths about something at the other end of the room, clearly not wanting to disturb Bethan, and she whispered, "You can't say anything."

"I won't."

She shot me a look. "You're Jack's now. That means your loyalties lie with him."

I frowned. "That doesn't mean that. It means that I'm loyal to him, but it doesn't mean I can't be loyal to you and Bethan too. Now, what's going on?"

"I went to the farm..." Her eyes glazed over with tears. "It was split into two. The front was a kennel."

"That was the part they let you see, right?"

She swallowed. "I went into the back room."

"How—" I rubbed my brow. "Never mind. You broke in."

"The police will probably want to talk to me about that at some point."

I snorted. "Honey, with what your family gets away with on the regular, I'd imagine Sean is pulling strings as we speak."

If they could work on getting Bash out of jail when he'd been arrested on suspicion of murder, then a little breaking and entering wasn't going to be difficult to throw out, was it?

Her voice choked as she said, "You should have seen the state of it, Beau. It was disgusting. I've seen pigsties that were cleaner. I started grabbing puppies, but—" She reached up and rubbed her brow. "—he... there was...it hurt," Rosie finished miserably.

Pity filled me.

Rosie had a hero syndrome worse than anyone I knew, but her heart was in the right place.

"At least the RSPCA know and can save the dogs now," I said, knowing that would cheer her up.

The tears faded. "Yeah."

Did I know my best friend or what?

"When did…" I sighed. "When did Bash come into the picture?"

"Bash? He didn't. He stopped by when I first got home."

My brows rose. "Oh. I must have misunderstood."

What the hell?

"Do you know where he is?"

"Who?"

"Bash, of course."

Of course?

I frowned at her. "Since when do you want to be around Bash?"

Her cheeks burned with hectic color. "Do you know where he is or not?"

"I don't," I told her, sharing the truth but only insofar that I didn't technically know where Bash was.

I wasn't about to lie to her. Neither did she need to know the whole truth. Not yet, at any rate.

"I'm surprised he's not here, that's all," she told me, her tone wistful.

"Do you want him to be?"

"Of course," she repeated with a snipe.

"You keep saying that, but the last time I saw you together you—"

"Not that again," she interrupted, scowling at me. "I *didn't* flinch."

"Sure as hell looked like that to me."

"You're wrong. I didn't flinch."

My lips quirked. "You really wanna argue right now, Ms. Rosie?"

I made sure to pronounce the 's' sound.

As I hissed at her, her nose crinkled which made us both cringe as the cut on the bridge creased with the gesture.

"Sorry," I rasped.

"Don't be." She touched her nose with tender fingers. "I'm sure Jack will tell me it's my own fault."

"You'd be right."

I grumbled under my breath as Jack stepped nearer to the bed, and I elbowed him in the gut as I peered up at him. "Stop living up to your old nickname."

He shook his head. "When are you going to realize you're not Robovet."

Rosie huffed. "I never thought I was."

"Apparently you do if you think you can go around stealing people's property without any repercussions."

My eyes flared wide. "You're victim blaming."

"No, I'm using common goddamn sense. You go onto someone's land, you steal their property, you expect repercussions."

I jerked to my feet. "You expect to get arrested." I quickly glowered at Rosie. "Which we'll talk about later. But what you don't expect is to have the shit kicked out of you, Jack."

Ignoring that, Jack demanded, "Did you know Goose was stolen?"

Rosie and I shared a look.

"You did?" Jack sputtered.

"He was abusing the dogs, Jack! Treating the mothers like—"

"Nobody is arguing that the puppy mill needed to be closed down, Rosie, sweetheart," Sascha murmured softly, wading into the discussion.

Immediately, Rosie and Jack calmed down.

I'd often noticed that was the case.

Sascha was like nitrous oxide—without the laughter. Calmed her kids right down.

"What we're saying is that you shouldn't have gone in guns blazing."

"You didn't go in armed, did you?" I cried, aghast.

Rosie scowled. "I'm anti-gun, anti-violence, anti-war, and—"

"Okay," I said, raising a hand. "You're right. I forgot my friend is a pacifist when she went and declared war on a puppy mill owner."

Rosie huffed. "I'm tired."

"No, you're exhausted from being beaten physically and verbally because you know you were a fool to do what you did," Jack retorted.

The lack of give to his voice pissed me off, but I watched as he leaned down and pressed a kiss to the one place on Rosie's forehead that wasn't bruised—the middle.

I followed the move, while Sascha plunked herself down on the other side of the bed, declaring, "I'm not going to sleep over there. Those Chesterfields make your butt feel like cement after a couple hours on them."

"You don't need to sleep with me," Rosie countered.

"If you're napping, I'm napping."

The stout response had her daughter grumbling under her breath.

"Would you turn off the lights, dear?" Sascha asked me.

I complied, flicking off the switch on the nightstand lamp then the one on the desk too, before shuffling out of the room as quietly as I could.

Goose danced around my heels as we headed into the hall, and when we'd made it about four doors away from Rosie's room, Jack rumbled, "Don't think you can start an argument over this. You should have heard what she did."

I glared at him. "You blamed her—"

"Bet your ass I did."

"Would you have blamed her if she'd worn a short skirt and got felt up at a bar?"

"Beau, that is a completely different scenario and entirely out of context. She went onto private property. She stole several dogs—"

"And she should have been arrested. *Not* beaten."

"Because of her, Bash is in fucking jail," Jack snapped, his eyes raging with fury. "Rosie's not a kid anymore. Her actions have consequences—"

"Why are you two arguing?"

My head whipped to the side, and that was when I saw Devon.

Three dogs either side of him, his usual pack, with a new puppy I didn't recognize on his knee, he was sitting on the floor, his legs splayed out in front of him, books and some travel tumblers dotted here and there. From experience, I knew they'd be filled with water and chamomile tea.

"Devon? Are you okay?"

If I'd been thinking about it, I'd have expected him to be sitting with Sascha, Rosie, and Bethan.

Goose stepped forward and investigated his pack of pooches, but not one of them stirred at his interest.

Devon stared at me and, like he'd heard my question for once, actually answered; "It's dark in Rosie's room. I can't see my notes. Plus, from here, I can see everyone who goes into her room."

I twisted back and found that he did indeed have a great vantage point from his position thanks to how the hallway was laid out.

"Where's Father, Dad?" Jack asked, dropping into a crouch by Devon's feet.

"In the kitchen with your daw and *Vati*. They're getting drunk."

I blinked. "They are?"

"It's not every day your little girl gets beaten." Devon's nostrils flared, and I saw a temper stir in his eyes that made Jack's earlier rage seem like a storm in a teacup. "Why were you two arguing?" he repeated.

"Because Beau thought I was being too harsh on Rosie."

"Were you?"

Jack squirmed, his shoulders hunching which hid his ears. "Maybe. She needed it."

"She's healing," Devon chided. "Give her hell when she's better."

"Devon!" I cried.

"What?" Devon stared at Goose who nuzzled into his arm. "Beau, Bash killed a man for her. She has to realize—"

"It isn't her responsibility that Bash is capable of those things. That's like blaming me for Jack being an adrenaline junkie."

He smiled. "What if I told you half of those stunts Jack pulled were to impress you?"

"Shut up, Dad," Jack hissed, jumping to his feet.

When he tugged on my hand, I stuck fast, demanding, "What?"

"Don't get me wrong, he was always a monkey. But he got worse when you were around. You know how boys are." His gaze turned distant. "Odd, isn't it? That we teach little girls it's okay for a boy to tug on their hair or to call them mean names because they like them..."

"What did you teach Jack?" I rasped, not looking at him, but his dad.

"I taught him natural selection."

"Huh?"

Devon angled his head as he murmured, "Why are peacocks' feathers so beautiful?"

He peered down at Goose who'd curled into a ball at his side and immediately went to sleep.

If Sascha was nitrous oxide for her kids, Devon was that for his dogs.

His question had me frowning. "To impress the peahens?"

He nodded.

As if that were an answer.

Frown deepening, I asked, "You mean you told him to impress me?"

"Yes, I just didn't realize I had such illogical children," he said with a grunt. "Tin decides he's G.I. Joe, Jack can't go around a racetrack without crashing, Rosie likes to dive headfirst into fights she can't win, and Bethan... well, she's the worst of them all."

My brows lifted at that. "Bethan's the least sanguine—"

Focused on his books, Devon smirked. "If you say so."

I shoved Jack in the side. "You've been trying to impress me with all the stunts you pull?"

Jack shoved his hands in his pockets. "Not always."

"Ha," Devon grumbled under his breath, his pencil scratching against the paper as he drafted something on the pad.

"You scared the living hell out of me," I cried. "Every race, I was terrified you were going to kill yourself. What's impressive about that?"

"That's the problem when your parent commits suicide, Jack," Devon rasped. "We always think the ones we love will leave us. We believe they *want* to leave us because we're not worthy of sticking around."

For a second, I didn't register what he said. Then I felt each of those words as if they were the hit of a hammer to my heart, squishing it like it was an orange in need of juicing.

"Y-Your—" I couldn't get the words out.

"My mother." Devon shared a glance with me. When we made eye contact, I realized that was the first time in years he'd ever looked me in the eye. "But their decisions don't define us, Beau. That's a life lesson that will take you until you're old and gray like me to figure out though." He tapped his pencil against the notepad. "Jack, are you going to stop trying to impress her now that she's yours?"

Jack cleared his throat. "I quit the team."

"Good." He reached for a book and flipped through it. "What are your plans?"

"I'm going to propose."

My eyes widened as I gaped at him.

"Good. When?"

"I was thinking New Year's Eve."

Devon hummed. "Nice idea. Will you say yes, Beau?"

For a second, I was pretty sure this conversation wasn't happening.

Jack didn't just propose via proxy, and Devon didn't expect me to answer in the same vein, did he?

Devon caught my eye again.

Whoa.

This was getting weird.

"Well?"

I swallowed. "Yes. He's a jackass, but he's my jackass."

Devon beamed a smile at me. "It's about time you became an official Dubois."

"Don't tell the others, Dad," Jack ordered, his hands still shoved in his pockets.

"I won't. Forget this conversation, Beau."

"How am I supposed to?" I half-wheezed.

"Well, you won't be surprised on New Year's Eve if you don't try to forget, will you? And this wasn't the most romantic setting."

"Whose fault was that?" Jack grumbled.

Devon, ignoring him, stated, "We'll renovate the East Wing."

"Why?" I queried, trying not to feel like I was in the Twilight Zone.

Jack's dad started to pet Goose's head. "You'll live here, of course, splitting your time between London, Surrey, and Madela." With his gaze in the near distance, he rumbled, "Jack wants to leave Formula One and head into management, but I know he needs to win another championship to get his new team off the starting post—"

Jack pulled a face. "How the hell you know any of this is beyond me."

Devon just smiled. "I know my children."

"What if I don't want to live here?" Jack argued. "What if Beau wants a change?"

He just wagged his pencil. "You're not going to be superglued here. But you wouldn't be able to stand living in Veronia full-time, Jack. You know they've put in speeding regulations, don't you?"

"What?!"

"On the highways." He mused, "Maybe Germany would be better. The *Autobahns* still don't have speed limits, and I'm sure your *Vati* has somewhere you could live."

Was my life really being planned around me as I stood in a hallway, beside a suit of armor, my turncoat dog sitting beside Devon while Jack and his dad argued about speed limits?

For a second, I just shook my head.

With the Dubois family, why was I even surprised?

TWENTY-ONE

JACK

A conversation with my dad often left a person feeling like they'd been dragged into a drive-thru car wash without ear plugs or goggles.

Beau, for all she knew my parents, and knew them well, was clearly in a state of shock.

When Dad stopped talking and started scratching more notes on his pad, I decided to leave him to it, and carefully, I guided Beau down the hall to my room.

Where she'd be staying.

Whether she was pissed at me or not.

I knew her well enough to know that she was silent because she was shocked, not because she was mad, so with Goose finally deigning to leave Dad's side and prancing around our heels, I stayed quiet too.

Once inside my bedroom, I left her to it. She knew the place as well as I did, after all.

Heading over to the small kitchenette that we had in our suite of rooms, I made myself a coffee and her a green tea.

I hated the stuff, but I always had her favorite brand in one of the cupboards because... well, I loved her. Why the hell wouldn't I get her something she favored?

It got me to thinking though.

How many decisions had I made with her in mind?

Dad had broken it down in a pretty facile way, but it wasn't facile. It was incredibly complicated.

I opened one of the French doors to let Goose out, but because it was cold, he darted into the garden, then a couple minutes later, returned, flinging himself across the room and returning to Beau's side.

That was where I found them both.

Beau curled up on the sofa, her feet burrowed under her butt, Goose on her lap, and the TV on. One of those weird spaceship videos she liked, the ones that were supposed to help you fall asleep at night, was on the TV.

Placing the cups on the coffee table in front of her, I moved over to the door, switched off the lights, and then returned to her side.

As I watched Earth through a spaceship's porthole, I didn't prod her to talk, just allowed my mind to wander.

"You will stop trying to impress me now, won't you? I don't think I could stand much more of it." Her voice was small, *scared.*

Guilt hit me like a punch to the gut. "Dad overexaggerated."

"Whether it was over, under, or somewhere in between, I don't care, Jack. You need to stop with the stunts or you'll break my heart."

Flinching, I rasped, "I told you I quit the team."

"And like your dad said, you'll need to cement your new team's standing by winning the next championship."

Contemplatively, I rubbed my chin. "I don't have a death wish."

"From where I'm standing, it looks like you do."

"Well, I don't. I want to win."

"No shit, Sherlock. I get it. I do. But fuck, Jack..." She swallowed. "I love you. I love you so much it hurts. I love you so much that even though I don't have an aggressive bone in my body—"

"Lies. You're always shoving me in the side."

She ignored me.

"—I could see myself doing something crazy like Bash did on *your* behalf."

My brows lifted. "Is that what you've been thinking about?"

She probably thought she'd shocked me, but I didn't come from the same world as she did.

My father had associates in the Bratva, for God's sake. That changed your perception of how shit worked.

But she broke into my thoughts with, "—that and you and all the crazy stunts you've pulled over the years to 'impress' me when what you really did was push me away and terrify me."

And like that, she did it.

Her words were the final nail in my coffin.

I was used to terrifying people. It was how I'd built my reputation: going further and faster than other drivers, willing to do shit no one else would because I knew my engines, knew what they were capable of with the right driver behind the wheel.

But I *had* pushed her away.

At the time, I'd missed her something fierce.

It was different now. I wouldn't just miss her if she left me in Veronia. I'd...

I didn't even want her sleeping at her dad's place tonight.

I wanted her here.

With me.

Al-fucking-ways.

"I'll tone it down."

Four words.

Who knew they'd mean more than three—'I love you.'

She hurled herself at me but didn't elbow me in the eye this time. Goose yipped as he went flying off the sofa, but Beau didn't care. She clung to me like a spider monkey. Her knees burrowed into my hips, the curvy thighs fitting either side of mine as she tightened them around me.

One arm went around my neck, the other around my waist, and her face burrowed into my throat as she sobbed.

Her terror ate into my bones.

My very heart.

Each tear she shed fell like acid as it dissolved the veins and arteries that kept it in place.

Slowly, as her pain seeped into me, I hugged her back as hard as she hugged me.

A part of me wanted to kiss her in thanks for loving me this much, but her fear wasn't something the union of two mouths could repair.

So I held her.

I hugged her.

And when she sagged into me, I rolled us up into a standing position and walked us over to the bed.

I didn't bother undressing us.

The way her legs were clamped around me told me she wasn't going anywhere, so I just dropped us to the mattress. As I rolled us onto our sides, I curled the duvet around us like we were the stuffing in a burrito.

She relaxed even more, and when I felt her soft breaths against my throat, I stared up at the ceiling, the soundtrack of the ASMR vid playing in the background, Goose nosing around, his claws tapping against the floor, and I whispered, "I'll never let you go, Beau. Never."

Which was how we fell asleep.

And that was how I'd fall asleep for the rest of my life.

No way was it going to be a short one, so I knew I had to hold fast to my promise.

Dad, much as he always did, broke everything down to the basics.

I'd fluttered my fancy blue feathers, and it had worked. My peahen was in my arms so there was no longer any need to preen, no need to impress her with stupid shit.

That might have gained her attention, but, as she'd said, it had pushed her away.

Away was the last place I wanted her.

TWENTY-TWO

BEAU

I was disappointed to wake up without Jack there, but when I checked my watch and saw it was almost lunchtime, my brows rose in surprise.

Stretching, I climbed out of bed, semi-relieved to find no 'accidents' on the floor, or, for that matter, no Goose hindering my steps so that I was tripping over him when I walked to the bathroom.

I felt no compunction in stealing one of Jack's tees or a pair of his boxers. It wasn't the first, neither would it be the last time I did so. I even used his soap and shampoo in the shower, and afterward, his deodorant.

Smelling like a boy, I drifted out of his rooms and, starving, went to the kitchen.

It was empty.

That wasn't altogether unusual considering it wasn't lunch yet. I'd been given the run of the house years before, so I felt no unease in making myself a cheese sandwich and a cup of tea.

As my tea steeped, I ate a bite of my snack, and that was when I saw Loretta Hardy.

She wandered into the kitchen, her gaze on her phone.

Because I was quiet, she didn't see me, but I watched as she bit her lip and muttered, "Oh, Julian, just drop it."

There weren't many Julians around here apart from my dad, so though it was none of my business, I murmured, "Do you want me to tell my father to back off?" When she shrieked, I winced. "Sorry. I didn't mean to frighten you."

She placed her hand against her chest. "You scared the hell out of me!"

"I wasn't hiding," I grumbled. "I was just standing here, eating a snack."

Her brow furrowed as she looked me over, then her cheeks burned. "I'm so sorry. I'm just jumpy."

Jumpy was an understatement.

I mean, I hadn't raised my voice or shouted, 'BOO' then leaped out of a corner at her...

"It's okay," I replied, but I nodded at her hand. "You mentioned a Julian... you're talking about my dad, right?"

She bowed her head. "I'm so sorry—"

"You don't have to be sorry," I countered. "I was the one eaves-dropping. If you want me to tell him to back off, I will. I know he..." Awkward. Wow. "...likes you."

Loretta blinked at me. "You know that?"

"Um, yeah. Don't you?"

"I guess." Her gaze started flying around the room. I understood why when she said, "He asked me out."

"Is everything okay?" I queried.

"Y-Yes."

I knew my dad wasn't the kind of guy to cause this level of fear in someone, but she was really nervous. It was making me edgy.

"Has he said something to upset you?"

Her eyes flared wide. "No! No, Julian's a gentleman. He—" She winced again. "Well, you know what he's like. He's your father."

"He is. But I never dated him," I tried to tease.

Her smile was faint. "True. You don't mind that he's..." She cleared her throat. "You know?"

"Wants to date?" At her nod, as I started to wonder how my father could like someone so anxious, I murmured, "No. I'm glad he wants to."

"You are?"

She was clearly surprised.

How to answer this while being truthful and not frightening her off...

As I pondered that, I slowly said, "He deserves to be happy again. He's spent a long time looking after and worrying over me."

"He still loves your mother."

I shrugged. "Maybe. Maybe not. It leaves a mark on you when your partner takes their life. I'm sure you can imagine."

Beyond the kitchen counters, there was the massive table where the family congregated for long, leisurely breakfasts. Resting her cell on it, she placed her hand on the back of one of the chairs, and her fingers tightened to the point where the skin turned white.

"I don't know if I..." Her brow puckered. "He's a good man."

"Yes. He is," I agreed. "But if you don't like him that way, and if he's messaging you..." Although, how she'd gotten his number if she hadn't asked was beyond me. My dad wasn't the kind of guy who'd push himself on anyone.

"I like him."

"Okay, that's good, isn't it?" I asked warily, half-wishing I hadn't gotten involved in this conversation.

"Yes, it is." She bowed her head but nodded so that her chin had to bump off her chest. "Thank you, Isabeau. I appreciate your help."

Before I even had the chance to tell her she should call me Beau, she scurried away like a frightened mouse.

Shaking my head, I started to take another bite of my sandwich when someone murmured, "That was very kind of you."

Recognizing the sharp, upper crust tones, I asked, "Sean?"

His head popped out from behind the wing of an armchair that peered over the land from behind a set of French doors.

"I didn't realize you were in here," I replied. "Sorry, I'd have made you a cup of tea."

"I was having a nap. It's been a busy couple of days."

When he pressed his hand to his forehead, I remembered what Devon had said last night.

"More like you need hair of the dog," I teased, stepping over to him with my plate and cup.

I loved this room. It was like an old banquet hall where food was made, eaten, and afterward, you could sit and lounge around the place because, at the foot of the table, there was a nook with comfortable seats—that was where Sean had tucked himself away.

Perching myself on the armchair opposite him, I asked, "Want the other half of my sandwich?"

He grimaced, and his cheeks bulged. "Thank you, Beau, but no."

"Any news on Bash?"

"Andrei, Tin, and Alice have yet to return home."

I bit my lip. "That doesn't bode well, does it?"

"Andrei has pulled off larger miracles, and all without the help of a crown princess and her husband."

"True." My brow puckered. "I'm sorry, Sean."

"What on earth for?"

I shrugged. "Everything."

"You always were a sweet girl." His tone said the opposite.

"You make that sound like a bad thing?" I queried warily.

"Hardly."

He studied me long enough to make me fidget. But because this was Sean, I slumped back against the armchair.

I was comfortable with him. With all of Jack, Rosie, and Bethan's parents, to be fair, because while they were my dad's bosses, they were my best friends' family first.

"You always made him happy."

His words were an odd declaration.

"I did?"

"Yes. It was only when Tin pointed that out I realized how short-sighted we'd been."

"Tin pointed that out?" I questioned, though I remembered one of the twins saying something about Tin and Devon being the only ones to realize there was a spark between Jack and me.

"He did. He said Jack's always been jealous of your girlfriends."

It was terrible of me.

Truly, I knew it was.

But I perked up at that.

"Really?"

Sean snorted. "Yes, really." Amusement gleamed in his eyes. "You like that he was jealous?"

"I've spent years jealous over him," I muttered. "All his girlfriends and the women he fuc—" I choked on the word.

"You can say it, Beau," he teased. "I'm not dead yet, and I'm well aware of my son's proclivities."

My nose crinkled. "Sorry."

"Don't be. Jack is... Jack."

Yeah.

That summed it up.

I fiddled with my earring. "I've loved him for a very long time."

"That's the only reason you'd put up with him," Sean retorted which made me laugh.

"True." I peeped a grin at him, but it slowly died. "It isn't the only reason. He's..."

"What is he?" he asked me quietly, kindly.

I'd always liked Sean.

There was something infinitely calming about him. His was a judgment-free zone.

"He's someone I didn't think I could ever have. I'm grateful for him. I keep waking up and wanting to pinch myself."

"You're going to make his ego even bigger."

I snickered. "No, I pinch him instead."

"And that deflates it?" He gave me a rare smile. "You don't have to question. Life will get in the way, as it usually does, and it will provide its random punches and kicks, but you have the strongest foundation imaginable.

"You know each other inside and out. You know each other's flaws and weaknesses. That means that when life *does* come calling, you'll be prepared."

"Life came calling yesterday," I rasped.

He heaved a sigh and rubbed his temple. "Bash is…"

I half-expected him to say, 'Bash is Bash,' like he'd done with Jack, but he didn't.

"He was terribly abused by his stepmother. It's a wonder he survived what she put him through."

My eyes flared wide. "Jack said she hurt him but I didn't realize his family situation was that dire."

"Why would you? You came after he was here, and by that point, Sascha had worked some of her magic on him.

"She'd gotten him to eat vegetables and he'd started eating foods that weren't doused in pints of ketchup." He tapped his fingers against the armrest of the chair. "I've always known he's had this in him. Sascha's been in denial, but I knew…"

"You knew?"

"I've dealt with too many people who've—" He sighed. "My job is to put away killers. Not free them from jail."

"You disapprove of what Andrei, Tin, and Alice are doing?"

"The professional side of me does. But the father?" Sean shook his head. "I want my boy home."

I swallowed. "You think he's dangerous?"

"I know he's dangerous, but he's on a leash."

"He is?"

"Rosie's his leash. It'll kill her when she finds out what he did. I'm concerned what will happen in the aftermath."

"Maybe if he's surrounded by family, and if she is, then it'll work out okay?"

"I doubt it. But you could be right." He blinked at me. "Are you staying for Christmas or returning to London?"

"Staying. I wanted to come back here anyway."

"Sascha told me that you were thinking of moving there full-time?"

"I was. But I'd still have come back here for the holidays."

He nodded. "It's good that you're becoming a part of the family, Beau. It never felt right, you being on the outside looking in."

I had no idea why, but that almost made me want to cry.

Choked, I whispered, "Thank you, Sean. You've no idea what that means to me."

Reaching forward, he patted me on the hand and said, "Thank you for taming my boy. If he'd have carried on the way he was going, he wouldn't have made it past thirty."

That had me gulping because I knew he was right. "I'll keep him safe."

I was graced with another rare smile. "I know you will."

TWENTY-THREE

JACK

When Tin and Alice arrived back home, I was standing by the Christmas tree, Mom directing me where to place decorations with all the patience of Stalin.

Having been roped into this against my will just so that it'd cheer her up, and with a Santa Claus in my hand, one that I'd made out of pasta shapes back when I was five—which I kept trying to throw away and which she fished out of the trash every year—I stormed over to the window.

Each step was like trying to cross a minefield as I attempted not to trip over Goose who was determined to play with every garland we retrieved from the many boxes littering the floor.

One glance out of the window, however, and my mood plummeted.

Bash and *Papa* weren't with them.

Dammit to hell.

Tin spied me in the window, and as he tucked his hand into Alice's, he raised the other and waved to me.

Frowning, I opened the window and called out, "Any joy?"

"Couldn't you wait to ask until I took another ten steps and made it inside?"

Tin's grumpy retort had me informing him, "You're a real stick in the mud now that you got married."

Alice huffed. "Hey, that's my husband you're talking about. He isn't a stick in the mud."

"He is," I argued.

"Where's Noelie?"

"Where do you think?"

Her lips twitched. "With Sawyer?"

"Yes. Glued to his side," Mom agreed as she tucked herself against me. "Where's your *papa?*"

"I'm literally ten steps away from the front door," Tin groused.

"This is too important to wait."

Alice took pity on us both. "We filed the appropriate forms, dotted the Is and crossed the Ts. Bash is currently sitting pretty with diplomatic immunity."

"So why haven't they let him out yet?"

I'd been dealing with Mom's impatience all morning.

This was the woman who'd been married to Devon Jerome for decades, yet she'd sniped at me when I put the star on the tree wrong and was grumbling about the placement of the string lights.

Tin, however, wasn't used to 'impatient Mom' so he frowned at her. "There's no need to bark at Alice."

Alice patted his chest. "It's okay. Tensions are high."

Tin wasn't appeased. "Apologize, Mom. Your daughter-in-law is the reason Bash won't be sitting in a jail cell for Christmas."

Mom stiffened but told Alice, "I'm sorry if I came across as curt."

"Who's taking my name in vain?"

I twisted around and found Kurt, my *Vati,* watching over the scene. He looked a little like Father, worse for wear after too many drinks last night, but he stepped into the brewing argument with the ease of a consummate diplomat.

That might not be his job, but in this household, it was.

"Mom's being a bitch toward Alice."

Mom gasped, Alice snorted, and Tin barked out a laugh. "Yeah, she is. Thanks, Jack."

Vati stepped forward and curved an arm around Mom's shoulder. "What's wrong, *Liebchen?*"

Now, you had to bear in mind that Mom wasn't a crier by nature, but when she whispered, "You have to ask me that?" and there was the clear sound of tears in her voice, I kind of felt bad.

But, I also kind of didn't.

Alice was cool.

Sure, we had to have a million guards around the place when she was staying, and I was pretty sure the Guard Elect—the Veronian Secret Service—had a shooter in one of the barns at all times, but she was nice, and it wasn't like she wanted guards to know whenever she used the bathroom.

It wasn't every day you had a future queen living in your brother's suite of rooms, one who could provide alibis and diplomatic immunity at will.

"Everyone is doing all they can," *Vati* crooned, tugging her against his chest and hugging her tighter. "He'll be home soon."

"It's that bitch's fault," she muttered into his sweater. Her condemnation stunned not only me, but Tin and Alice too.

Had she just called Rosie a bitch?

Vati hushed her under his breath and rasped, "You got him away from her."

So, not Rosie.

"Not before she broke him," she said with a sniffle. "After the last time, we said—"

My brows lifted. "The last time? Bash has done this before?"

Vati sighed. "Yes."

I heard the crunching of footsteps, then a door bang, and wasn't surprised that Tin and Alice had raced in here to discuss what we'd just learned.

"Is he dangerous?" Alice asked grimly.

"Of course he isn't," *Vati* rumbled.

I eyed him and slotted in, "Unless Rosie's in danger."

Vati nodded. "Her safety is his blind spot."

The news that Bash had killed for Rosie more than once didn't come as a shock.

What agitated me was that Rosie had been in two situations where her actions had necessitated Bash react that way.

After four years in the Army, he'd left at twenty-two, but I was pretty sure he worked for the government, having followed in Tin's footsteps at some point.

Maybe his body count was a lot higher than the two we knew about.

Rubbing my chin, I asked, "Who was the last guy Bash killed because of Rosie?"

"A boy in St. Andrews." *Vati* shrugged. "He saved Andrei from doing it."

"St. Andrews... isn't that where Rosie went to school?" Alice asked.

I nodded. "Yeah. What happened?"

"Bash was visiting—"

"Since when did he visit Rosie? They're always arguing!" Tin countered.

Unease creased *Vati's* expression. "He never said why he was there. At the time, I thought he'd been sent there."

"By whom?" Alice demanded. "The mail service?"

Vati harrumphed. "No. You know he does odd jobs."

"What kind of odd jobs are we talking about here? There's a difference between fixing a leaky faucet and taking people out assassin-style."

"You're not helping, Alice," Mom grumbled. "He does things for the Army."

"I thought he left a couple years ago," I queried.

"On paper, yes," was her answer.

"But not in real life?" Tin asked.

"Yes. Anyway, Rosie was at a club. Someone spiked her drink." *Vati* hesitated. "As far as either of them have explained to us, Rosie managed to contact Bash. He found her, stopped... she wasn't raped. Bash saved her."

Well, talk about a million holes in *that* story.

Like how had Rosie even known Bash was in the area for one?

I didn't say that, just mocked, "So, what you're saying is that we have to wrap Rosie in cotton wool to make sure that she's never in danger or Bash will turn into Batman?"

Vati sniffed. "It isn't ideal."

"Damn straight, it isn't."

I wasn't sure why I was angrier at Rosie than I was at Bash though.

"That's why Rosie's frightened of him."

The words had me blinking, but I turned and found Beau standing in the doorway, her brow puckered as she clearly processed what she'd overheard.

Beckoning her over, I watched as she darted to my side, her hand tangling with mine.

She looked more freaked out than anyone else in here because most of the room's occupants, including myself, were pretty calm about *Vati's* confession.

"Yes," *Vati* agreed with her. "She knows what he's capable of but he's her brother and she loves him all the same."

"He protected Rosie. Twice now," Mom grated out. "She doesn't need to be wrapped up in cotton. She needs to stop acting like her actions have no consequences.

"Take Bash out of this picture and what would have changed? She'd have been beaten because she shoved her nose where it shouldn't have gone. The police told her to back off, but she didn't. She refuses to listen—"

"You taught us to stand up for what we believe in," I argued, even if I partially agreed with her. "You taught us to fight for it."

"I did, but not to the point where you'd find yourself being beaten with a pipe on farmyard land," she shrieked. "I also taught you common sense. I taught you that there are ways and means of doing anything.

"You do not put yourselves in danger. You fight fire with fire, but you do it smartly!"

As she took a second to catch her breath, her cheeks as bright red as her auburn hair, a small voice chimed in, "You're right. I reacted, and I shouldn't have."

My head whipped to the side, and maybe I shouldn't have been surprised with how loudly we'd all been yelling, but I saw Rosie was there, leaning against Bethan, and so were Father and Daw. She had her arm in a sling and wore a contraption on her chest that I knew was for a broken clavicle.

How did I know?

I'd broken mine once, and it hurt like a motherfucker.

Noelie giggled from within Daw's embrace until she crowed with glee as Alice collected her and propped her on her hip.

"This is a mess," I rasped.

"Bash's actions are not Rosie's fault," Beau argued, and Alice nodded, piping up with:

"You can't put a pause on your life because Bash has issues."

Rosie's battered face was even worse in the light of day. The bruises were bright red with purple tinges around the edges.

Mottled and sore, her eyes swollen and her cheeks puffy, Mom's words made sense.

That bastard *had* hit her with a pipe.

It was the first time I'd seen her in the full light, but it staggered me. Made me plop backward as I took a heavy seat on the sofa.

My sister acted like she was untouchable, but someone *had* touched her.

Twice.

Bash had saved her.

Twice.

I owed him a drink and a handshake.

Maybe even my Aston Martin.

In fact, no maybe *about it.*

"I think I failed you," Mom rasped, turning in *Vati's* arms so she was facing Rosie.

"No, of course you didn't," my sister retorted, but her face puckered with pain as she shot her a frown.

"I did. I let you think you're untouchable because I wanted you to feel that way. I wanted both of my girls to know that glass ceilings were meant to be destroyed, that the sky was your only limit.

"I was raised in a world where, for every step forward I took, I was dragged back by how society functioned.

"I never wanted that for you, and the moment I could, I raised you all knowing that you could be whatever you wanted to be." She sucked in a breath. "But the world is a cruel place. We knew that before Bash came into our lives."

Vati squeezed Mom's shoulder. "You can't raise children to limit themselves because of how society works, *Liebchen.*"

"You can if it means not only your daughter, but all *three* of your sons as well, keep diving headfirst into trouble." Her nostrils flared as she pointed at Tin. "Shoots first, asks questions later." To me, she grated out, "You almost kill yourself on the track every time you're out there.

"It's reached the point where I can't even watch your races on the TV anymore without thinking I'm going to witness my son's death along with tens of millions of spectators." She wafted a hand at Rosie. "And you, my darling, so earnest in your desire to help but so impervious too. Then there's Bash. God.

"None of you are immortal." Mom released a breath. "We live in this fancy house, and we give to as many charities as we can, and we're blessed with more than most could ever dream of, but I can't buy your lives back if you get yourselves killed."

Father stepped over to her, and finally, so did Daw. As they clustered around her, Beau perched beside me on the sofa, while the others remained standing.

"We made brave kiddies, Sascha. That's nae somethin' tae be ashamed of."

"I'm not ashamed. I'm incredibly proud of everything they've achieved, but they need to realize that life is *not* kind." She pressed her fingers to Daw's shirt. "How many times have we almost lost you? And Kurt, your heart..." She swallowed. "Every year we're granted is a blessing, and they squander it."

"We don't," Bethan argued.

Which was amusing because she was the only child Mom hadn't mentioned.

She cast a look at Bethan and whispered, "You're the only one who's frightened of life, and at this moment, I'm beyond grateful for that because if you leaped headfirst into danger too, I don't know what I'd do with myself."

Bethan did *not* take that as a compliment. "I'm not frightened of life."

No one said anything when she looked around because Mom was right.

It was never verbalized, but Bethan toed the line at all times. She was risk-averse and not adventurous in the least.

Then, Beau, God bless her, got to her feet and walked over to her. "We're the same, you and I, Bethan. Tigers, but no one can see our stripes."

But from her scowl, it was clear to see that Bethan wasn't appeased even as she accepted Beau's gentle hug.

"This is getting us nowhere," Father intoned, his calm voice a soothing balm that eased the tension in the room. "We all have our flaws, and we all have our strengths. Perhaps this year, we need to recognize that everything must be balanced.

"Your mother's right, children. We raised you to believe in yourselves, and we've watched you flourish and grow.

"I know I speak for all your fathers when I say that we're beyond proud of you. What you've accomplished is more than anything we could have dreamed of, but at the end of the day, those accomplishments mean little to us if we can't have *you*.

"We love *you*. Not what you've achieved. Not who you've become.

"Rosie, we're proud that you want to fight for the rights of creatures who have no voice. But what does pride give us when we're standing over your hospital bed, wondering if you're going to survive?

"It's only by luck that he didn't crack your skull open and that you're standing here, able to tell your tale.

"Bethan, you're an incredible lawyer. You're like your sister, willing to fight for those who have been canceled.

"The pride I have for you, darling, is more than you could know. I'm grateful for your common sense, for your ability to argue until you're blue in the face, but your mother's right. We all know about Matthieu—"

"You don't know anything about Matt and me," she snapped.

"Who the hell's Matt?" I muttered under my breath.

"He used to be a footman at Masonbrook," Alice explained quietly.

"A footman?" I repeated.

Masonbrook was like Veronia's version of Buckingham Palace.

She just nodded.

"As for you, Tin, what you've accomplished in your years is nothing short of incredible. But your mother's right. For all your brains, you shove yourself into danger like it's your job."

"He has a point," Alice grumbled, knocking Tin in the side.

"And you have a daughter now and another on the way," Father continued. "Your responsibilities are to your children first."

When Father turned his gimlet stare on me, I braced myself for the storm, but he shook his head like he knew and rasped, "You're well aware of your flaws, my boy. You know you terrify us, but you persist anyway."

His disappointment hit me square in the chest.

It wasn't even a guilt trip. It was the truth.

"I didn't mean to," I mumbled.

"You did." Father's gaze never left mine. "I just hope you'll learn your lesson before it's too late."

Mom's bottom lip quivered. "This sounds like a lecture. It isn't. You have to know we love you, each of you, for what makes you so uniquely you. But no one is perfect."

"We're not murderers though," Bethan sniped.

Rosie's voice was small as she whispered, "Whatever Bash did, he was protecting me."

With the pain etched into her expression how it was, I got the feeling she'd overheard *everything* Bash had done for her.

I hoped she felt bad for all the years of arguing and shit she'd doled his way.

"Father, you strived for years to put men like Bash away," Bethan interjected. "I'm dedicating my life to—"

"That's just it, sweetheart. Bash is not like the men I put away. He's Bash.

"Bash has issues. I won't say that he doesn't. But he belongs here. At home. He doesn't belong out in the cold."

Mom started crying, and I was reminded of what she'd told me over the phone.

Don't worry, Mother Hen. I'm going where I was born to be.

Uneasily, I started to say, "Bash is..."

"My protector." Rosie's chin tipped up. "He's looked after me for years. It's time I looked after him."

"You don't have to do that," Beau argued. "Not if he frightens you."

"She's right, Rosie," Mom agreed softly, but I saw the hope in her eyes for peace among her children. "If he frightens you, your fathers and I will figure something out."

Her mouth quivered. "It's time I grew up."

"You're already grown up."

God, the voice of logic was here.

Dad stepped into the room, glanced at everyone's faces without making eye contact, then declared, "Our children *are* perfect."

Like magic, a gleam of amusement appeared in Mom's eyes.

It was almost predictable.

"Nobody's perfect," she countered.

"Our children are perfect," he repeated. "They make mistakes, and they might kill people from time to time, but I'm sure those people needed to die."

I rolled my eyes.

Daw rumbled, "Feck's sake, Devon, shut yer trap. We dinnae need nae talk of more murder in this house."

Dad merely shrugged but demanded, "Where's Bash? He wanted to see the paper I'm writing."

"He's still in jail, Dad," Tin explained.

"I thought you were fixing that."

Alice coughed, but I thought it was to hide a smile at his complaint. "We did, Uncle Devon. He'll be home soon. There were some formalities to finalize."

"Why didn't you come together?" Dad grumbled. "Have you never heard about carpooling? It's much better for the environment."

Tin snorted. "I had to come back for Alice yesterday evening, Dad. *Papa* didn't want to leave the car in London."

His disapproval clear, he wandered over to Mom and stopped in front of her. His hand cupped her cheek while his thumb wiped away the tear tracks, and he murmured, "They're perfect, Sascha, because you made them."

A soft laugh huffed from her. "I'm anything but perfect, but thank you, sweetheart." She reached up on tiptoes and pressed a kiss to his lips. "You always know the right thing to say."

Which was amazing because he usually said the wrong thing but it always ended up making Mom feel better.

Still, as I stared at them, all of them, as they congregated around her, as *Papa* fought traffic to bring the fifth and final child home, a sense of rightness filled me.

We were not normal.

If anything, we were strange.

But we were us.

And under this roof, in this circle, we were, as Dad said, perfect.

When Beau slipped onto my lap, one arm coming around my shoulders, I stared into her eyes and knew that my family's secrets were as much mine as they were hers.

Because she'd become a part of this craziness years before.

Much as my dad had with my mom, I reached up and cupped her cheek and, amid the chatter as everyone talked over each other, I rasped, "Thank you."

She blinked up at me. "What for?"

As we looked into each other's eyes, as the uneasy tension in the room ebbed and flowed around us, all I knew and could see was her.

"For being you and for accepting me."

TWENTY-FOUR

BEAU

For being you and for accepting me.

Over the rest of the afternoon, those words stuck fast in my mind.

He'd meant each and every one of them, and because we were still so new, I didn't realize how badly I'd needed to hear that.

When he told me things like that, it made it so much easier to have faith in *us*.

Not because I doubted, but because he'd loved me a long time as a friend, apparently as a woman too, but now, that had merged, become something else entirely—

"Beau?"

"Sorry, Dad." I grimaced. "Lost in my head."

He gave me his patented shoulder pat. "No worries, sweetheart. Everything okay?"

"Yeah. Well, no. I'm worried about Andrei and Bash. Haven't you heard from him?"

"Got an email about an IPO this morning he's interested in..." He hesitated.

I frowned. "Nothing else?"

"He mentioned a few other things, but it was a couple hours

before Tin and Alice arrived back, too, so I'm guessing he was checking his emails before they went to the police station once it reopened or something." He squeezed my fingers. "It'll be okay, love."

"Will it?" My brow puckered. "It's insane, Dad."

"Yeah, it is." His lips twisted. "I'm used to insanity in this house. Maybe not murder and mayhem, though. That's definitely new."

Snorting, I tugged on his hand. "Don't make me laugh. This isn't funny!"

"I never said it was, Buttercup," he countered immediately, but then he shrugged. "I'm a father, so from my position, it's difficult to condemn Bash. If you were Rosie, then I'd want to kill that bastard for hurting you too. Sadly, that isn't how the laws of the land work."

"No. I have a feeling that Bash works to his own laws."

"He does, but everyone has to toe the line at some point." He scrubbed his chin with his other hand. "Unless, of course, you know a crown princess who can erase your criminal record."

"Is that what she did?"

"Granting him diplomatic immunity? Yes. That's a 'get out of jail free' card." He shot me a wary look. "Is…"

"Is?"

"Would you say the family's aware that he'll have to move to Veronia?"

"What? No!"

He admitted, "Andrei told me that Alice's father would only agree if Bash became a Veronian citizen and enlisted in the Guard Elect… I'm not sure Sascha understands that yet."

My mouth rounded. "Oh, my God, that's going to kill Sascha."

Pain hit my heart for her.

"Yes, I fear it will. She loves the boy like he's her own. *But* they summer in Veronia, so she can see him then. Better for him to be in Madela or Laurela than in a prison cell."

I thought about how wistful Sascha had been this afternoon as she decorated the tree in the main room.

After Thanksgiving, trees darted up around the house, but

the main living room was always kept until the day before Christmas Eve. I had no idea why, just knew that it was a family tradition.

Jack had known how down his mom was, too, because he'd actually been helping decorate and hadn't tried to toss the ornaments away he'd made as a kid.

Sascha had stared with soggy eyes at Bash's ornaments, to the point where all of her men and children had taken to gathering around in there to wait things out with her.

Even Devon had stayed.

I plucked at my bottom lip. "I don't like this."

"Me either, sweetheart."

My mind wandered, and maybe it was only because my eyes were kind of unfocused that I saw it.

I batted my lashes a couple times to make sure I wasn't losing my mind or the power of sight, but nope.

Dad had a hickey.

Brows high, I asked, "Loretta talked with you, huh?"

He tilted his head to the side in confusion. "What?"

Trying to hide a smile, I wafted my hand at the general area of his face. "You might want to wear turtlenecks for a while."

He frowned, but then realization dawned and his cheeks blossomed with color.

My self-assured, confident father blushed.

I'd have laughed if he hadn't appeared so mortified.

Clearing my throat, I squeezed his fingers and told him, "You owe me one. I spoke with her earlier. She's kind of jumpy."

"Her husband was a monster," he said simply, but some of the hectic color faded from his cheeks. Mostly because my dad always turned pale when he was furious.

"Figured as much."

A part of me wondered if Dad had a thing for fragile women, if they were his type, but who the hell was I to judge?

Apparently I liked risk takers... apparently, I shared the same kick of taking risks because I'd definitely pulled some of 'Jumping Jack's' moves on the track yesterday.

"You don't mind?" He wafted a hand that seemed to encompass everything and nothing.

"I'm twenty-three next February, Dad. I don't think you have to worry about me disliking the wicked stepmother," I tried to tease. "Plus, I want you to be happy. If she gives you that, then I'll love her more than you do."

He shot me a smile that was both sheepish and dopey—definitely lovesick.

"Thank you for talking to her."

"You must move fast," I teased again, "I only spoke with her this morning."

Dad patted my hand. "I loved your mother, Buttercup. I want you to know that."

"Of course you did," I said easily. "You didn't leave her, Dad. She left us."

He sighed. "You keep saying things like that."

"It's Christmas. Why wouldn't I?" Dad rubbed a hand over his face, but I saw his guilt etched into his expression, and it prompted me to say, "You did nothing wrong, Dad."

"I worked long hours. The day before... I told her my boss wanted me in the office because China doesn't celebrate Christmas."

Yes, Mama had hung herself on Christmas Eve.

Was it any wonder I was bitter?

But though my feelings were valid, Dad's were too.

His guilt was real, and it made me realize that my bitterness was affecting him. Amping up *his* guilt.

I plucked at my lip again, and while my mind raced, it didn't get me anywhere.

This was something that would haunt us both forever.

Still, that was an old chapter. A really old one. We both had new ones starting.

Clearing my throat, I rasped, "I'll try to keep my thoughts to myself about Mama."

His brow puckered. "You can't help how you feel, and I'd prefer you to express yourself to me than to bottle things up inside."

"I'm not a child anymore. I can work through stuff on my own, and if I can't, then I'll get another therapist."

Nose crinkling, he told me, "I can't see that lasting long."

I shrugged. "Maybe you forcing me to go was something you had to do as a parent, but it wasn't the right thing for me. At the time. I clearly have issues still. Issues that aren't good for either of us."

"This time of year always drags everything back up again." A soft breath hissed from between his lips. "There were times that..."

"That, what, Dad?"

"I loved her, Beau," he repeated, like by saying it over and over I'd believe he did. "I loved her so damn much, but it wasn't enough to put the broken pieces of her back together again." He swallowed. "All those years of self-loathing and training and eating disorders from the dancing, I couldn't fix those things. But I loved her all the same."

"That wasn't what you were going to say."

"No, I was going to say that there were times I hated her for choosing to do what she did so close to Christmas. Losing her, finding her... both were a scar." He closed his eyes. "But to scar that as well? Does Jack know yet, Beau? Have you told him?"

"I told him I found her."

"But not around Christmas?"

"No."

"Maybe you should."

I hummed. "Maybe I will. Maybe we can make nicer memories together."

His hand reached for mine. "I hope so, sweetheart."

My lips kicked up in a half smile. "Bash looks set to ruin that though."

The hope in his eyes was dashed a little. "Yeah."

"Will you tell me if Andrei calls?"

"Of course."

I got to my feet and dipped down to press a kiss to his cheek. "You really are an awesome dad."

He snorted and patted my hand.

That patented pat.

I made to leave, but he grabbed a hold of my fingers and rasped, "Does he make you happy, darling?"

I smiled. "More than I knew was possible."

A breath escaped him. "Good." But for all that the word was simple, it was spoken with such feeling that I felt it in my heart.

I kissed his cheek again. "I'll leave you to get on with work."

As I left the office, I tried to shrug off the blanket of grief and anger that I often carried, but I knew it was easier said than done.

Change wasn't just coming, it was *here*.

Something that was only confirmed over the next couple hours.

Sascha was frantic when Andrei didn't come home that night, and I'd admit, I was nervous too.

We all went to bed late, but that didn't ease up our concern.

Jack was on edge, tossing and turning, while the rest of the house was up and about as well.

"Why won't he answer his phone?"

I wasn't surprised that he asked that out of the blue. Neither of us were sleeping.

The question had Goose shuffling around the mattress, stepping from the bottom corner and over to the top half. When he pushed his way between us, I stroked his head, but it wasn't me Goose wanted to comfort—it was Jack.

He tweaked Goose's ears and muttered, "It's not like him not to check in."

I bit my lip, unable to deny that I had a thousand thoughts racing through my head.

None of them good.

"Mom said today that Bash was in the Army."

"Still?"

"Apparently."

I blinked at that news. "I wonder if Rosie knows."

Though he shrugged, he asked, "Do you think she loves him?"

"Yes." I pressed my face against his arm. "I don't think she realizes she does. You know how she is. Blind to herself but hyperaware of everyone else."

"When did everything get so complicated?"

Goose's tail started wagging, and as it thumped against my stomach, I replied, "When she took Goose from the guy who..." I sighed. "We don't even know his name. Don't you think that's crazy?"

"Bastard. That'll do."

"I won't argue."

"He hit Rosie with a pipe," he ground out. "Can you imagine?"

"No. She's lucky to be alive."

"She really is. Did Rosie tell you what happened?"

I shook my head. "Not the details. Do you think Bash stalks her or something?"

Hearing my unease, he touched my arm. My feelings were all over the place where Bash was concerned.

What he'd done, *twice*, was insane to me.

But love was insane.

Love had the power to change lives and break them.

End them, even.

Patting me there, he said, "I don't think he's stalking her."

"Rosie didn't know Bash was there at all. How would he know where Rosie was if he didn't track her or something?"

"'Find Friends?'"

A snicker escaped me, one that morphed into an outright laugh.

Maybe we were both feeling the tension because he started chuckling too.

Eventually, his amusement faded, and he admitted, "I'd kill for you. Even before we became this..." He grabbed my hand and squeezed my fingers. "I wanted to hurt anyone who hurt you."

That was the bitch of it—I knew what he meant.

"There's saying it, and then there's doing it," I pointed out, trying to be rational.

Trouble was, I didn't feel rational about this.

"You're right."

We both fell silent.

"I already told you that I could do what Bash had if it meant protecting you, but even when we were just friends, I wanted to hurt anyone who hurt you," I admitted into the silence, staring up at the ceiling, grateful for the dark. "Why do you think I got so mad at you? *You* were the one hurting yourself. *You* were your own worst enemy."

My voice broke, and he tightened his hand around mine again, but didn't reply.

Clearing my throat, I told him, "My dad says that if Andrei gets in touch, he'll tell us."

The pillow rustled as Jack nodded. "I just don't understand what's taking so long."

"Me either."

"Did you talk about us?"

"With whom? The twins?"

"No. Your dad."

"Oh. Not really." A tad awkwardly, I told him, "He asked if you made me happy."

"What did you say?"

I heard the vulnerability behind the question, otherwise I'd have teased him. "I told him that you do."

My simple words had him releasing a gusty breath. "I'm glad that I do, Beau. No way it would be fair that you make me feel as fucking alive as this if I didn't make you feel the same."

Lips curving at the admission, I nuzzled into him and whispered, "I need to tell you something."

I hadn't intended on saying anything.

Not at all.

But Jack had something about him.

He made me feel safe. He didn't make me feel like I was kooky.

"What, sweetheart?"

"Mama..."

He tensed. "What about her?"

"She killed herself on Christmas Eve."

A sharp breath escaped him. "Jesus."

"Yeah."

We were silent.

Only, I didn't mind that.

With someone else, I might have apologized for burdening them with that truth, but not with Jack.

Then, he curled into me deeper and whispered, "Thank you for telling me."

My eyes closed as relief pricked me.

He understood how much trust that had taken; he understood that I didn't want to talk about it.

Swallowing, I rasped, "Thank you for listening."

He squeezed me. "Always, Beau. Always."

Legs tangled in a knot, arms clinging to each other, Goose mixed in, a soft bundle of fluff with a habit of standing on soft squishy parts like they were his personal trampoline, we relaxed.

Though things with his family were up in the air, and while I wished that weren't the case, what ping-ponged between us made me so grateful for what we had, and we drifted to sleep like that.

Until, of course, life intruded as it kept on doing so far this holiday season.

As far away from the front hall as it was, I still heard the booming sound of someone pounding on the front door like the Devil himself was there...

I just hoped he wasn't.

TWENTY-FIVE

JACK

I jolted awake at the sound of someone's fist slamming into the door.

Scrabbling to my feet, I grabbed the jeans I'd deposited on the floor before bed and told Beau, "Stay here."

She snorted, of course, and said, "Yeah, okay."

Then followed me.

Of. Fucking. Course.

"Just stay back."

"I've taken self-defense classes too," she said with a huff as we rushed down the hall where the banging sound was even louder than before.

"What the feck is that?" Daw boomed from the other end of the hallway.

Seeing him covered up with just a sheet, I rolled my eyes. "Can't you go to bed with pants on?"

"Like ye dae, boyo," Daw countered. "What the feck's goin' on?"

"Who the hell is that?" Tin snapped, and I peered at him and found him standing at the top of the staircase, staring down at the hall.

"If someone opened the frickin' door instead of asking who was behind it, we'd know," Beau sniped, doing the exact opposite of what I told her and heading over to it.

She stared through the peephole. "I have no idea who that is."

I joined her there and gently pushed her aside. "Who the fuck is he?"

Dressed in a green padded vest under a large navy coat with a flat cap on his head, I didn't recognize the stranger until he hollered, "Where's that murdering bastard?!"

"Well, I guess we know why he's here," Beau intoned. "He must be the brother of the guy Bash... *you know*. The one your mom didn't want you to kill?"

"Jesus."

What a conversation starter.

Before I could drag open the door, Dad was there.

He moved toward us with a serenity that belied the lateness of the hour, looking as bright and cheery-eyed as if it were late morning instead of the early hours.

"I'll handle this," he told me pleasantly.

I frowned at him. "Dad—"

I didn't have a chance to answer.

The door was opened. Dad stood in the way.

"Good morning," Dad greeted as if the mailman had a habit of showing up this late at night.

"Good morning? You bastard." Through the peephole, I saw him tilt back his head to roar at the house, "Where are you? You killed my fucking brother—"

"No. I didn't kill him. My son did."

"Your fucking son—"

"He isn't 'fucking' anything," Dad retorted. "He's quite brilliant, actually. Very good at compartmentalizing."

"Compartmentalizing?" the stranger spluttered.

"Yes. Well, aside from where my daughter's concerned. He's quite in love with her, you see."

I didn't have to stare at the man to know his eyes were bugging out of his head.

Tin groaned, loud enough for me to hear.

"Your son and your... daughter? Jesus Christ, man. And you're okay with that?"

"Well, of course," Dad replied, his confusion clear. "They're quite well suited."

"Well suited?" he cried, and Beau released a snort.

I glowered at her and watched as she clamped a hand over her mouth.

"Yes, well suited," Dad repeated. "I just said that."

"That's incest."

"Hardly. If anything, it's *faintly* taboo. My wife reads me some of her romance books, you know. Taboo can be anything now."

The guy wheezed, "Taboo? It's illegal."

"No. It isn't. Is it, Sawyer?" Dad called out. Then, in aside, said, "That's my wife's other husband."

"Other husband?"

"She has five. Haven't you heard of us? We're quite famous."

"Famous?" The stranger gulped. "You're fucking lunatics is what you are. No wonder your bastard son killed my brother."

"Your bastard brother," Dad replied calmly, "beat the living shit out of my daughter."

"She stole our property."

"Whether she did or not, he didn't have to beat her with a pipe. Would you like me to beat you with a pipe?" His voice changed. Morphed. Turned frosty. "I can. I'm younger than you, and very fit. I could probably bench press you if I wanted to, so I'd consider your strategy before you take me on."

"I want justice, that's what I fucking want. He got out last night. Out! My brother's dead, and that sick bastard is roaming the streets."

"Who's the sick bastard who's raising dogs just to die giving birth to endless litters?" Dad demanded. "Who's the sick bastard who trains pit bulls to attack each other in front of sicker bastards who pay to watch and gamble on the outcome?"

A short, sharp gasp escaped the man. "What the hell are you talking about? We just breed Corgis."

"Liar," Dad rasped, then he leaned into the opening. "I wouldn't worry. You won't be 'out' for long, my man."

"Is that a threat?"

"No. It's a promise. And this time, no lawyer in the land will be able to get you out because I'll make sure you suffer in a jail cell for as long as is legally possible.

"Whatever it is, it isn't enough for what you put those dogs through."

Just when I thought he was about to close the door, he didn't.

His arm snapped back.

But Daw, racing out of nowhere like a bat out of hell, was there, just in the nick of time. He grabbed Dad's arm mid-swing and said, "Let's nae be adding an aggravated assault charge tae matters, Dev."

Dad huffed. "He deserves it. He called Bash sick."

"Well, the boy ain't right. I love him, but he's a wee bit odd."

"He's perfect."

"Aye, aye, you can talk that shite with Sascha and she'll suck your cock over it, but I willnae. I like that my kiddies ain't perfect. They'd be feckin' boring if they were." Daw sniffed then turned his focus on the front stoop. "Yer still here? I'da thought ye'd be fleeing by now?"

"Fleeing? I haven't done anything illegal!"

Daw guffawed. "My brother is never wrong."

"Your brother?" the guy cried. "What the hell is going on in this house?"

"All kinds of sin and wickedness," Daw crowed, sounding like he was enjoying himself. "Now, I'd be running along if I were ye. I'll give ye a twenty-minute head start before I call the police on ye."

Devon sniffed. "You could have let me hit him."

His wistfulness was clear, as was the sound of the man's boots in the gravel as he rushed off, followed promptly by the roar of his engine as he sped back down the driveway.

"They were breeding fighting dogs?" Rosie squeaked.

Not surprised by her sudden appearance, not with all the racket, I cast her a look as Dad turned around, but his shoulders were hunched.

"I didn't want you to know."

She swallowed, looking wispy and frail and not like my sister at all in an oversized robe that drowned her. "How did you find out?"

Dad sighed. "Your *papa* and Bash learned the truth tonight and shared the information with me."

"They called you?" I growled. "Why didn't you tell us?"

"Because you were all sleeping."

"You should have woken us," Tin hissed, stomping down the stairs to join us.

"Why would I do that? You couldn't do anything." Dad raised an arm and beckoned Rosie, "Come here, child."

She blinked at him but stepped over to his side. "What is it? What's wrong?"

Beau huddled into my side as Dad hugged Rosie.

When she burst into tears a few moments later, I wasn't far off.

Daw and Tin looked stoic with their grief, but it was clear they'd understood the ramifications of what had happened in a way that I hadn't.

Bash wouldn't be coming home for Christmas.

Maybe never again.

TWENTY-SIX

BEAU

Christmas Eve was never a great day for me, for obvious reasons, but with Bash a political exile, the only upshot was that Andrei came home.

He didn't say why he'd been gone an extra fifteen hours.

He didn't say where Bash was, and neither did we ask.

He looked drawn and fatigued, and as soon as she saw him, Sascha led him away to their private rooms.

It was a subdued breakfast as a result.

Tin, Alice, and Noelie on one side, with Devon sitting so he could stare at his granddaughter like she was giving a lecture on higher order math. Jack and I on the other with Rosie and Bethan, then the remaining dads—mine included—dotted here and there, all lingering over breakfast.

Was I surprised when Jack drew out the bunch of letters and photos we'd found in the attic?

Not really.

It was in his nature to try to cheer people up, but I wasn't sure if it was going to work today.

"When we were putting up the tree in London, we went digging in the attic and we found these." He tossed the letters to Sean then gave the photos to Devon, Kurt, and Sawyer. "Care to explain yourselves?"

Sawyer snorted as he looked down at the newspaper clipping. "That president was an asswipe. In fact, I've seen toilet paper with more use than him."

My lips curved. "Why were you there? The article was cut off."

"Sascha didnae like my reason for being there, so she pouted and only took the clipping."

"Why? What were you doing?" Alice asked.

"It was all of us really," Sawyer said sheepishly. "Only Devon wouldnae attend the feckin' party because he was being an ass-kisser—"

"I see no shame in kissing Sascha's ass," was all Devon had to say.

"Dad!" Bethan grumbled. "TMI."

Sawyer just continued, "And Andrei had this feckin' cold. Ye ken he's the one who deals with all the politicians and such."

"Did you have to talk to the President for long?"

"Too feckin' long. They were having a wee problem with their debt ceiling, and we slipped in and tried to help."

"Did it work?"

"What dae ye think?" he retorted, cuffing Jack on the back of the head.

He grinned then asked Kurt, "What's with the Lederhosen, *Vati?*"

"Knees are nothing to be ashamed of, Jack," Kurt chided, his brows furrowed as if he were disconcerted Jack didn't know that already. "It's the traditional dress of our region in Germany. I'm sure we have pictures of you and Tin in a pair somewhere."

"You're joking? I need to see these photos."

Jack glowered at me. "Don't encourage him."

"You can't haul out embarrassing photos of the dads and not expect payback," Bethan argued, ever the Devil's advocate.

"Who's embarrassed?" Devon asked calmly as he looked down at his photo, a faint smile curving his lips as he took in the shot of him clearly wearing no clothes, holding a newspaper in front of the goods, and with a pair of boxers on his head.

In this household? Why the hell not?

Sean chuckled as he started leafing through the letters, but his amusement faded as he read a couple lines. In silence, he passed them out, leaving only one behind—Andrei's, I assumed.

"Bittersweet," Kurt rasped as he read his.

"That was a horrible time," Sean agreed.

"The worst," Devon muttered, his gaze anywhere other than on the letter.

Did he have X-ray vision?

How the hell did he even know what the 'worst' was?

Before I could ask, Sawyer murmured, "Ye girls were our rainbow babies. Afore ye three heathens, we had Camilla, but we lost her and almost lost ourselves yer ma. Until we brought her back to us."

"We'll always do that," Devon said sharply.

"Aye," Sawyer said, his voice relaxed, purposely, to counter the tension in Devon's. "There's nae need to worry. We havenae lost Bash. Yer forgetting, we're spending more and more time in Veronia anyway because of Noelie. We'll see the lad plenty."

Devon's mouth tightened. "He should be here."

Rosie sniffled. "It's all my fault."

That was when I felt the depth of the family's grief.

I'd known it was there, but seeing it was believing.

No one, not even Bethan or Devon, argued with her.

TWENTY-SEVEN

JACK

"Papa?"

I'd knocked on the door but hadn't gotten an answer, so I traipsed inside and headed toward the massive bed.

It wasn't massive because all my fathers slept in there with Mom. It wasn't strange that I knew that—I'd been a kid once upon a time, and I'd often crawled in with them.

It was massive because they all liked their space.

Dad was usually in here on the floor somewhere—I swore he had a problem with soft furnishings—but Father had his own suite and never came in here as far as I knew. As for Daw, *Papa*, and *Vati*, they usually populated this room, but not always.

Their dynamic was weird, but it worked for them.

Who was I to argue with what brought them joy when I had the best parents in the world?

"Jack?" *Papa* rubbed his eyes. "Is everything okay?"

I stepped over to the bed and clambered onto it. "Want your advice."

Sucking in a sharp breath when my shoulder twinged hard

enough to almost trigger a cramp, I flopped onto the bed and tried not to cry out.

It hadn't been right since that crash with John.

"What about?" he rasped, his exhaustion clear.

Grabbing the covers, I dragged them over me too, much as I'd done when I was a kid, and I told him, "I put a thirty percent stake in an F1 team."

"Without asking me?"

"I wanted to—" I sighed. "I know it was a dumb move."

Not because I needed to ask his permission, but it was like having a psychic who always guessed the lottery numbers and never calling her up for them until two days after the draw.

"It was. Very dumb. What's happened? Has it folded?"

"No," I chided. "I'm not that stupid. I knew whom I was investing with."

"Then what's the problem?"

I turned onto my side. "I don't think thirty percent was enough."

He yawned. "Is it too late to invest more?"

"Maybe. Unless it's your hedge fund group."

"Sneaky. Is that wise? Who is it?"

"It's new."

"How new?"

"Brand new."

Papa stared at me. "You're starting as the driver?"

"Yeah."

"Okay. I'll arrange with Julian to approach the team if you give him the details."

His faith in me had me smiling.

"We won't tell your mother this though, *niet?*"

"I'm turning over a new leaf."

I half-expected him to mock me, but he didn't. His gaze was measured as he said, "Ah. *Da.* When you meet the right one, suddenly priorities change, hmm?"

"I met her a long time ago."

"Devon said you were trying to impress her. I just thought you were trying to terrify us."

"That was a byproduct."

He grunted as he scrubbed a hand over his face. "What's your plan?"

"Race for a year, win, put the team on the map, poach some big names, get them to take over."

"You only want to race for one more year?"

"Yeah. I want to manage a team." I sighed. "I'm tired, *Papa*."

"Of course you are. And your body's exhausted."

Grunting, I admitted, "I have physio later on."

"On Christmas Eve?"

"Beau worked some kind of miracle to get Jensen here."

Papa eyed me. "Your back?"

"Hips and shoulders." My nose scrunched. "It's all good. Just one more year."

"You could die. It isn't one more year of sitting at a desk. You race, you take risks, and you don't approach the track like a driver, but a warrior."

"It'll be different."

"Why?"

"Because Beau will be there."

"She was there before."

"I got worse when she stopped traveling with me."

"What kind of logic was that? Were you trying to impress her long distance?"

I just huffed. "Everyone's a critic."

"This is true." He eyed me. "You die, your mother will haunt you."

"Shouldn't that be the other way around?"

"Sascha is capable of miracles where her children are concerned." That had him clearing his throat as if his words triggered thoughts of the state of our family.

I couldn't condemn him for that—it was why I'd come here, after all. Not just about the team.

"What happened with Bash, *Papa?* Why were you gone for so long?"

"Bash did not want to leave with the dog fighting ring still intact."

"You took it down?"

Papa snorted. "I appreciate the vote of confidence, Jack, but *niet.* I got some people to help him." Then, his jaw clenched as he shook his head. "The conditions those poor beasts were kept in."

"I'm surprised you didn't bring one home for Mom to adopt."

"They were crazed. Half-starved. I had a vet come and tend to them, but he had to put down several. Very tragic day." He stared up at the ceiling, which was a canopy of fabric suspended by the four posts. "Then Bash..."

I swallowed. "You took him to the airport?"

"Yes. When Tin and I concocted the plan, we knew he'd have to leave. Freedom comes with a price to pay." His mouth twisted. "It was a shrewd move of Edward's. Bash is very good at what he does."

Quietly, I asked, "Do I want to know?"

"You don't," was his taut reply.

"Were they holding the dog fights here?" I asked.

"No. London. But they were breeding them here. Your sister was right to question what was going on in Bishop Linden."

"I don't even know *what* she questioned."

"She came to speak with me before I slept and explained that she went to tend to one of the mothers of a new litter who wasn't doing very well. She knew that it was a puppy farm."

"They're not illegal," I inserted.

"No, and they had all their paperwork." He grimaced. "She broke in later because she wanted to inspect the back room after she heard a strange noise..."

"What kind of strange noise?"

"I'm assuming it was one of the pit bulls."

I grimaced. "So she broke in and started stealing puppies?"

"Yes. But she got caught. And in her words, she started *saving* them."

"Of course." I couldn't even roll my eyes. That was Rosie to a tee.

"The back rooms were horrendous, but that was nothing to what was happening where the fighting dogs were kept." His voice turned cold. "Bash made the first brother pay. I'll make sure the other rots in jail."

"Good."

We were silent for a second, then *Papa* rasped, "Now he's in the Guard Elect, he won't be able to..." He heaved a sigh. "Your mother won't like that he can't come and visit her here as much as she's used to."

"No. She won't."

Bash, for all that he hung on the outside of our family, visited often.

More than I had in the past year.

"Where's the new team based?" *Papa* asked out of the blue.

"Veronia."

"Good, that's good."

"Why do you think I bought thirty percent of the shares?" I gibed.

"With yourself as the main driver, you were very shrewd."

"Hardly. I should have invested more."

He wafted a dismissive hand. "I already told you to leave that to me."

"*Spasibo, Papa.*"

His lips twitched because I rarely spoke with him in his mother tongue. "You're welcome." His eyes narrowed on me. "You're happy with her?"

"It's like a piece of me was missing and I didn't even know it."

"This pleases me. Devon told me you're proposing on New Year's?"

"Dad wasn't supposed to say anything," I grumbled.

He just smiled. "Be grateful that he did. I stopped at the bank."

Papa twisted onto his side and dragged open the nightstand drawer. Because I had no desire to see whatever they kept in there, I kept my focus on the canopy overhead.

He tossed something at me that landed with a plop on my stomach.

Frowning, I stared down then found myself looking at a ring box.

"Your great-grandmother's ring."

When I opened the box, a smile curved my lips. "It's beautiful."

"She had hair like your Beau's." He eyed the sapphire. "It will suit her."

"Thank you, *Papa*. You didn't have to do that."

He shrugged. "Why didn't I? She's going to be my daughter, isn't she?"

Love for him filled me. "Julian might argue with you about that."

"He can argue all he wants."

"*Papa?*"

"Yes?"

"*Schastlivogo Rozhdestva.*"

"Very good, very good. Merry Christmas, my boy."

TWENTY-EIGHT

BEAU

I smirked when he teased my nipples, tweaking the piercings rather than the tender skin. When he twisted them anti-clockwise, I grumbled, "Thought I was the sadist?"

Only, he wasn't in a laughing mood.

He'd been grouchy since Jensen had left, and I couldn't altogether blame him.

Jack had been limping worse *after* physio than before it. Sadly, that was all too common for him.

He dropped his head and tested the tip with his teeth which made me shiver as sensation washed through me, forcing thoughts of the tense day aside.

My hands raked through his hair, nails dragging along his skull as I hissed when he bit down harder. He carried on teasing me, focusing on the hypersensitive area, before he pulled back.

When he grabbed a lock of my hair that hung loosely around my shoulder, then stroked it over the tip, he rasped, "I've always been obsessed with your hair."

"Obsessed is a strong word."

He peered up at me. "It isn't. Do you know what I want my Christmas gift to be?"

"Okay, I'll bite—"

"So will I."

I grinned. "What do you want for Christmas?"

"Your first blowjob and for you to jack me off with your hair."

Arching a brow at him, I retorted, "Possessive much?"

"Possessive a *lot*. I admit it. Are you going to give me what I want for Christmas?" he asked in a low, rumbly voice as his hand slipped down over the curve of my belly and his fingers started playing with my clit.

A moan escaped me as I widened my legs to give him free access. When he rubbed the tiny nub, we both started breathing like we'd been running.

"Fuck, you're always so wet for me," he groaned, pressing his forehead between my tits.

For a second, I thought he was going to motorboat them, but he didn't. He just slipped a finger inside my pussy. It clung to him, as much as I did, my arms and legs curving around him where they could in the position he was in.

Thrusting another in, he scissored his fingers, making me moan, before he paused and whispered, "What about my Christmas gift, Beau?"

"You owe me six orgasms," I ordered.

"I do."

I whimpered when he ground the butt of his hand into me. "No arguing?"

"Never. But this is Christmas..."

I cast a glance at the clock on the wall. "In three minutes."

"It'll take exactly four to get me off."

Snorting, I said, "I'm bad for your stamina."

"I knew that already. Don't worry. I'll fuck you into next Friday afterward."

"Tease. Why are you so angry anyway?" I rocked my butt back into the mattress when he thrust his fingers harder and faster.

He grunted. "Not angry. And I mustn't be doing this right if you can think."

"Lies," I rasped, moaning the word.

His mouth dropped to mine and his teeth went to my top lip. He teased the curve of one side with his teeth then treated the other to the same torment. I moaned at the prickle of pain then sighed when he soothed the area with his tongue.

"Jensen said you were hot."

I blinked then hissed when he bit down on my bottom lip.

Before I could complain, he thrust his tongue into my mouth, but because he'd pissed me off, I wrangled control from him, clutched my legs around his hips, and wrestled with him until I was on top.

I knew I only won because he'd already experienced an elbow to the eye, so out of self-preservation from my poor coordination, he undoubtedly allowed me to straddle him.

The hair he loved falling into a curtain around us both, I rocked my pussy against his dick as I whispered, "He can think I'm hot, but I'm not his, am I?"

"Jude was checking you out too."

"Are you pouting?" I frowned. "When was she even here?"

"Earlier. She brought a bunch of groceries for dinner tomorrow."

She had?

"I didn't see her."

"Well, she saw you."

"You're jealous."

After what Sean told me, and knowing what my spiteful exes had done, his jealousy didn't come as a surprise, but what did stun me was that I didn't want him to suffer through that anymore.

"Bet your ass I am."

"Why though? My pussy's on your dick."

His nostrils flared, and I swooped my hair away to let in some light so I could see his expression.

Before I had a chance to read it, I yelped as he twisted us back around so he was looming over me again, and that was when I heard someone clear their throat.

"Merry Christmas. I did knock."

For a second, both of us froze.

Then, Jack rasped, his back to the doorway, "Dad, that isn't you?"

"Who else would it be?"

"Who else? That's the fucking answer."

I snorted out a giggle as I clapped a hand over my face.

"I heard you so I thought I'd wish you—" He huffed. "Are you going to get all pissy with me like Tin did?"

"Tin? You mean you've barged in on him and Alice too?"

"What was I supposed to do? Wait for them to answer the door when I'd solved another government crisis."

I snickered again, and Jack muttered, "You're not helping." He twisted around. "We're all going to pretend that this didn't happen. You can't see us; we didn't see you."

"I can't lie to your mother, son."

"You can't lie to her about what?"

"When she asks me in the morning if I wished you a Happy Christmas, I can't lie and tell her I didn't wish it to you and Beau."

"Why would she ask?"

"'Because ET always forgets,'" he quoted.

That was it.

I was done because I knew ET was Sascha's nickname for Devon.

Outright chuckling as I died on the bed, Jack snapped, "Just tell her you did. You can leave out the—"

"Sex stuff," I choked on the words.

"Helpful," he said with a grimace. "Anyway, why are we having a conversation about this? Just go, Dad."

"I'm going."

"Don't tell Mom in the morning."

"I'll tell her that you were indisposed."

"Indisposed?" At that, Jack plopped off me and dragged the

covers to his chin. "Dad, I'm not ill. You tell her that, she'll think I had a stroke or something."

"That's statistically unlikely at your age and fitness levels. Although, if you think it's a possibility then we need to call in the doctor."

A giggle escaped me.

Jack groaned. "Just tell her I was sleeping."

"And that I wished it to you while you were sleeping? That won't work."

"Why won't it?"

"She says that conversations that happen when people are asleep don't count."

My eyes widened at that, at the many and varied rules Sascha had clearly had to implement in her relationship with Devon. He was admittedly odd, and yet, I knew not one of her men was capable of breaking down her guards like he was.

Case in point the other day. Amid the tension and the sorrow, Devon had made her smile.

My heart warmed at what each man brought to their individual relationships with her, and I almost missed Jack huffing as he compromised, "How about you wake us both up early so that you can wish it to us then?"

"That I could do," Devon agreed. "Do you want some tea, Beau?"

"Why would she want tea, Dad? I was about to—"

I whacked him in the side.

"—never mind," he ended with a grunt.

"She sounded like she had a sore throat."

Okay, so I'd thought I was done before, but I was wrong.

Very. Very wrong.

I knew from experience that, in this household, you had to laugh or you'd explode, and it was only compounded when, down the hall, I heard a hissed, "Daddy? What are you doing?"

When Rosie barged her way into our bedroom, and the pair of

them started talking about boundaries and how Devon had to be better at knocking on doors, I had to smile.

Even as, in Jack's ear, I whispered, "Rain check on the handjob with the hair?"

He grunted. "I think Dad just ruined that fantasy for me forever."

TWENTY-NINE

BEAU

"You said you didn't get me a gift."

He snorted. "Yeah. Right. It's Christmas. Our *first* Christmas together at that."

Staring at the key fob in my hand, I swallowed. "You didn't have to do this."

I thought about what I'd gotten him and cringed inside.

"Anyway... I have to be honest; this is my gift to you and Mom's too. It's her old Caddy."

My eyes rounded. "Your Mom had a Caddy?"

He grinned. "She did. But now *you* do."

"Holy shit," I breathed. "I only got Sascha some perfume."

And that had nearly busted my bank account.

Jack had a massive family, and most of them were my friends and needed gifts—that was hella expensive.

"She'll love it," Jack disregarded as he pressed a kiss to my lips before he shoved his phone at me. "You can't drive it yet because it's in the shop. There were some safety issues and I'm not about to let you into a death trap even if I know you'd love it."

"Reassuring," I teased.

His eyes gleamed. "Safety first."

"Since when?" I gibed, but before he could answer, I murmured, "I feel bad because it wasn't anything like this..." Grabbing the box from my pocket, I shoved the gift at him.

His grin widened. "I'll love it whatever it is. You give weird gifts but they're always brilliant."

I guessed that was a compliment.

"Remember that time you took me to the zoo because I said I'd never been?"

My lips curved. "Yeah, I remember."

My gift to him had been the treat of us acting like we were five all day.

That meant he'd puked later on from all the ice cream he'd eaten, and he'd gotten bubblegum in his hair when I blew a massive bubble that had popped on his face.

I'd been saving up all year for this gift, which money-wise was nothing to him, but I hoped he liked it...

The Italian leather had cost me a small fortune, but I'd embroidered it with JD to mimic the GG of the Gucci brand. The detailing alone had taken hours, and I'd almost stained it with blood because leather of that quality was hard to work with.

On the back, there was a photo of us.

On that day.

When we'd been acting like five-year-olds.

We'd been at a park, dicking around, eating a picnic that consisted of cake and cookies, and both of us were riding a sugar high.

As he stared at it, he rasped, "I want this back." Then he swiped his thumb over the photo, and that was when my nerves died because I knew he loved it.

"What back?"

"This. You and me. I missed this. Missed doing random shit with you. I want it back."

I grinned. "That can be next year's Christmas present."

He put his hand to the back of my neck and dragged me against him. "I think we should start now."

THIRTY

We ate.

A lot.

We drank.

Too much.

We watched shitty TV and played board games that were no fun because Dad always won.

Julian joined us, as did two of Alice's guards at Mom's insistence, though they drifted away after dinner, and still, Bash's place was a glaringly empty space that should have been filled.

Not even a video call with him slotted into the gap because he didn't answer, and of course, that broke Mom's heart, and Rosie darted away to a corner of the kitchen, looking a lot teary-eyed and in desperate need of a large wine.

Or maybe a *whine*.

I wasn't sure yet.

Rosie wasn't much for self-pity, but with the state she was in, and the repercussions on a family level being what they were, I couldn't say that I blamed her for being down.

I was used to joyful Christmases, but this year just wasn't the same.

As *Vati* served up some traditional Christmas pudding, Mom declared, "Next year, we're doing this in Veronia."

She said it like she was preparing for war, and because I was a smart child even if I was the dumbest of my siblings, I knew that tone was not to be ignored.

Or argued with.

Bethan, being a typical lawyer, had to grouse, "That's not practical."

"You'll just have to take vacation time," Mom sniped. "I'm not doing this without all my kids here. Next year, Alice and Noelie won't be able to come and visit, anyway. It's her turn to be with Perry. Plus, they'll have the new baby."

My brows rose at her inclusion of Alice. Normally, she just said Noelie, but Mom was clearly feeling nostalgic right now.

"I wouldn't leave Alice and Noelie alone at Christmas."

Daw clapped Tin on the back. "There's my good lad."

I rolled my eyes. Tin saw, of course, and smirked at me.

Bethan grumbled, "We can't move to Veronia just because Bash is there. We didn't move to Boston when I lived there two years ago, and we didn't move to Paris when Jack was based there when he was eighteen."

"This is different," Mom argued. "Bash is safe in Veronia. We need to celebrate there."

Before a family argument could start, Father, ever the voice of wisdom, asked, "Why would you mind being in Veronia, Bethan?" He arched a brow. "It doesn't have anything to do with Matt, does it?"

Her eyes narrowed on him. "Are we doing this now?"

Dad asked, "What are we doing now?"

"Arguing," Beau chimed in.

"Arguing? On Christmas Day?" He rubbed the back of his neck. "That doesn't seem right."

"It isn't," Mom agreed. "Bethan, stop arguing. Christmas will be in Veronia—"

Bethan's chair scraped against the floor as she started to walk away, but before she could stalk off in a snit, Daw clasped his hand to hers and said, "Lassie, dinnae be getting yer knickers in a twist. There's nae problem with being in Veronia. You probably willnae see the lad."

"I don't care if I *do* see Matt. You're the ones always going on about him."

"Only because he made you happy, *Liebchen*," *Vati* reasoned.

Bethan growled under her breath and moved over to the kitchen where Rosie was still licking her wounds.

"The only rational daughters I have are at the table," Mom mumbled, clearly annoyed.

Beau blinked. But that was nothing to Alice. Her mouth gaped, and her head whipped from side to side as if she were seeking confirmation that her ears weren't deceiving her.

I couldn't blame her. Mom always gave her a hard time even if Tin nagged her about it.

"Who?" Alice sputtered.

Mom winced. "This is years too late, Alice, but I should have told you that from the start. My only excuse is that you stole my firstborn—"

Tin grumbled, "She didn't steal me. I was always hers."

"You were my baby first," Mom snapped with a huff before she made a show of trying to calm down. "I'm going to make a better effort at being—"

"Kinder?" I inserted.

"Nicer?" Tin added at the same time.

Her cheeks turned bright pink. "I didn't realize it was so obvious."

"Just a bit."

She cleared her throat. "Then I have to apologize to you, Alice."

Alice gaped even harder at that but quickly rasped, "There's no need to apologize, Sascha."

"*Mom.*"

Still looking shell-shocked, she gulped. "Mom."

"And there's every need," Tin argued. "Even with this Bash situation, you gave Etta crap, Mom. She was the only person who saved him. Because Edward wouldn't have gotten involved otherwise."

Edward was the King of Veronia, Alice's father.

Mom squinted at him but straightened her shoulders and said, "Thank you, Alice."

"You're welcome..." Alice licked her lips. "Mom."

Beau whispered, "That's so kind of you to say, Sascha."

"Mom, dear," was her pointed reply.

"Mom," Beau agreed.

"If this Christmas has taught me anything, it's that we shouldn't take each other for granted." Her gaze drifted over the dads. "We were blessed with many things, my loves, but not a lot of family."

Father nodded his agreement but said, "I didn't give you those letters to make you maudlin, Sascha, darling."

My ears pricked up at that. "You gave her the letters?"

"Of course they did." Mom cast me a glance. "Thank you both for finding them. Camilla's always on my thoughts at Christmas—what might have been, what could have happened, *but* I don't have to think that way with any of you." Her tone might have been stern, but I saw the glassiness in her eyes so I knew the letters had made her teary. "You're all here, thank God, and I'm beyond grateful to have you at this table—even if the girls are being stubborn and are pretending they can't hear me."

"We already said our thanks at Thanksgiving, Sascha. You're mixing your holidays."

Mom merely shrugged at Dad's snipe. "I'll be mixing a lot of things in the future. Yule with Christmas and Thanksgiving and... do you do anything Polish, dear?"

That was directed at Beau who sputtered, "Um, no."

Julian tutted beneath his breath, but there was a pleased smile in his eyes that told me he was grateful Beau was being inducted into the family. "Beau, tell them what we do on Christmas Eve."

She winced. "Well, I mean, we fast for the day."

"You do?"

My brows rose in surprise.

Especially considering the secret she'd shared with me. But I guessed her dad had done his best to get her to celebrate even on that most difficult of anniversaries.

My respect for him soared.

I knew I'd always liked him.

"It's a Polish thing. I didn't do it yesterday, but normally, yeah. You fast and then gorge on a feast at night. There are twelve dishes, each one kind of representing an apostle, and beneath the dish, there's always a gift, and sometimes, the table has hay stuffed under the tablecloth." The excitement in her eyes made me vow that next year, we'd be going the whole Polish hog. In a rush, her eyes gleaming, she finished, "Dad always made sure we did that even though he's as British as Big Ben."

Daw guffawed at that; *Vati's* chuckle wasn't exactly quiet either.

"It's also a tradition to have an empty space at the table for an unexpected guest."

"That's perfect because we'll always be waiting for Bash to show up, won't we?" Mom's eyes were loaded with a sorrow I wished I could resolve. "But the fasting and the feasting, we can do that! How wonderful," she declared, clapping her hands together. Her joy was fierce, resolved. *Determined*, even. Not much held Sascha Dubois back. Not when she had a plan. "We're already a multicultural family, but the ties that bind us are going to deepen. What with this new feast, and Three King's Day for Alice, Kurt's Advent wreaths, and *Svyatki* for Andrei—"

My lips twitched at that.

Russian Christmastide meant that the family celebrated the holidays pretty much from Thanksgiving until January 17th, which, to the Russians, was when Jesus was baptized.

"If we're going to Veronia, *Papa,* for the holidays, then you can dive in Lake Encharne—"

Papa squinted at me. "Are you trying to get into my bad books?"

I shot him a cheeky grin. "Aren't I always there?"

He huffed.

"Why should he dive in a lake?" Julian asked, his brows high.

Clearly, Beau hadn't shared this family tradition of ours with her father.

"It's something the Russians do to celebrate Jesus's baptism," I explained.

"They dive into lakes?" His mouth gaped. "But they're freezing."

Papa sniffed. "Only for the British."

Finally, Mom's lips curved in a genuine smile as she drawled, "Baby, you've been more British than Russian for a long time."

He wagged his finger at her. "Next year, we shall all dive into Lake Encharne, and we will see which nationality will win."

Daw grumbled, "I'm a Scotsman. Yer feckin' crazy if ye be thinking I'm nae gonnae win that round."

And somehow, amid the bickering, as Mom invited Julian to Veronia for next Christmas, and while Daw and *Papa* shot the shit about who'd had it colder growing up, Rosie and Bethan returned to the table, and Bash's space there felt a little less vacant.

Not because we were forgetting about him, but because we made plans to ensure that, next year, our family would be complete once more.

JACK

"Beau loves fireworks."

I blinked at Julian. "Excuse me?"

His lips twitched before he repeated, "Beau loves fireworks."

"Yes, sir. I know she does."

"To be fair, you *should* know that, but I was just checking you did."

Confused, I asked, "Sir?"

He wafted a hand. "Are you going to keep pacing outside my office all day? I didn't realize I was so terrifying."

Shooting him a sheepish smile, I told him, "You're not."

"No? So why is it so hard to knock on my door?"

He wasn't wrong—I'd been pacing outside it for about twenty minutes now.

Asking for permission for anything wasn't my strong suit.

I was a firm believer that you should apologize after the fact rather than request permission beforehand.

Where was the fun in being told no?

But Beau deserved for me to do this the right way.

My shoulder twinged again when I straightened up and asked, "May I speak with you?"

"Aren't we doing that already?"

"We are." I cleared my throat. "I mean, inside your office?"

"Sure." He stepped back, but I saw the gleam of amusement in his eyes and figured he knew what was happening.

Heaving a sigh, I asked, "*Papa* told you, didn't he?"

His smile appeared. "He did."

Shit.

I scrubbed the back of my neck. "Are you averse to the idea?"

"Averse?" He leaned back against his desk and folded his arms across his chest. By body language alone, I felt like he was going to say no on principle. But he was also smiling, so that shot off mixed signals. "Only if you're going to continue being reckless on the circuit."

Ah.

My goddamn track record was biting me in the ass again.

Julian continued, "I've watched Beau sweating bullets through every race for the past couple years, Jack. I don't want that to happen again."

"It won't. I have one more year ahead of me, and then I'm ready to retire."

"So young?"

I shrugged, and the pain in my shoulder made itself known, underscoring exactly why I was retiring. "I've got a lot of injuries that I've been pushing to the side that I need to heal. I'm in a lot of pain all the time."

He frowned. "I'm sorry to hear that."

"It's okay, but I just... I think racing and driving were always in my blood, but I started to really get into it when Beau came along. She seemed to dig it, and it was... she traveled with me. I liked that. I wanted her with me."

It seemed so simple now, but back then, I'd just wanted her away from Penelope.

I'd wanted her by my side.

Selfish but true, and it sure as hell didn't paint me in a good light with her dad.

"You pushed her away by doing crazy stuff."

"I did." I nodded. "I was a fool."

"And you're not anymore?"

"Well, yeah, I am, but not now I have her. She'll keep me on the straight and narrow." I tipped my chin up. "I'm not going to put her through what her mother did. She won't ever have to deal with losing me."

His gaze softened. "I'm glad to hear it." We stared at each other a second until he questioned, "Well? Are you going to ask me or what?"

Okay, so he wasn't going to make this easy on me.

I blew out a breath, more nervous now than when I was neck and neck on the track and the championship was on the table.

"Can I have your daughter's hand in marriage?" I gulped. "Please." Then quickly tacked on, "Sir."

Julian smiled. "Fireworks. When you propose. Remember them. It'll make her smile."

I guessed that was as good an answer as any.

THIRTY-TWO

BEAU

NEW YEAR'S EVE

It didn't come as a surprise.

How could it after Devon ruined it?

But that didn't take away from the joy I felt when Jack dropped to his knees amid a pile of fluffy snow, a ring box in his hand, a sapphire sparkling from within its silken confines.

As impossible as it was, this was happening.

This was my life.

We'd feasted as if it were Christmas Day again, and the women had watched the men washing the dishes until midnight had approached and we'd gathered around, with champagne in our hands, talking about our hopes and dreams for the new year.

At the count of twelve, we each popped a grape into our mouths as was the Veronian way that ensured good luck for the following year, and then we moved around, kissing and hugging and wishing everyone a happy new year.

It was amid that chaos that Jack drew me outside into the dark, frigid night that spontaneously lit up with fireworks which, from this vantage point, we could see for hundreds of miles into the distance.

Into that magical scenery, Goose chased after his own tail,

flouncing around the snow drifts that had made the estate picture perfect, all while Jack said, "I know Dad spoiled this. I know he took away the surprise, but let's be honest, Beau, this was always going to happen.

"The second we kissed, we were always heading to this moment. In two weeks, two months, or two years, this was always going to be the next step for us.

"You, my beautiful Isabeau, are it for me. I want you at my side, I want you fighting in my corner, and I want you back in my ears when I'm racing.

"I want you with me. I don't ever want to go through these last fourteen months again.

"We don't have to marry this year. It can be ten years down the line, but I want this ring on your finger. I want the world to know that I love you. That we belong to each other—"

It was that that hooked me.

That had me dropping to my knees in the snow as well.

No way in hell was I going to say no, but his proposal wasn't a simple, "Will you marry me?"

It was us.

In a nutshell.

Difficult and complicated and full of feeling.

So I clasped my hands around his neck as I pressed myself into him to offset the cold. "I will call the physio even if you don't want Jensen to come."

"That's 'in sickness and in health.' A wife's right."

I snickered but informed him, "I'll bitch at you if you take corners too fast."

"That's the 'until death us do part' bit, no? I think it's a good thing you don't want me to die."

"We need to agree that I won't let you pay for everything—"

"'For richer or poorer,'" he argued.

"That's not how I work."

He huffed.

"I promise I won't miss a single race—"

His arms tightened around me. "Do you mean that?"

"'To have and to hold,'" I promised, pushing my forehead against his. "But you have to stop scaring the shit out of me."

"I meant it when I said I want you in my ears, Beau. I want you helping guide me, strategizing with me. You are *not* a scrounger. If anything, you're imperative to my life, my happiness. Hell, my safety. That's why I want you to be my race engineer."

My lips parted. "You can't be serious."

"I am. Deadly. You might need training, so we'll figure that out, but my life matters to you. My safety is your safety," he rasped, breaking and rebuilding my heart in one fell swoop. "I don't want to die, Beau. Not when I'm so ready to start living, and being with you is more exhilarating than any race—"

I joined my mouth to his, unable to do anything other than kiss him.

Kiss him long and hard and wet.

In the background, I heard cheers and rounds of applause and knew that our family was watching us.

Something that was confirmed when a couple of fireworks lit up the night sky a good twenty minutes after midnight directly above our heads.

"Those were your dad's idea," he whispered in my ear so I could hear over the noise.

I blinked at him. "My dad's?"

He smiled. "When I asked for your hand in marriage."

My eyes blurred at that. "Thank you, Jack."

That beautiful smile of his deepened. "For what?"

I was capable of only one answer.

And they were his words, only amended.

"For being you and for accepting me and for loving me as much as I love you."

The second I spoke them, I knew those were going to be our marriage vows.

Yet he was right—*there was no rush.*

Ten days, ten weeks, ten months, ten years, whenever we decided to get hitched, those would be the promises we'd make to each other.

Something he confirmed when he pressed his lips to mine again and sealed our deal with a kiss that drowned out the noise and that made me forget there were witnesses...

This was, I realized, the best night of my life.

A life, I knew, that was only just beginning.

BEAU

ELEVEN MONTHS LATER

My hands were sweaty.

My forehead beaded with perspiration.

My back was drenched beneath the uniform I wore.

And my eyes?

They stung.

I couldn't blink.

I just couldn't.

The black race car whipped around the track, faster than ever, using slipstreams to surge ahead of the other competitors as it flew around the circuit.

"How many laps to go?"

Jack's voice was barely audible over the beat of my heart, but I focused on it and rasped, "Two."

"Shit. These inters are getting worn."

"Is it affecting speed?"

It seemed a ridiculous question when the car was performing like a charm but Jack knew this car better than anyone.

It still boggled my mind that he'd helped build it.

That he'd poached staff from Sabre who were sick of being

treated like shit, and who wanted to work for a man who cared about his team.

With the help of some backers, Jack created Team Dubois.

It was crazier still that, in its first season, he'd won eight of the twenty-two races, with this last championship of the season being the deciding factor between him and Sabre's current boy wonder.

"No," Jack grated out, but the long delay told me he was having to focus.

And because I was nervous, horrifically excited and terrified all at the same time, I couldn't remember what he was talking about.

Oh!

Tires!

They weren't affecting his speeds even if the tread was wearing down.

"Jack, the *Monver* hairpin on the back straight is coming up. Will the inters last the sprint?"

"Yeah. I'll make them last."

"Remember, they reprofiled the last chicane," I warned.

"Copy."

The black beast seemed to whip along the lap as if it took my words as a challenge. He didn't just sprint, he soared toward the finish line, zipping past it to the roars of the crowd chanting 'JUMPING JACK' over and over.

For a second, I just stared, unable to compute that he'd done it.

One season.

A new team.

And he'd forged our future.

My throat felt thick as an arm suddenly appeared around my waist and hauled me into him.

"HE DID IT!!" Sawyer screamed at me, jumping up and down, which was when I saw Andrei, Kurt, Devon, Sean, and Sascha were all leaping around like fools in the stands that Sawyer had clearly vaulted over to reach me in the paddocks.

Bethan and Rosie were hugging and squealing while Alice

shrieked and stunned the Veronian crowds by kissing Tin without a thought for decorum.

Only Bash remained still.

His gaze watchful.

Not on Jack.

Not even on the race.

Just on the crowd around Rosie.

"WE DID IT!" Jack yelled in my ears.

We.

We had.

We'd done it.

Together.

My knees buckled.

He was still alive.

I'd kept him alive.

He'd raced harder than ever, pushing his vehicle more than he had before, but he'd done it differently.

He'd once told me that every risk was calculated, but that wasn't the truth.

Not in comparison to this year's strategies.

Sawyer caught me before I could fall, but the relief was too strong.

My eyes were blurry as I looked up at him, and I whispered, "He's safe now."

Sawyer beamed a smile at me. "The second ye two got yer act together, he was safe, lassie."

His faith in me, to protect his son, shone through bright and clear, and I knew they all felt that way.

Each of them.

Jack wasn't exactly on the straight and narrow because of me, but he no longer courted death, and that was more than I could ask for.

I hugged yesterday to myself.

This was the grand finale.

The deciding race that, last year, would have been full of his crazy stunts that'd ensure he'd win come hell or high water.

But yesterday was the one piece of proof I had that I trusted him not to take risks anymore.

Not to endanger himself or our future.

Reaching up, I tugged on the necklace that housed the wedding ring he'd put on my finger yesterday morning.

It too was proof.

He hadn't let me down.

And I knew he never would.

BASH & ROSIE

Hello darlings!

You will notice that there is no preorder for any future Quintessence books... I think we all know we'd like Bash and Rosie to get together.

If you want that to happen, then you need to go to my Diva reader group and tell me you do! www.facebook.com/groups/Serena AkeroydsDivas Only if I see interest in their stories will I go ahead.

While RH might not be your thing, you might like to dip your toes into those books?

To enjoy Sascha, Andrei, Sawyer, Devon, Kurt, and Sean's story, you can find start here: www.books2read.com/HersToKeep

They're live on audio too, and the final book in the series will be dropping in audio with the marvelous Shane East and Hollie Jackson narrating on the 14th December! www.books2read.com/HersTo Hold

And if you feel like meeting up with Micah and Devlin, the neighbors Beau wanted to see get it on, ha, you can read all about them in THE INTERN. www.books2read.com/TheInternMMRo mance

I wish you all the happiest of holidays, and sending all my love from my family to yours,

Serena

xoxo

FREE BOOK!

Don't forget to grab your free e-Book!
Secrets & Lies is now free!

Meg's love life was missing a spark until she discovered her need to be dominated. When her fiancé shared the same kink, she thought all her birthdays had come at once, and then she came to learn their relationship was one big fat lie.

Gabe has loved Meg for years, watching her from afar, and always wishing he'd been the one to date her first and not his brother. When he has the chance to have Meg in his bed—even better, tied to it—it's an opportunity he can't refuse.

With disastrous consequences.

Can Gabe make Meg realize she's the one woman he's always wanted? But once secrets and lies have wormed their way into a relationship, is it impossible to establish the firm base of trust needed between lovers, and more importantly, between sub and Sir...?

This story features orgasm control in a BDSM setting.
Secrets & Lies is now free!

CONNECT WITH SERENA

For the latest updates, be sure to check out my website!
But if you'd like to hang out with me and get to know me better, then
I'd love to see you in my Diva reader's group where you can find out
all the gossip on new releases as and when they happen. You can join
here: www.facebook.com/groups/SerenaAkeroydsDivas. Or you can
always PM or email me. I love to hear from you guys:
serenaakeroyd@gmail.com.

ABOUT THE AUTHOR

I'm a romance novelaholic and I won't touch a book unless I know there's a happy ending. This addiction is what made me craft stories that suit my voracious need for raunchy romance. I love twists and unexpected turns, and my novels all contain sexy guys, dark humor, and hot AF love scenes.

I write MF, menage, and reverse harem (also known as why choose romance,) in both contemporary and paranormal. Some of my stories are darker than others, but I can promise you one thing, you will always get the happy ending your heart needs!